MW01488962

AGAINST THE WIND

A.W. BALDWIN

ISBN979-8-9884895-3-5Hardbound
ISBN979-8-9884895-4-2Paperback
ISBN979-8-9884895-5-9ebook

Cover art by Daniel Thiede.

For Dad – father, mentor, pilot, legend

AGAINST THE WIND

"…a perfect, spell-binding book."

"This entertaining thriller will have you hooked from start to finish with its upbeat tempo that never let's go."

"The writing was absolutely stunning."

"Teenagers and adults should read it because each will feel represented and accommodated."

"Two people from different backgrounds with different goals are brought together on a treacherous journey to an unknown destination."
    – OnlineBookClub.org 5 Star Review.

****

"…a powerful reminder of the positive impact that human relationships can have on our lives."

"…a page-turner and a must-read for anyone who enjoys thrilling adventure novels with memorable characters."
    – Readers' Favorite 5 Star Review.

****

"An exhilarating adventure from the opening salvo, *Against the Wind* follows a global race for next-generation quantum computing technology replete with hitmen, spies, scientists, and a headstrong runaway orphan suddenly thrust into the center of a global threat to national security. Ideal for fans of aviation, espionage, and adventure, Baldwin's writing is crisp, emotive, and atmospheric. The steadily escalating stakes and relatable characters make for an engaging, enjoyable read from start to finish."

— **Award Winning Author Nate Granzow** *(Black Cordite-White Snow, Get Idiota)*

Award-Winning Novels by A.W. Baldwin

MOONSHINE MESA

Criminal clients, a pollution mitigation scam, and a million-dollar double-cross make Moonshine Mesa a dangerous place for an aspiring lawyer, an intrepid deputy, and a moonshining hermit.

"witty dialogue and humor…[with] vibrant characters whose personalities leap off the pages"

"…a sleuth murder mystery, crime-drama thriller, and action novel all rolled into one page-turner"

"…a fascinating dynamic… If you enjoy crime capers, dry humor, and quirky characters, you won't go wrong with Moonshine Mesa."
    *— **Readers' Favorite Five Star Reviews***

THE ANTIDOTE

Can a botany student, a couple of old-timers, and genetically modified seeds provide the antidote for climate change? The cross-hairs on those million-dollar seeds are on them, too…

"This harrowing techno-thriller is an impressive achievement – timely, and rich with research, intrigue, and a main character you will be rooting for from the beginning all the way to the exhilarating climax. Highly recommended!"
>   *– #1 Amazon Best-selling author Landon Beach (The Wreck, Narrator).*

"The chemistry between Harry and Keaton is electrifying."
"…there is never a dull moment…The Antidote [is] a gripping novel."
>   *– Readers' Favorite Five Star Reviews*

BROKEN INN

The mob, undercover agents, and secret payloads make *Broken Inn* a dangerous place for a fresh reporter, a newspaper photographer, and a moonshining hermit.

"The desert bakes while the danger scorches in another outstanding mystery from A.W. Baldwin."
   — *#1 New York Times Bestselling Author Dirk Cussler.*

Winner of awards from the Grand Master Adventure Writer's Competition, New York City Big Book Awards, Independent Press Awards, Global Book Awards, and Books Shelf Writing Awards.

WINGS OVER GHOST CREEK

Can a moonshining hermit, a reluctant pilot, and a misfit student uncover the truth and escape an archeology field class that hides assassins and dealers in black-market treasure?

Baldwin has a "gift for capturing the reader's attention at the beginning and keeping them spellbound."
   — *Onlinebookclub.org review*

Winner of awards from the Grand Master Adventure Writer's Competition and Global Book Awards; Reader's Favorite Five Star Review.

RAPTOR CANYON

Armed with a full box of toothpicks (and a little dynamite), can a moonshining hermit, a big-city lawyer, and a student with secret ties to the site monkey-wrench a corrupt land deal and recast the fate of Raptor Canyon?

"A gem of a read…"
> — *#1 New York Times best-selling author Dirk Cussler*

"[You'll be] holding your heart and your breath at the same time…"
> — *Peter Greene, award winning author of The Adventures of Jonathan Moore series*

"A hoot of an adventure novel…"
> — *- Reader's Favorite.*

Grand Master Adventure Writer's Finalist Award and Screencraft Cinematic Book Contest Semi-finalist; Reader's Favorite Five Star Review.

DIAMONDS OF DEVIL'S TAIL

When diamonds appear in a remote canyon stream, white-water rafters and artifact thieves set off in a deadly race to the source.

"Relic is a unique and intriguing character…passionately interested in preserving the ancient archeological sites and conserving the land and water…[We] enthusiastically recommend it to readers who enjoy thrillers, action-packed adventure, and crime novels."

> – *Onlinebookclub.org four out of four Star Review.*

"Another rollicking Relic ride from A.W. Baldwin…a bunch of double-crossing, dirt dealing, diamond thieves run into Relic's trademark wit and ingenuity. Enjoy!"

> – *Jacob P. Avila, Cave Diver.*

"…an adeptly written thriller…the excitement and tension are superb…the entire plot [is] compelling"

> – *Readers' Favorite Five Star Review.*

"When everything seems to be going against you, remember that the aircraft takes off against the wind."

– Henry Ford

CHAPTER 1

At times, a single moment can radically alter our lives. Chloe knew that this one would be pivotal.

If she could keep up her nerve.

She wrung her hands together, her fingers stiff, palms wet despite the desert heat. She leaned against the outer wall of the airport terminal, an uninspired cinder-block box that housed a bathroom, a tattered leather couch, and a do-it-yourself coffee maker—a place she'd never visit again.

She shaded her eyes and stared across the open ground.

A 1946 Aeronca Chief airplane sat on a grass airstrip, its fuselage the anemic yellow of a number-two pencil, a flash of fiery red wrapped around the windows that narrowed to a point near the tail. Long wings, curved downward at the tips, loomed above the cockpit; the old craft was an albatross among the modern Skyhawks and Pipers that shared the small airport.

She could reach the Aeronca in mere minutes—just walk across the low-cut grass like she always did, check the wings and tail, and get in. Just go.

Peter, her flight instructor, had left the rural airport fifteen minutes before. When he wasn't looking, she'd pocketed the extra key that he kept in his flight bag. She was ready to fly solo, of that she was entirely certain. Well, mostly certain.

Whether she could steal his old Aeronca was another question.

Colossal cottonwoods shaded hangars along the north end of the airstrip, trees she'd climbed, boughs she'd swung from, shadows she'd hidden behind as a child. But she was leaving this place now.

She'd only borrow the Aeronca and only for a week or two. Right? Her flight instructor would understand, wouldn't he? Her heart ratcheted tighter against her ribs.

Now was not the time to doubt herself. Now was the time to escape that ghastly house she was in, and it was ghastly, wasn't it? Chloe had other ideas about her future, and her new life was beginning right now. She wiggled her fingers, rolled her head, and took a slow breath. Time to stiffen her spine, ignore the worry in her head, and get on with it.

She touched the small stone on her necklace, a gift from her grandpa. She straightened her daypack, lifted her tent and sleeping bag from the ground, and stepped away from the building.

Roger, the airport mechanic and part-time manager, walked out of a hangar forty yards away and strode across the tarmac to his workshop. She dropped back behind the terminal, her heart pounding like she'd run a sprint.

A blast of fever prickled her cheeks and she tried to imagine ice on her forehead, mountain snow in her face, anything to cool her skin and focus her back on task. Was Roger's appearance a sign that she should cancel her plans? She peeked around the corner. He was already out of sight, inside the hangar that served as his shop. She shook the blood back into her fingers.

If anyone asked, she'd tell them she was flying her first solo today. Only her flight instructor could contradict her, and he was gone, probably for the weekend. No sweat, really.

Chloe took a slow breath and walked across the grass as casually as she could, tripping once on a low bump in the ground, willing herself not to care if anyone noticed.

She opened the side door and placed her pack, tent, and sleeping bag on the floor behind the seat. She moved to the wings and untied the ropes that held the plane to the ground. She did a cursory pre-flight, checking the ailerons and tail, furtively searching the airport for any movement, her eyes crammed right, then left, as far as they would go in their sockets without turning her head. Straining mightily to look cool and casual.

A dirty orange windsock fluttered halfway down the runway, spinning slowly to the right. Would the quiet morning air hold long enough for her to take off?

She had to stop searching for excuses to turn back.

Chloe made sure the front wheel was blocked by wood chocks to keep the plane in place. She straightened her shoulders, opened the pilot's door, and inserted the key. She leaned into the cockpit, turned the magnetos on, and gave the carburetor a pump of fuel.

She stood outside the plane and searched the grounds again, the sound of a distant engine buzzing in her ears. A macadam strip ran north and south a few hundred feet away, but she'd been practicing take-offs and landings on the grass strip that ran northeast and southwest. No one else was out in the open. No other planes were on the taxiway or in the air nearby. No excuses here.

Because the old airplane didn't have a starter, Chloe had to turn the propeller to hand-crank the engine. She placed her fingers on the edge of the propeller and leaned back. Using her weight to help, she pulled downward and twisted away from the plane as the prop turned once, twice, then stopped.

Chloe glanced toward the terminal but saw no one.

She tried again, falling backward into the grass, and this time the prop turned once, twice, then the engine pounded into life, idling as she dusted off her pants. She lifted the chocks from the wheel and placed them behind her seat. She hopped into the cockpit and pulled the door shut. The fuel tank looked full. The tachometer hovered where it ought to, the compass bobbed, the oil pressure was good. She adjusted the throttle until the engine hummed.

The yoke was a metal tube shaped like the top half of a steering wheel used by pilots to turn or to gain or lose altitude in flight. She moved it forward and back, watching the tail's horizontal move up and down, then turned it left and right, watching the wing's ailerons rise and fall opposite each other, just as they should.

She swallowed hard and checked again for anyone or any other aircraft, any final sign from the heavens that she should stop. Seeing none, she pushed the throttle forward and the Continental engine roared, jostling her across the bumpy field and onto the grass airstrip.

This was it.

CHAPTER 2

Richard Dochauser, Ph.D., was a walrus of a man, meaty without much muscle, a long mustache framing his saddened lips, eyes droopy with fatigue. The lead researcher in a quantum physics laboratory at the University of Azteca just west of Phoenix, he'd had three restless nights in a row worrying about a thorny quantum computing problem. He'd woken to a ringtone and a message to attend an early morning meeting that had started five minutes ago.

As ranking Ph.D., "Doc" advised and directed several students, including his lead assistant, Ph.D. candidate Belle Smith. Belle had sent him the invitation. Brilliant but impetuous, Belle had declared their latest protype an unqualified success. Doc was not convinced. Tests showed promise, to be sure: the ion-trap module approach to providing quantum particles for computation was a great leap forward. But the quantum state was unstable in moderate temperatures, a fatal flaw for any meaningful computations. Belle had insisted that victory was at hand and that they must use their big win to gain additional funding and expand their project.

Her message said the meeting was with Robert Morozov, a freelance reporter for the Scientific Times, a popularized science magazine. The publication featured stories on legitimate research but was also known for promoting fringe ideas that captured public attention. And sold magazines, he presumed.

Declaring victory too soon could shrink their annual grant from the University Board of Regents, not increase it. Worse yet, declaring it to the *Scientific Times* could shrivel their professional reputations forever.

He zipped his fleece jacket against an early morning chill and hurried down the sidewalk toward Abbey Hall, a stout brick building with classrooms on the first and second floors. His physics laboratory filled the entire basement. A pair of students, books under their arms, crossed the greens toward the Douglass Dormitory. A low-flying airplane buzzed behind him, swinging into view for a landing on the university's private field on the other side of the campus.

Doc shuffled through the doorway and down the hall to the staircase. He unzipped his jacket and trotted to the bottom of the steps. He rounded the corner and through the entrance into the lab. A locked steel file cabinet on his left held the prototype when it was not in use. Stopping at a long table, he tried to slow his breathing and his thoughts, preparing to curb Belle's improvident call to the Scientific Times and redirect any ideas the reporter had for a story about their project.

A small conference room was behind another door

and, as he approached, he could hear some of the conversation between Belle and the man who he assumed was Morozov.

"…currently requires operations at or near absolute zero," Belle said.

"So, you want to manipulate quantum particles for computing purposes without the need for extreme refrigeration?"

"Exactly. And we've developed a prototype that can do it."

"That's the modular approach that some other researchers are developing?"

"It's built on that approach, yes, but it goes much, much further." Belle's excitement was obvious. "Here's a model of the prototype…"

Doc moved closer to the door.

"The actual prototype?" Morozov asked.

"That's in the lab. What you're holding is a model of it."

"Amazing!"

Doc swung open the door and stepped into the room, hands on his hips. "What the hell?" Despite his best efforts, he'd lost his cool.

"Doc!" Belle turned to greet him but stopped cold by the sheer force of his disapproval.

Morozov slid the model behind his back, a man protecting a prize. A loose dress jacket hung from broad shoulders, his pale eyes tight. A scattering of pumpkin seed shells circled his feet, detritus from an old habit.

"We're not ready to take this to the press."

Morozov set the model on the table behind him. Doc glimpsed a leather strap beneath the man's jacket.

"Our research is confidential," Doc continued, his cheeks flushed. "Until the university or I release it."

"Doc…" Belle began.

"No." Doc lifted his hand to silence her.

"But you've solved the problem!" Morozov held his arms wide and smiled. "Your success should be celebrated."

"Belle." Doc forced his next words from behind his teeth: "I think this meeting is over."

Belle looked at Doc, then Morozov, then back to Doc. "No." She shook her head. "This will revolutionize quantum computing." She pointed a finger at Doc. "Medical researchers, astronomers, and universities all over the world will have it. It will help find the cure for cancer, extend healthy lives for decades, and offer new solutions for climate change. Our prototype is literally going to change the world."

Morozov stepped closer to them, interrupting. "She's right! It's the quantum advantage, the Holy Grail. Whoever has this first will take the lead in every area of scientific research and space exploration. Once in the lead, no one else will ever catch up."

Doc swiveled toward Morozov, surprised the man was so well informed. He was exactly right about the "quantum advantage." Whichever nation developed it first could take and maintain its scientific lead over every other country on the planet. Mankind would advance exponentially, but a single nation could very well dominate the political and military landscape in the process.

Morozov moved closer to Belle but kept his eyes on Doc. "Please, Dr. Dochauser, you need to share your prototype with the world."

Doc shook his head. The discussion was over.

Belle's arms went limp at her sides, defeat on her face.

Morozov reached for something beneath his jacket.

Doc pointed toward the door. "Time for you to leave, Mr. Morozov."

"No." Morozov pointed a black pistol at Belle's stomach. "If you won't share your discovery with the world, then you will share it with me."

CHAPTER 3

Chloe flew the old Aeronca a thousand feet above and slightly behind a silver semi-trailer as it rolled down State Highway 85, a two-lane route west of Phoenix that ran between the Mexican border and Interstate 10. A hand-held radio system had been attached above the instrument panel so she could talk with local air traffic, but the plane was not authorized to fly into controlled airspace. The partially restored Aeronca had no modern navigation equipment – no GPS or other systems for finding your way across the country. Chloe used the old technique of following rivers or major highways, aiming at recognizable landmarks, and relying on the compass.

Slowly, almost gently, the Aeronca began to overtake the semi-trailer. Without a headwind, she could cruise at about 80 miles per hour. With 15 gallons of fuel, she could fly up to 4 hours and 300 miles, but the calculation was not perfect. Winds, engine performance, passenger weight, and how precisely she stayed on course all affected the distance she could reach before refueling. Her first planned stop was a small airfield near Wikenburg, northwest of Phoenix.

If her bladder lasted that long. She hadn't really thought about that issue until now.

A sudden pocket of air dropped her a few feet and bounced her back up, refocusing her on a pilot's priorities: aviate, navigate, and communicate, in that order. Don't let your mind wander too far away.

She glanced at the radio. She'd already decided not to announce her tail numbers to other pilots in case her flight instructor or the police were looking for her. Or, for that matter, her social worker, a stubby little woman whose empathy had been wrung out of her like a sponge.

Chloe's parents had been killed in a car crash more than six years ago, though the memory still felt like yesterday. Her grandfather had moved from Spokane to stay with her, and they'd grieved and survived together for more than four years. A retired Navy pilot, grandpa had rented a Piper Cub and taught her all he could, soaring over the desert, landing in remote spots for a quick lunch, then back in the air. He'd shown her a few maneuvers he'd performed in the Navy, moves best left to professionals. She'd learned to love it and began lessons with a licensed instructor at grandpa's expense.

Last year, her grandpa returned to his own home in Washington for a few days. While there, he had a stroke that kept him from traveling back to Chloe. It nearly broke her heart. They emailed or spoke to each other almost every day, but it just wasn't enough; he was her anchor, her family, her direct connection with her parents. Grandpa sounded better now, but his rehab was slow, and the separation was torture. She had been all alone, the house dry and barren.

Then the local social worker swooped in, found her a room in Mary's house, and got her enrolled in a charter school. Chloe called the proprietor "Mascara Mary" because the woman's eyeliner was so heavy Chloe thought it would slide off her face if she ever smiled. Mary's ghoulish husband gave Chloe the creeps, leering at her when he thought no one was looking.

Static gurgled from the radio, a pilot too far away to hear clearly.

She and Mary had had a terrible fight yesterday. As if she had the right, Mary had forbidden flying lessons, insisting that no one staying in the same house as her should engage in anything so reckless. Apparently, Chloe's flying was an unhealthy influence on the young foster children in Mary's care. Ha! When she discovered that Chloe had continued her lessons, Mary's face turned purplish, her thick makeup threatened to peel off her cheeks, and she roared about the rules of the house, even whipped Chloe's cell phone out of her hand and refused to return it.

That's when Mary's husband grabbed Chloe's wrist and began sliding his belt from out of his pants. Mary quickly left, leaving the two of them alone. He'd threatened a beating, but it was more than that, too. She'd pulled away and run to her room, blocking the door. He'd pounded outside, demanding to be let in. She'd tossed essentials into her daypack, grabbed her tent and sleeping bag, and slipped out the window. She'd spent the night on the couch in the little airport terminal, worried about what he might do if he had another chance. The fresh memory seemed to slide her stomach across an ice rink, spinning into curlicues.

She gripped the yoke and pulled a deep breath.

She'd thought about taking a car to get away, but a stolen vehicle would be too easy for the police to find. A bus would be better, but she'd have to buy a ticket the police could trace. Plus, she'd probably have to show some identification to buy it. Social services could easily find her along an established route or at a station. But an airplane? By the time they realized it, she'd be half-way across the country, sticking to rural airports with no security.

She'd worked part time at a fast-food joint, spending all her money to continue her flying lessons and learned to appreciate the slow Aeronca. She patted the metal dashboard. "You'll get me to Spokane, old girl, won't you? To grandpa and then a whole new life?"

The thought of flying cross country on her own and recapturing a sense of home buoyed her, wingtip to wingtip.

Ahead, she could see a steady stream of dots crossing the horizon. She was coming up on Interstate 10, the main freeway running west of Phoenix. She adjusted her heading toward the east, a route that would pass over the interstate and eventually cross State Highway 60, which would lead her the rest of the way to Wikenburg.

She suddenly felt starved, the sides of her stomach

touching each other. She craved a hot, double cheeseburger with extra ketchup, but a stale, dry protein bar would have to do. She reached behind her seat for the snack and ripped off the wrapper with her teeth.

She'd planned her route carefully, going from small airfield to small airfield to avoid any kind of air traffic control or scrutiny by the FAA, the Federal Aviation Agency. Rural airports relied on a "self-announce" approach to avoid mid-air collisions. Each pilot was responsible for announcing her position and flight path to other pilots in the area. She could announce herself as "Aeronca" without including the tail number, and no one would give it a second thought. In that way, she could traverse the country, literally "under the radar."

She climbed a few hundred feet higher and crossed the busy interstate at an angle, glancing from her instruments to the matchbox cars below and then toward the horizon. A swath of sagebrush seemed to roll beneath her like a slow-moving treadmill as she levelled the wings. The morning sky seemed warm and thin, a pallid teal stretched across the horizon, and she lost herself in the moment.

The four-cylinder engine abruptly coughed, then caught itself and resumed its natural hum.

Odd.

The cylinders sputtered and jerked again, now shaking the plane like a cheap carnival ride.

What the hell?

She toggled the magnetos, making sure a spark was

firing in the cylinders, but it made no difference.

She pumped the throttle, but the old engine continued to wheeze and jerk and then stopped entirely, slowing them as if they'd leapt into a deep pool of water.

Instinctively, she pushed the yoke forward, keeping the nose of the plane down and her airspeed above 60 miles per hour. Aviate. Don't let the plane go into a stall, when it would lose lift over the wings and tumble from the sky. A deathly quiet filled the cockpit, and she was gliding now, the propeller frozen in place, the engine useless.

She tapped the fuel gauge and it dropped to zero.

Damn.

She'd miscalculated the rate of fuel consumption. The tank was empty. She'd flat run out of gas, 1,400 feet above the crusted Sonoran Desert.

CHAPTER 4

"Oh, oh, oh, oh." Belle stepped backward into a chair, stumbling onto the seat, her eyes on the barrel of the gun.

Morozov kept his aim on her.

A fog seemed to cloud Doc's vision, the event unclear and perplexing. Nothing in his experience had prepared him for the kind of threat Morozov presented and he simply stared at the man, confused and confounded.

"You have the prototype in your lab?" Morozov stepped closer to Doc.

Belle gripped the arms on her chair, her soundless mouth open.

Morozov spoke again: "Prototype. Where is it?"

Doc tried to clear the fog. "You're a journalist…"

"Bring me the prototype."

"…why would you want it?" Then Doc realized this man was not a journalist at all.

"Where is it?" Morozov moved the pistol closer to Belle's head.

"The lab." Doc pointed behind him. "A file cabinet

in the next room."

"Go and get it now or I will shoot your colleague."

"But…"

Belle's body stiffened and her eyes grew wider, pleading with Doc to do as he was told.

"Hurry along." Morozov nodded his head toward the door. "But leave your phone on the table."

Doc pulled his cell phone from his pocket and set it down, as instructed. He took a step back, turned, and walked through the door, his knees rubberized, his vocal cords in a vice grip.

He hurried through the laboratory, listening, looking for the presence of anyone else, someone he could ask for help, but all was quiet. He went to the metal file cabinet and fumbled with the keys in his pocket until he found the right one. He unlocked and slid the drawer open and stared at a waterproof, dust-proof box. He opened the container and stared at the quantum processor inside as if committing its design to memory, all over again.

Could he remove the prototype and give the gunman just the outer box? No, no. Of course not.

He closed the container and lifted it from the cabinet.

The prototype hadn't been perfected. But it was still the most advanced processor system developed to date and must be worth a lot of money to someone, or some government, for Morozov to pull this stunt.

Losing the prototype would set his team back for months. And help whoever was buying it to move way ahead of them.

But there was a modular component on the prototype, a recent modification. Could he remove that? He re-
opened the container, lifted the unit, and wiggled the flat
component free. He slipped that piece in his pocket and
returned the prototype to its container.

He shut the file cabinet and searched the room for
anything he could use to help Belle or avoid surrendering
the prototype. The door across the lab was closed; beyond
that lay the main hall that ran along the basement. Could he
run there, up the stairs, and yell for help? He didn't have the
time. Behind the cabinet was a stack of chairs that blocked
the door to a utility tunnel, one that connected Abbey Hall
with administration, across campus, but he had no time for
that, either. He began walking back toward the conference
room, listening for the sounds of any students in the hallway, but no one else seemed to be in the building this early.

Doc reached the entrance to the conference room,
container in hand.

"Set it next to me, on the table," Morozov said.

He did as he was told and then returned to the doorway, watching Belle. She sat on the edge of the chair, hands
tense on the armrests as if ready to leap. Morozov stepped
away from her and unlatched the container one-handed,
keeping his pistol aimed at her. He flipped open the top and
peered inside. Then he lifted the prototype in his left hand,
turning it, examining it, a faint smile on his thin lips.

Then Morozov scowled. "This is missing something.

Something on the back has been removed."

Doc shook his head. The man seemed exceptionally well versed in the current technology, the latest approaches to quantum computing. Did he actually know about the new modification? Who was he?

Morozov slid close to Belle and aimed the Glock at her stomach. "Where is the rest of it?"

"That's it," Doc pointed, "the prototype you wanted." He prayed that Morozov would not notice the tremble in his voice.

Morozov cocked the hammer on his pistol.

"No, no, I'll--" Doc said.

Belle leapt at Morozov, pushing the gun away. It fired, blasting the chair across the floor. Morozov turned his left side toward her, blocked her wild punch and fired again, this time the bullet diving straight into her stomach, knocking her backward, and he fired a third time, another slug puncturing her chest, and she dropped to the floor in a heap.

Doc stared at Belle for a split second, the alarm in his head warping normal time, his muscles trembling, his heart thumping like a hundred little birds scattered into flight.

Morozov, red-faced and breathing hard, turned toward Doc.

Doc spun around the door frame, into the open lab, and ran as fast as he had ever run, pounding across the concrete floor toward the file cabinet and the exit beyond. He heard Morozov scuffle into the room and stop, and Doc sensed the man was bracing to fire, so he dove behind the cabinet. Gunfire erupted in the lab, bullets piercing the metal above his head, one, two, three of them.

Distraught, Doc searched the room for an escape, but the door to the hallway lay across an open expanse he could not possibly traverse without being hit. He turned behind him and saw a simple wooden door. He tore at the stacked chairs that blocked the way, shoving them across the floor, the sound of clashing cymbals. Two more shots pounded through the metal cabinet above his head. He yanked open the door and leapt through it, forgetting to close it or try to block it, losing all sense but that of an animal frantic to escape.

CHAPTER 5

Chloe searched the ground, knowing she could glide only about a mile before she would have to land. A patch of verdant green flashed behind and to her right, so she turned the plane in that direction. Her best hope was an open field, irrigated and worked, or a well-used dirt road, one without large rocks or deep ruts.

Her stomach dipped with the plane as she aimed toward a set of white-roofed buildings on a rug of grass. Alongside them lay a ribbon of tarmac, straight and true, parallel to the cluster of rooftops. She searched for power lines, telephone poles, or any other obstacles—all of them deadly to a flying machine without the horsepower to avoid them.

In the time she'd looked and made her turn, she'd dropped to 1,100 feet above the ground. She had to make a final decision.

A major roadway led to the grounds, a compound of some sort. Power lines stretched toward the buildings from the highway, but the campus ended abruptly on its northern end. The grand Sonoran Desert surrounded the well-watered peninsula.

The plane had dropped to 980 feet above ground.

She focused on the strip of black pavement and, as it grew, she could see a dotted line of paint down the middle. A square building sat near one end and two domed structures faced south, toward the tarmac.

She'd found a local airstrip. She could read the number 03 on the nearest end of the runway.

The plane had dropped to 700 feet above ground.

Chloe searched the sky for any other traffic then announced on the radio: "Aeronca landing on 03, straight in." Nothing could be in her way, nothing could cause her delay, or she would crash land in the rocky, arid dirt.

She angled the plane toward the end of the strip.

The plane had dropped to 550 feet.

A light wind shifted the Aeronca off course. She quickly corrected, aiming again for the big white 03.

The plane dropped to 425 feet, and she was still a quarter of a mile away, her heart racing, her palms sweating against the yoke.

She watched her speed, dropping the nose, then lifting it, willing the plane to glide farther.

The plane dropped to 205 feet, the tarmac straight ahead of her now and rising fast.

She reacted to another gust of wind, one that misaligned the plane from the runway, correcting again, and this time the tarmac filled her entire vision. She focused on the farthest end, lifting the nose carefully, carefully, aiming at the sky as the wheels jarred against the pavement, rose briefly, pounded again, then settled. She rolled farther, solidly on the ground, adjusting the rudder to remain on the center line.

The Aeronca shuddered and wobbled as she applied the brakes and turned from the runway to the taxiway and toward an open area near the terminal. Beside the runway, metal tie-down loops were anchored into the pavement and marked by yellow paint. She rolled to the nearest one and came to a full stop.

Her hands shook, her breath fast and shallow. She stared at the cockpit dash, the tachometer, and the fuel gauge, letting the silence and the absence of motion sink into her consciousness and slow her heartbeat. She touched her necklace against her chest.

She'd done it. Barely.

By much more luck than skill, she'd landed at a private strip of some sort, maybe a giant country club. She rested a few more minutes then opened the door and stepped out of the plane. She stood there for a moment, holding the strut, steadying her knees.

Across the tarmac rose a square, brick building and beside that, a fuel pump covered with a metal roof. She walked slowly to the terminal, steadying her gait, and went inside, the air cool and quiet. The sheer normality of it all rattled her, made her question her sense of reality. She'd just made an emergency landing that could have been a five-alarm disaster, that could have been her very last landing, ever. Yet here she stood, alive, staring at a bulletin board with a B-52 calendar, yellow post-its, and notes for items for sale: chairs, used books, airplane parts. She'd returned to a normal timeline. A casual, everyday affair.

A young man entered from a different door and waved at her.

"Good morning! Need fuel today?"

She saw the restroom sign ahead of her. "Yes, please!"

"Fill her up?"

"Yes."

"95 octane okay?"

"Yes, yes." She hurried to the bathroom and ran inside.

CHAPTER 6

Doc's shoes clomped across the concrete floor, a faint light behind him fading into gray. The tunnel was about eight feet wide and just as high, musty and dank, old boxes of stuff stacked along the right side. Ahead, the ceiling lines merged to a solid point, like railroad tracks converging in the distance. He wanted to run, but he had to go slow. The shadows engulfed him. He put his left hand on the side of the subway and kept pushing into the void, into dark matter itself, he thought, unknown and unnavigable.

He listened for any sounds other than his own breathing, his own footsteps, but heard nothing. All things seemed to disappear in the black, a ghostly feeling like he was walking through walls, one of his beloved quantum particles slipping between the atoms of solid matter.

Clunk.

Morozov was behind him.

He walked faster now, feeling his way deeper into the unknown, one blind step after another, each one taken on faith, pushed by desperation. A drop of sweat rolled from his armpit to his waist. God, he hated the dark.

Where the hell was he? Still under Abbey Hall? He remembered that the passage was some sort of emergency space, somewhere to go if there was a tornado, but he'd never been here before. He'd run into this concrete shaft purely on instinct and now here he was, sliding farther and farther away from anyone who could help him.

Suddenly, his hand lost the wall, swinging into empty air. He'd come to a corner in the tunnel. To his left he could sense a tiny glow and, like any moth, any life at all, he moved instinctively in that direction. Once past the corner, he could not hear him, but he knew that Morozov was still on his trail.

Who the hell was this guy, really? Not just some random journalist.

He patted the component in his pocket, not sure whether he should have taken it or given it to the man. Maybe Belle would still be alive…

He choked on his own breath, an involuntary shudder passing through his throat.

Ahead, the light was a little brighter, the shape of the tunnel more defined and solid. To his right, he could see the shape of a door—the entrance to the administration building. He moved quickly, feeling for the handle.

There!

He turned the round knob, but nothing unlatched, nothing resisted, and he spun, pulled, and yanked against the latch to no avail. Locked. From the other side. He searched for a keyhole and found it beneath the knob, realizing at the same time that it would not help him. He had no key for this.

Shush. A footstep dragging across the concrete.

Doc twisted and pulled again and again but still the door would not unlatch. Should he pound against it? Scream for help? Would there be anyone in the basement to hear him at this hour?

He turned back and spotted another faint glow on the opposite side. An alcove branched away from the tunnel. He hurried toward it, feeling the wall as he went. The alcove ended at a set of stairs and at the top he could see daylight leaking beneath the exit.

He went quickly up the steps, feeling the way with his feet, until he stood at the top. An emergency bar ran below the latch, so he pushed it inward, feeling it unhook the door. The sun filled his view, stinging his eyes, and he raised a palm to shield his face. As he stepped outside, he heard feet running toward him from behind.

Ahead, maybe thirty feet away, sat a yellow and red airplane, its propeller spinning.

CHAPTER 7

Chloe stared at the map on her lap, tracing Highway 60 until it became Route 93, moving northwest toward Kingman. A slender, red-headed young man had attached a tow bar, moved the Aeronca to the fuel pumps, and filled the tank. Chloe paid with cash, disappointed at how much it cost and how fast her reserve had depleted. Did she have enough to get all the way to Spokane?

She'd looked at a brochure in the airport terminal and learned that she'd landed on a college campus that encouraged students in aerospace engineering and piloting.

She'd acted like she knew what she was doing, that she hadn't made an emergency landing, and the young man who refueled her didn't ask. Maybe he was new to flying, too.

Autumn was on the way, but the Arizona desert still cooked in the early morning. Though she hadn't made it to Wickenburg on her first tank of gas, she had plenty to fly past it now. The highway looked lonely between here and Kingman, which suited her purpose but made finding an airport and fuel problematic. On this leg of the trip, she'd have to keep a lookout for places to land, maybe even ranches where she might buy some gas. She'd keep the Prescott National Forest on her right and the Hualapai Mountains to her left, Route 93 within sight beneath her. She folded the map and tucked it under her seat.

She turned on the magnetos, generating voltage for the spark plugs, and pumped some fuel into the cylinders. She hopped out of the cockpit and placed the chocks behind the left wheel. Then she moved in front of the propeller, placed her feet on the ground, and pulled. On the second try, the engine popped into life, chugging a slow idle. She tossed the chocks behind her seat and climbed in, checking oil pressure, tachometer, and compass. She added power until the engine ran its fastest then pulled the throttle back to idle.

Her passenger door swung open suddenly, smacking against the side of the plane, and there stood a man with a long mustache, his face red and splotchy, eyes beseeching, hands reaching into the cockpit.

"What!" she gripped the yoke with one hand, the throttle with the other.

"Help me!" the man shouted, jumping into the seat, arching toward his right, searching for something behind them. "I'm being shot at…he has a gun!"

"What?"

"We have to go—right now!"

"Get out, you creep…"

"There!" He nodded toward the building and turned to face her again, lips tight, eyes wide, a man in sheer panic.

She leaned forward to see outside his window and there on the tarmac ran a man with a pistol, but he skidded to a stop and knelt. She saw him aim the gun at the Aeronca and a surge of broiling heat hit her heart, her lungs, her cheeks, and she shoved the throttle forward as fast and as far as it would go.

The plane leapt forward then began a slow acceleration down the pavement and toward runway 03.

Pop!

Pop!

Their speed increased down a slight incline and she lined up with the center of the runway, holding the throttle at maximum, pushing the sixty-five-horsepower engine as far as it would go, hoping the gunman hadn't hit anything vital on the plane.

The man's added weight slowed their acceleration, but still, within seconds, the Aeronca's tail rose behind them. They hit 46 miles per hour and the albatross rose slowly from the ground. She turned immediately away from the gunman's position, six feet, ten feet, above the grass, dodging the windsock, soaring twenty feet, then thirty, until they crossed into the barren desert, only a hundred feet above the cacti and rocks.

CHAPTER 8

Chert vozmi. Damn it.

Morozov returned his Glock to the shoulder holster beneath his jacket. He stepped back to the doorway, searching the lot and hangars for any sign that he may have been spotted, but saw no one. A shadow moved inside a distant hangar, but if it was a witness, he was too far away to identify Morozov. He pulled a cloth handkerchief from his pocket and wiped the outer doorknob, then stepped inside and cleaned the exit bar.

He'd have to work fast to finish and get out of the building before it began to fill with students.

He ran back down the tunnel, confident he hadn't touched anything there when he'd chased the professor. When he reached the door to the laboratory, he wiped the handle, then the handle on the conference room door. The caustic smell of iron filled the room, blood pooled beneath Belle Smith's body.

Too bad. He hadn't thought it necessary to kill her, but she'd made a move against him. After that, he'd had no choice. He looked around the room, assuring himself that he hadn't handled anything there.

Morozov walked through the lab to the outer door and cleaned the surfaces he might have touched. Voices echoed from above the stairs, students on their way to classes on the first floor. He had no idea when any of them would come to the physics lab, but he was pushing his luck as it was.

He stepped out of the lab and closed the door, using his handkerchief again. He moved quickly up the tiled stairs and onto the main floor, where he kept his head down and slowed to a natural walk. A heavyset student held the door for him, and he nodded a quick "thank you" without looking at the young man's eyes.

Outside, the air was already warming, and he took a slow breath. He set a casual but purposeful stride toward his car in the parking lot.

Morozov really was a freelance reporter for the *Scientific Times*, the perfect cover for his work with the FSB, the Russian Federal Security Service, which had replaced the old KGB. His press credentials let him move freely from one scientific research facility to another, asking questions, occasionally stealing or copying files. He'd kept his Russian surname because who would think an actual Russian spy would do such a thing? He'd even joked about that with a researcher at the Arizona Science Center of Phoenix last year. Besides, most of his sources refused to reveal any data that could be considered classified or top secret. But their layman-style discussions about physics often pointed him in the right direction. And several sources had pointed him to Richard Dochauser, Ph.D. and Belle Smith. They'd developed something new and highly promising—a modular approach to stacking qubits, quantum processors capable of complex computations that normal computers couldn't touch.

He reached his silver Toyota and searched the campus again. More people had entered the parking lot, staff and students beginning their classes for the day. Nothing seemed out of place.

He slid behind the steering wheel and started the car.

Belle Smith had been an excellent source, spilling details she should not have. He was sorry to have lost her.

Now he had a model of their latest work, which he'd photograph and send to Moscow, but the main prize was the prototype itself. He would arrange to hand that off to another operative, who would get it to Russia. But the prototype was missing a component of some sort, something that had been attached to the top of the unit. Dochauser's reaction confirmed it. The prototype was incomplete and Dochauser had the missing piece.

Dochauser was a hair faster on his feet than Morozov had expected. And he hadn't anticipated a tunnel in the basement, let alone an airplane waiting for him at the other end.

He pulled out of the parking lot and was soon on the freeway back to Phoenix. He needed a pilot's map, something showing airports all over the state. He had to follow an airplane now and he had to do it from the ground.

At least he had a description of the aircraft and remembered the first two symbols of the tail number: N and 4. There must be a database of planes, owners, or where they are stationed.

First, he'd get an encrypted message to his handler, Ivan, and see if he could help him track the little plane as it flew across the September sky.

CHAPTER 9

The man stared ahead, mouth open, a touch of drool leaking from his lips. He hadn't spoken since they'd lifted off. Who the hell did he think he was? She felt like shoving him out the door. What in God's name was he doing, jumping into her airplane like that? Well, her instructor's airplane, but still…

Chloe had turned gently to the northwest; a course set to intercept Route 93 and avoid a jet pilot training area. The man seemed to rouse himself from somewhere else and looked at her.

"I am so sorry," he said, "but thank you. Thank you. You saved my life."

She pointed to a headset beneath his seat. He pulled it out and placed it over his ears. She plugged it in and motioned for him to adjust his microphone. She switched the radio setting to "intercom." Even with the headsets, the roar of the engine made speaking a little difficult, so she raised her voice. "Why was that guy shooting at you?"

"Long story. Can I tell you when we've landed?"

"Well…" Maybe she had saved his life.

"Can you land somewhere where we can get help?"

The question stumped her for a moment. "You want to land to get help?"

"Yes."

"No. Not yet."

"But it's urgent. We have to get help." His voice had become more commanding now.

"Not yet."

"We have to!"

"Hey, bud, I just saved your ass down there and I am the pilot, here. I am the pilot in command." She pointed toward the instrument panel, asserting her authority, reminding him that she was flying the aircraft, not him. It was a rule her instructor had drilled into her. A pilot could even override an order from an airport control tower if, in her judgment, it was needed for safety.

"I need protection. Police protection."

"And you can get it at the next airport," she said.

He took a breath and sat back. "Yes, right."

She gripped the yoke and pulled gently. They were at nearly 900 feet above the ground and she wanted more. The higher the plane, the more time she had to find a spot to land in an emergency. Like a "running out of gas" emergency.

"They call me Doc." He extended his hand toward hers.

"Chloe." She shook it briefly.

"Where are we going?" he asked.

"Northwest. Toward Kingman."

His eyes tightened, a look of concern on his face, then he seemed to stifle it. "I see. Thank you, again."

Doc looked like a man who avoided the gym. He wore a blue fleece jacket and no hat, graying hair, longish and receding. He seemed haggard, exhausted.

Well, someone had been trying to kill him. What could he possibly have done to deserve that? But what if the gunman was a policeman? Or the FBI? Suddenly, she realized she may have let a killer on board.

But no. A policeman would not have shot at the airplane. Right? And a policeman would find a way to track them, despite the lack of GPS or other system in the antique plane, so she began to hope that the shooter was not, in fact, a cop or an FBI agent.

Doc's gaze flitted from the instrument panel to his feet, to the roof, and back to the panel.

"You ever fly before?" she asked.

"Sure." He kept his eyes on her now, avoiding the view below them. "Phoenix to Seattle, all the time."

She repeated her grandfather's saying: "That's not flying. That's a cattle car at 30,000 feet."

"Yes." He finally turned and glanced at the ground.

"Do you work at the college?" she asked.

"Professor of quantum physics."

That seemed to fit. "Why would someone want to shoot a physics professor?"

"That man was trying to steal a prototype from our lab. It's new. Valuable."

She nodded.

"And you?" he asked. "Are you a student?"

"A pilot."

He stared at her for a moment, then asked with a hint of disbelief: "Are you eighteen yet?"

Even under the radio headset, she could feel her ears redden. She shot him a withering look and refused to answer. He raised his hands in defense, a message that he was backing off, then stared out his side window, letting the steady rumble of the engine dampen the agitation between them.

A patch of rooftops spread to their left, doll houses for miniature people. She lifted the nose a little farther and they climbed higher above the earthen realm. Pine trees filled a horizon along the national forest, black in the distance, and they both fell into the uneasy hush of troubled thought.

CHAPTER 10

Chloe wanted to relax into the flight, but she had urgent questions for her intruder. She turned to face him. "Now, you need to tell me. Who the hell are you, really?"

"I've told you. I'm a professor of physics and I run a quantum computing research lab at the college." He folded his hands in his lap.

"Right." She leaned away from him. "And I'm a Christmas elf."

"Hey, no need for that."

"So, why was someone shooting at you? At us, I mean. I want the full story."

"That's, well…"

"Yes?"

Doc's eyes seemed to search the sky and he released a puff of air. "I know some of the answer. The rest is speculation."

"Try me," she searched his face for any sign of deception.

"We—my lab partner and students," his voice trailed

away, and he stared at the horizon for a moment. "We've developed a new approach to quantum computing. Belle— my research partner—called in a reporter to do a story on it. Well, he was supposed to be a reporter. She thought that a published story would help keep our university funding and lead to more outside funding, too, but she did it without asking my permission and we have this new approach, yes, but we're not quite ready for publicity."

"Go on."

"We were set to meet with this guy—Morozov's his name. Well, maybe it's his name."

"And?"

Doc wrung his hands together, his eyes pinched shut. "And the man shot Belle in the chest. She's dead, I'm sure of it."

Chole straightened her back. "What? And you saw him do that?"

"Yes." Doc sucked a deep breath of air.

"Oh, no."

"Yes. I think I was a little out of my mind. I saw your plane and just ran to it, opened the door, and hopped in."

"I nearly threw you back out."

"But you didn't, thank god…"

"I saw the man start to kneel down and shoot, so I gunned the engine and just kept going. You didn't give me much choice."

He reached out and touched her arm for a moment.

Doc had seen his partner, probably a close friend,

shot and killed right in front of him. She believed him. The same man had shot at both of them. Doc's head bobbed up and down a few times, eyes glazed, watching those fresh events all over again in his head, the nodding some kind of reaction to the trauma. Her anger evaporated.

"Right." She stared at the landscape ahead of them.

They sat quietly for a while.

"What do you want to do about it all?" she asked.

He tugged on his mustache and squinted at the ground below them. "I don't know what I'm dealing with, but I assume it's a threat to national security."

"Oh?"

"Whoever develops quantum computing on a large scale will leap ahead in scientific development of all kinds, including encryption of computers, state secrets, corporate secrets, that sort of thing. Morozov works for somebody and it's not the United States."

"So…go see the FBI? CIA?"

"Or the National Security Agency, yes."

She tightened her grip on the yoke. "First, we have to put some miles between us and the college. And find a place to refuel."

What had she gotten herself into?

CHAPTER 11

Three hours later, fatigue weighed on her shoulders like a leaden blanket. Chloe's unplanned passenger had settled against his door, leaning into it, eyes unfocused on the hills below them. They'd passed a well-known airpark thirty minutes ago. She'd been searching the ground for another option, specifically one that was private and unmarked. Some of the spreads out here were huge and ranchers often relied on small planes, even ultralights, to search the range for cattle. They might have grass runways and fuel.

The terrain had changed, rising nearly 3,000 feet from where she'd started, and the air had cooled. Saguaro cactus dotted a desert full of smaller cacti, brush, and rocks the size of truck tires.

The fuel gauge on the old Aeronca was the same type used on Model A Fords. She tapped the outside glass, making sure the needle made no sudden drops.

A dirt road wound in the distance toward a couple of buildings to her left, so she turned gently in that direction. She dropped them to about 700 feet above ground and Doc seemed to notice, shifting in his seat. One of the buildings looked like a Quonset hut, the kind of structure sometimes used as a hangar. A small building sat nearby and an RV, a pull-behind camper, rested near the building. As she approached, a street-wide strip of dirt became obvious to her as a private runway. She circled, searching for signs of anyone present, but the area seemed to be empty.

Then, someone strode out from the hut and waved at them. She smiled and waved her wings back and forth, a return greeting. A windsock hung limp on top of the building next to the hangar, the wind light and favorable.

She lined up for a left-hand pattern and readied herself for the final maneuvers needed before landing. Once turned, she quickly dropped again and aligned with the runway. Sliding downward, they reached 400 feet above ground, then 200, 100, 50 feet, and she adjusted against small gusts of air, keeping the wings levelled and the prop pointed toward the Quonset hut. The nose lifted higher, higher, the wheels skimming the grass along the edge of the strip, blowing it downward. They jarred onto the sunbaked field, bounced upward a bit, then stayed on the ground as she wrangled the Aeronca down the strip.

Dust blew past them as they rumbled to a stop. Chole shut down the engine and relaxed a beat before opening the door and stepping out. A thin old man, his hair white and wavy, approached her with a salute and a smile. He wore battered work boots and a five o'clock shadow that would qualify soon enough as a bona fide beard.

"Hello there! I'm Lewis."

"Hello," she stepped toward him and shook his out-stretched hand. "I'm Chloe."

"Nice looking Aeronca you have."

Dochauser walked around the front of the plane, shook Lewis's hand, and said, "Doc."

"Sorry to drop in unannounced," Chloe began, "but we missed the airpark and I'm not sure I can make it to Kingman without some more fuel."

"Hey, I'm glad to have the company. I work for the Howell Ranch, fixing Mr. Howell's ultralight, and it's quiet as a mouse in church all the way out here." Lewis hooked his thumbs in his pants and meandered toward the Aeronca, examining it with interest. "Scout model?"

"Well, I think it's been modified." Chloe walked with him as he circled the tail.

"Yours?"

"No. My instructor's." Well, that was completely true.

"You're a newbie?"

"Pardon?"

"New pilot."

"Oh. Yes. Flying my friend and me to Kingman." Also partially true.

"Well, your instructor has a hole in his fabric." Lewis pointed at the fuselage in front of the tail.

She leaned forward and saw it—a hole the size of a bullet. "Oh, yeah, he's been meaning to repair that…"

"Odd place for a hole like that." Lewis rubbed his chin.

"Do you have a bathroom here?" Doc interjected.

Lewis looked at him and nodded. "Well, yeah, the hangar has a little apartment in the back, complete with water, toilet, stove. My boss is planning to turn this into an airpark and put it on the maps. It's a good location between Kingman and Wickenburg, and the hills are prettier than most. He's already got a nice trail cleared in the desert in a loop around the place so you can stretch your legs. The apartment will be turned into a bunk house. But that's a couple of years off from now. Come take a break, out of the sun, and I'll get us something cold to drink."

"Oh, yes, you're a life saver." She smiled.

"And I can sell you up to twenty gallons if you need it. Belongs to the boss, but I can refill them over the weekend and until I get the carburetor on the ultralight rebuilt, he's not going anywhere anyway."

Lewis turned and strode back toward the hangar.

Chloe took a slow, deep breath and followed behind. As she passed Doc, he spread his hands and rolled his eyes toward Lewis, his unspoken question clear: what the hell do we say to him?

She whispered: "Someone's shooting at you, so let's keep him out of it. We'll get you some help at the Kingman airport, where there's security and a pay phone. Tell him you teach a physics class I'm taking. You want to see a friend in Kingman, and I offered to fly you there."

"But now we have to deal with the guy…" he nodded toward Lewis, who walked well ahead of them.

"Be nice, Doc. At least he hasn't tried to shoot us out of the sky."

He pursed his lips, his mustache closing in on itself, his face an eclectic mixture of confusion and resignation. "We should talk some more," he said under his breath. "Privately."

That much was also true.

CHAPTER 12

Morozov sat in the rear corner booth at The Ratchet, a dark, blue-collar bar on the western outskirts of Phoenix. He turned a glass of whiskey and ice in his hands, wiping the dew from the glass, waiting for Ivan. He thought of the man as a part-time "handler" or a middleman of sorts, a source for payments when Morozov had a lead on something of scientific interest. But he knew the man could be dangerous. Ivan may or may not be his real name, but he used it to invoke the reputation of the Russian tsar, Ivan the Terrible, who was said to have tortured animals as a child and killed his own son in a fit of rage. The Ivan who Morozov was waiting for was also known for being ruthless. He had a scar that traced his jawline to his chin, the real deal, said to be a wound from a fight against three thugs. Ivan promoted the rumor that he'd killed all of them with his bare hands.

It seemed fitting to meet Ivan in a dingy bar. In years past, barmen in Russia were required by law to cooperate with the KGB. Alcohol loosened lips. Clandestine meetings were not uncommon there. Pretty barmaids picked up all kinds of intelligence.

A thick-set man in a black shirt slid into the seat across from Morozov, startling him from his thoughts.

"Ivan," Morozov blurted. He hadn't recognized him at first because today he wore a short beard on his grizzled face, an attempt to soften his features. But a long scar under downy white hair only seemed to make the man more threatening, a timber wolf in a sheepish beard. All impressions of anything gentle disappeared whenever the man spoke, his vocal cords a rasping baritone.

Ivan squinted at Morozov, waiting for him to begin.

"Good evening, Ivan. Can I order you a drink?"

Ivan ignored the question and glanced behind them. Morozov knew that Ivan never traveled alone. An arm of the old Russian mafia, Ivan stayed close to his trusted lieutenants, linebackers with short clubs and machine pistols.

"What do you have for me?" Ivan's voice rolled out on a bed of gravel.

Morozov lifted the small box Dochauser had surrendered and slid it across the table. Without looking at it, Ivan set it on the bench seat next to him.

"Now, tell me."

Morozov explained what he'd learned about Belle Smith and Robert Dochauser, their laboratory at the college, and their breakthrough in quantum computing. Ivan snorted when Morozov said he'd shot Belle and frowned when he explained that Dochauser had a piece of the protype and had escaped in a small airplane.

Ivan clasped his hands in front of him and leaned toward the table. "Word has come down. Dochauser's new chip, or whatever it is, is high value."

Morozov's eyes widened.

"As you well know, the so-called space race between nations has become the quantum race. Whoever wins that, wins it all." Ivan folded his hands on the table. "Our compatriots have realized this and are working around the globe to put our homeland in first place."

Morozov nodded.

"So right now, you are in very hot water for letting this professor get away with part of the prototype."

Morozov swallowed.

"If you hadn't done away with Dochauser's assistant, our friends would have interrogated her and gotten what they needed that way. That was your second mistake. So, if you can't get the device itself, then bring us Dochauser. Alive."

"Yes, yes. I understand."

"I have access to resources reserved for high value objectives." Ivan leaned back against the booth.

Morozov nodded. "I could use some help finding that airplane. I need a pilot, someone who knows about airports and such."

"And you will have it."

"Yes, good."

"And if you can retrieve the thing, we both will be

rewarded handsomely for it. Your share could be as much as half a million dollars."

Morozov straightened.

"If you cannot retrieve it, your time as a roving reporter will be over."

Morozov knew the threat was serious.

"I have contacts in many places. I will pass on to you any leads that we uncover." Ivan pushed away from the table, stood, and walked away.

Morozov shot the last of his whiskey down his throat.

CHAPTER 13

Chloe and Doc followed Lewis to the side of the hangar, where he showed them a string of carburetor parts lined along a workbench. The ultralight aircraft rested near the east wall, its wings covered with parachute fabric, its engine in various stages of reconstruction on a table nearby. Aluminum tubes formed the frame and a lone seat with flight controls perched just below the wings. Chloe and Doc each used the restroom then joined Lewis at a wooden picnic table where he'd set out a pitcher of water and glasses filled with ice.

"Hey, folks, I've got to get to an appointment. I'm going to be late as it is. It'll take me about forty-five minutes, so I'm going to leave you to rest up, then we can visit some more when I get back."

Chloe and Doc shared a glance with each other.

"Of course, you know not to touch anything here in the hangar, not while I've got some of the engine spread around. Right?"

"Oh, of course," Chloe nodded. "We know not to

touch anything. Thanks again." She raised her glass of water in the air.

Lewis smiled and hurried out the back door of the hangar. "I won't be too long. And I'll bring my iPad so we can check the weather between here and Kingman."

"iPad?" she asked.

"It's got the latest flight planning program on it, complete with winds aloft, temperatures, and detailed weather briefings. You haven't been using that?"

"Well, it's expensive."

"Not really. You'll learn to love it."

"Cool, and I hate to ask," she cringed, "but do you happen to have anything to eat?"

"I can get something for you when I get back."

"Thanks. Oh, and the gasoline?" Chloe asked.

"It's here. If you want to refuel, we can do that when I get back, too."

"Thanks again," she called after him as he closed the door behind him. They heard a truck start and drive away, tires popping on gravel.

She turned to Doc. "You want to keep going? Get to Kingman and then get to someone there for help?" she asked.

"That's an offer to take me?"

She nodded. It didn't seem right to just leave him here.

He rubbed his forehead, worry in his eyes. "I need to report the shooting, but I'd rather get to someone in the NSA."

"Sure."

"Well, we're sure as hell in the middle of the desert here. I'll take you up on that offer, thank you."

"You want to tell Lewis anything?"

"No, no. Like you said, for his own sake, let's keep him out of it."

"Yes, okay."

"Are you flying just to Kingman?" Doc asked. "Or back home after that?"

She thought about it for a moment. She'd already said she was flying her instructor's airplane. She may as well admit that she was flying to Spokane to see her grandpa.

CHAPTER 14

An hour later, Lewis returned to the hangar and joined them at the picnic table. "Bad news." He handed an iPad to Chloe. She studied the forecast carefully, but she didn't know much about the program Lewis was showing her.

"See this?" He switched to a chart showing temperature, winds, and other information by the hour.

"Yes."

"High winds are already at Kingman and coming east. Do you want to fly in gusts of up to 35 miles per hour?"

"Yikes."

"Yeah, but you're lucky you stopped here. You're welcome to stay in the apartment, two beds, overnight. Like I said, my boss is working on making this a private airpark, so we're getting ready. Unexpected weather changes are a way of life out here." He changed the view to a visual weather map.

Doc scooted closer to see.

"This front is going to dip down tonight, but it moves on tomorrow before sunrise. You can head out in the morning, no problem." Lewis held the iPad so Doc could see the blue line across the screen.

"You absolutely can't fly in this?" Doc asked. "Are you sure?"

"Be crazy to." Lewis shook his head.

Chloe sighed.

Doc rubbed his forehead. "I'm exhausted. I can't even think about this anymore. Maybe we really do have to stay over tonight…"

She clamped her lips together and glanced at Doc. They didn't have much choice. She knew her journey would be subject to the whims of weather, but she'd hoped to get into Nevada before she hit delays. The farther she could get from her home airport by the time her instructor realized his Aeronca was missing, the better. She'd packed changes of clothes, water, and food for nights she expected to camp in the desert. Here, she'd get a hot shower at least.

"I guess it's on to Kingman tomorrow." She nodded.

"Well, let me get you a beer, then," Lewis said.

Doc stared across the airstrip and Lewis went inside the apartment.

"May as well accept it." Doc put his arms on the table and laid his head on them, a man ready for a nap.

Lewis returned with three opened beers and set them down. Then he went back to the apartment and returned with three microwaved breakfast sandwiches on paper plates and a bag of pretzels.

"Dig in." He handed the food and drinks to each of

them. Chloe thought she saw a moment of hesitation when he slid her the beer but appreciated Lewis's decision to let it pass. She knew she didn't look twenty-one, but the man respected her enough to let her decide whether to have a drink or not.

Doc sat up and eagerly devoured the hot sandwich.

"What got you interested in flying so young?" Lewis asked between bites.

"My grandpa had a Cub and we'd fly it out over the desert." She took a sip from the bottle, the sting of it scouring her throat.

"Cool." Lewis seemed energized, enjoying his new-found company, ignoring the carburetor spread on the workbench behind them.

Doc crunched on pretzels.

"What about you? You teach physics?"

"Mmm." He swallowed. The food and beer seemed to give him a second wind. "Some teaching. More research."

"What are you researching?"

"Quantum physics."

Lewis released a low whistle. "Neutrinos, particles, that kind of stuff?"

"Yep." Doc wiped his mustache. "Quantum particles so small they pass right through matter without stopping." He raised the palm of his left hand. "They're passing through my hand right now." He wiggled the fingers of his right hand, simulating the passage of particles through his left.

"Amazing stuff." Lewis smiled. "You know, as a kid I

used to believe in ghosts—things that could pass through walls. I got talked out of that years ago, but now I'm coming back around again. Something so out of our everyday experience, something we can't see or hear. Or taste." He raised his beer. "Floating right through us like magic."

"They say that magic is just an observation that science hasn't decoded yet." Doc released a low belch.

"Once it's decoded, it's not magic anymore." Chloe took a bite of food.

"Yeah, and that's a shame." Lewis shook his head. "I mean, what's life about without some magic in it all?"

"There's plenty of magic left." Doc raised a finger. "Every time we push the limits of knowledge, we seem to discover whole new worlds, whole new aspects and intricacies to life."

Lewis canted his head.

"Like the fact that quantum particles can exist in two places and in two states simultaneously—as a particle, a piece of matter, and as a wave, a state of energy. They pop in and out of existence. How can that be? And if they are linked to each other in something called quantum entanglement, they can exist galaxies and light years apart from each other and still, they are linked. Move one particle down, the other moves up. Instantly. Faster than the speed of light."

Chloe leaned closer to listen.

"So, scientists are working on how to harness quantum particles to compute some of the most complex mathematical problems in the universe. Because quantum particles can exist in more than one state simultaneously, they can be used to compute problems simultaneously."

"What does that mean?" she asked.

"Digital computers calculate using zeros and ones. Like two-dimensional computer bits. They have to calculate each possible problem one at a time. Imagine a maze for a mouse with cheese at the end. Digital computers try one route until it fails, then another route, then another, in a linear fashion. Quantum computers calculate all possible routes simultaneously, using what we call qubits. They can be one hundred million times faster than a conventional computer. A problem that would take a digital computer 274,000 years to calculate will take a quantum computer one day to solve."

"Whoa." Chloe pushed her beer away, finished with the bitter tasting stuff.

"So, why don't I have one of those on my desk?" Lewis asked.

"Because the biggest problem in creating a quantum computer is keeping the particles in the correct state, in a quantum state. We have to refrigerate to nearly absolute zero so that other particles or atoms don't collide with them and collapse them out of that quantum state. But even then, we can't get the number of qubits we need to tackle the big computations."

"Fascinating." Lewis stood. "I'm getting another beer? You two?"

They shook their heads. Lewis left to get another

drink from the apartment.

Chloe leaned toward Doc, her voice low. "You've told us about the general problem, but you haven't told us about your research on it, have you? What you've figured out?"

Doc swallowed and aimed his gaze outside the hangar.

Chloe stared at him. "They want your research, huh? That's why that guy was shooting at us."

Doc seemed to struggle with a decision then gave a quick nod. "We have a new computer module," he whispered, patting the unit in his jacket pocket.

She leaned even closer. "It's some kind of breakthrough, isn't it?"

CHAPTER 15

Morozov found a quiet corner in the Western Edge Café, a little place on the highway west of Phoenix with Formica tables and a black-and-white checkered floor transported in time from the 1950s. The sun had lowered on the horizon, glaring against the restaurant glass. He ordered a regular coffee and a slice of banana bread and waited.

A wiry, middle-aged man with a deep tan walked through the entrance, looking for someone. Morozov guessed it was Carl, the pilot Ivan had promised would help him find Dochauser. Carl looked like a guy who shaved every morning but needed to again by noon, a five o'clock shadow darkening his jaw. He approached Morozov and they exchanged quick greetings. The waitress delivered Morozov's order. Carl sat and ordered a coffee and peach pie.

"Ivan pretty much filled me in," Carl began. "So, we're looking for an airplane?"

"Right." Morozov sipped his coffee.

"Describe it, please."

"Yellow, maybe a bit of red on the side. Seemed like

an older model."

"Tail number?"

"N 4 is all I can remember."

Carl rubbed the stubble on his chin. The waitress placed his coffee and pie in front of him and left. "We really need that tail number. Think of it like a license plate that's in big letters for everyone to see. We need that."

"How do we get it?"

"Is there anything else you remember about the plane? Did it have a tricycle gear?"

"What?"

"A wheel in the front, under the engine?"

Morozov took a bite of banana bread and thought. "No."

"Okay, then, it's a tail dragger. Wheel is on the tail, which rests on the ground."

"Yes," Morozov mumbled. "But I don't have a clue what kind of plane it is. Other than yellow."

"There must be thousands of small planes in this part of the country that are yellow, so we're still going to need that tail number." Carl drank his coffee.

"Ideas?"

"Yeah, I figured we'd need something to help." Carl glanced around the café, reached into his shirt, and pulled out a sheaf of papers. "Here is a fake I.D. card, no photo of course, and some official looking papers from the Federal Aviation Administration, the FAA. And some business cards. You can write your cell number on the back in case someone wants to call you with information. We're going to say we're FAA inspectors called in from our regular desk jobs to help find a missing airplane."

"Missing?"

"It's a way for us to ask local pilots which planes are not in their hangars. We say that the FAA only has a partial tail number and a general heading the last time the pilot used his radio."

"Wait." Morozov set his coffee down. "If the owner called it in as missing, wouldn't we have gotten the tail number from him?"

"In that instance, we would, yes. But we say that the FAA got an emergency transmission that was garbled, partly cut off. All we got was a heading and a partial tail number. We're afraid the pilot may have crash-landed somewhere. Others are out searching and our job—we're normally desk jockeys—is to try to find a tail number and maybe a better description of the plane."

"Aren't there radio beacons or radar systems or something like that? To help find a plane that's gone down?"

"Not necessarily. Not on older planes or light sport planes, and I'm counting on that. It's possible we'll find out that the missing plane has that kind of system, but it's not all that likely. And even if it has it, the lack of radar contact might just mean the system was turned off or not working right. If anyone asks, that's all we need to say. We shrug it off, we're just doing our jobs, we'll report it back up the line."

"We're just a couple of cogs in the wheel of bureaucracy?" Morozov wore an ironic grin.

"Yep. Just a couple of paper pushers called to duty."

"How do we know where to start?"

"You said they flew northwest. We start there."

"How do we find the airports?"

"There's an air map here." Carl pointed at the papers on the table. "I've circled the ones we'll start with in red. You should start at the northernmost air strip. I'll start at the southernmost, and we'll work our way to the middle and coordinate as we go."

"Should we go now?" Morozov asked.

"No, it'll be dark soon. Unless that small plane is equipped correctly, and the pilot is certified for IFR, flying only by instruments, he's not going to fly at night. We start before the sun comes up, though."

"Won't we need to have a plane of our own? Dochauser's flying somewhere. How do we catch him without an airplane?"

"Ivan's got people checking on rentals all over the state. Once we have a clue where they went, we'll meet up, rent a plane, and get in the air." Carl took a bite of pie.

Morozov stared at his coffee. "So, we split up until we have a trail to follow, then meet up and fly after them?"

"You got it."

Morozov smiled, a glint in his eye. Carl knew what he was doing.

The two men touched their mugs together, a toast to success.

CHAPTER 16

Sunrise flashed across his desk, as harsh and sharp as the early hour. Deputy Yazzie closed the blinds in his office, softening the light. He sipped a cup of fresh coffee with cream and turned on his computer. The Mohave County Sheriff logo popped on the screen, then prompted for a passcode.

Yazzie sat back in his chair and took a long breath, pondering a list of tasks he'd been avoiding. Revising his budget, for one. And selling his double cab Dodge pickup, only eighteen months old. Massive V-8 engine, high-end suspension system, fire-engine red. Damn, he was going to miss it. But if he didn't sell it soon, he'd have to turn it back to the bank or have it repossessed. He still had his '15 Tahoe, beater that it was. A bachelor's life on a deputy's salary was a real pisser, and between the trips to Vegas and the new truck, he'd overshot his income yet again.

A rap on his door rattled the quiet air.

"Come in."

Marsha entered with a nod. "Morning."

"Morning."

"Got a fresh BOLO, kind of unusual, and an Amber Alert today." She handed him several papers.

"Be On the Look Out," Yazzie read from the top page. "Oh." He raised a brow.

"Yeah. Don't get a lot of BOLOs for an airplane," Marsha said.

"This comes from the owner?" he asked.

"Yep. It's got the description, a photo, and the tail number."

"What makes them think it will show up here?"

"I'm not sure."

"Okay. I'll take a copy up to the Kingman airport and ask around."

"And an Amber Alert."

"I hate these." He'd had a missing child report in May that turned tragic. A fifteen-year-old girl found dead in the desert. The coroner concluded she'd died of dehydration after a night of partying and drinking. Someone must have left her there, miles off the main road. Maybe a friend, maybe a boyfriend. They never caught whoever abandoned her.

Yazzie scanned the pages. "Foster parents reported her missing late last night."

"There's a full description there. Copies already distributed through the county offices." She pointed at the document in his hand.

"Good. Thanks. Anything else?"

"You want more?"

He dipped his chin to his chest.

CHAPTER 17

Lewis had spent the night in the RV, letting Doc and Chloe take one bed each in the efficiency apartment at the back of the hangar. She'd luxuriated under a hot shower and a clean set of clothes rejuvenated her. Doc showered after her and had to wear the same pants and shirt he'd had on yesterday, but he seemed refreshed. Lewis served them microwaved breakfast sandwiches again, this time with yogurt and strong, fresh coffee.

Pale sky hung over the Hualapai Mountains to the west. Lewis combed his white hair with bony fingers, eyes checking his iPad again for weather and wind reports.

"You should be good to go anytime, but if you wait," he glanced at his watch, "for about a half hour, you'll be sure to miss the high winds and gusts around Kingman. But you'll still have a head wind at about ten miles an hour."

Chloe studied the map of terrain, airspace, and airports. She pulled her paper map from her daypack and spread it across the table, comparing places there with information on the iPad. She took a pencil and made a few notations on her map.

"Hey, Doc, I have a question for you." Lewis sipped his coffee. "If you don't mind."

"Sure."

"Is this quantum stuff you've been working on a whole new deal? I've never heard so much about it until you told us last night."

Doc explained more about quantum physics and how it's already in use in GPS equipment, MRI technology, and more. "But quantum particles are hard to control for computing purposes. Keeping temperatures near absolute zero helps control them, but that's expensive. Chemists have shown some quantum effects in biomolecules at room temperatures, but we don't know much about how that works yet."

Lewis listened intently.

"Biomolecules?" Chloe asked.

"Plants."

"Sounds more than a little strange," Lewis said.

"An electron can be forced into a quantum state—it can literally be in two places at the same time—but it ends up in only one place after just a short while, or after even the tiniest interaction from outside forces. They're everywhere around us. But controlling enough of them for long enough to use as a sizeable computer is the challenge."

"Are there small quantum computers out there already?" Lewis asked. "I mean, that are usable right now?"

"All the really big tech companies and several universities have them. But, again, their computational power is still pretty limited because you can't get enough quantum material to stay in a quantum state long enough. It's really expensive to maintain even a small level of computational power." Doc put the last of his egg sandwich into his mouth, the lecture over.

"Hmm." Chloe drank the rest of her coffee and stood. "Time to hit the bathroom again then get in the air."

Lewis closed his iPad.

"Thank you again for all your help, and the food, and the bed last night," Chloe said to Lewis.

"Do we owe you anything for it all?" Doc asked.

"No, no. My boss will be thrilled to say we've had our first guests and that you liked it, rough as it still is."

"Thank you." Doc stood.

"We should be in full swing as an airpark in a year or so, so please recommend us. Leave us a review on our website."

Not until we're long gone, she thought. But it had been the perfect getaway for a getaway. "Of course."

CHAPTER 18

The Aeronca jarred them across the narrow airstrip, rattling their teeth, until they reached 42 miles per hour, when suddenly the smoothness of flight lifted them, and their spirits, into the air. Doc waved as they rose above Lewis's hangar and aligned on their northwestern route.

Last night's storm had moved east of them, out of sight and out of mind. They climbed steadily to about 600 feet above ground then rose more gently, following the contours of the desert for a while. The sound of the engine kept them from starting a conversation, Chloe checking the altimeter, tachometer, and gas gauge. She continued to lift them higher and leveled the plane at about 1,500 feet. Mountains on their left lay like rumpled blankets, rough and wild. They flew over some high hills, and Highway 93 suddenly appeared below them.

Chloe turned gently toward the paved route, ant-sized cars moving in opposite lanes. She kept the road in sight as they flew on.

Two and a half hours later, the land rose from the valley to a flat plateau, the geological feature where she knew the town of Kingman perched. Just beyond lay the historic Route 66, an iconic road that ran 2,448 miles from Chicago to Santa Monica, a primary migration route during the Dust Bowl of the 1930s. The two-lane highway had been made famous by authors and later by Hollywood and television shows.

It took them another 45 minutes to reach the outskirts of Kingman, where Chloe announced themselves on the radio. The airport was easily visible, two solid macadam strips, one an impressive 6,800 feet in length. Hangars and buildings sat near the airport entrance.

"Airplane graveyard," she yelled to Doc and pointed below.

"It's huge." He nodded.

Next to the active runways sat rows and rows of large commercial airplanes and private jets, forever parked in a boneyard of sorts, old planes stripped and de-commissioned years ago. Storage Depot No. 41 was established after World War II, when 5,500 airplanes were flown to Kingman for resale, refabrication, or disposal. Scrapped aircraft were reduced to aluminum ingots for recycling. Though Chloe thought she saw the outline of an old air force bomber, most of them these days seemed to be turboprops and jetliners from modern commercial airlines.

She turned into the pattern for landing and broadcast her plans on the radio. Only two other aircraft radioed their locations and intentions. There was no control tower at this airport, which suited her just fine; an air traffic controller would have insisted that she provide the tail number of her instructor's plane.

Chloe lined up with auxiliary runway 35, immensely longer than needed for the small Aeronca. She landed smoothly and crossed the main runway, stopping first to check for other traffic. They rolled farther down then turned left onto the taxiway and toward the terminal and a building where fuel was sold. She slowed to a stop near the fuel pumps and shut down the engine.

They sat for a moment, adjusting to the silence of pistons at rest.

"Let me buy you a tank of gas." Doc opened his door and stretched one leg outside the tight cabin. "It's the least I can do for all your help."

"Thanks, I'll take it. What do you plan to do now?"

"Use the restroom, grab a drink, then call for help. I'll see if I can borrow a phone inside the terminal. I think I'll start with the nearest NSA office."

Chloe nodded. "Good. But do you mind paying first?" she grimaced. "I lost time yesterday and want to get fueled up and out of here right away." She did not want to be here when the feds arrived.

"Oh, sure. Where do I pay?"

"Inside, I guess." She opened her door and climbed out. She was going to miss Doc, in a way. It was nice to have some company and his work with quantum physics had piqued her interest. She chocked the wheels and waved at a lineman, an employee who pumps fuel for aircraft. He drove a portable tank to the front of the Aeronca and began filling it. Chloe went inside, where Doc was paying for the gas. She made her way to the pilot's lounge, a comfortable area with a recliner chair and couch, coffee pot, and restrooms.

There, front and center on the bulletin board, was a Be on the Lookout notice, complete with a grainy color photo of the Aeronca, its tail number on the bottom of the page, a police contact number, and the name and telephone number of her instructor.

She glanced around the empty room and tore the paper from the board. She went inside the women's restroom, wadded it up, ran water over it in the sink, and stuffed it in the waste can.

She had to move faster than she'd thought. And she'd have to avoid even medium-sized airports like the one here at Kingman. She finished in the restroom then hurried to the front desk just as a man in a dark blue jacket left the terminal to go toward the taxiway. Doc was nowhere to be seen.

"All paid up?" she asked the woman behind the counter.

"Yes, dear, all set to go."

She nodded and left the terminal. The lineman had finished and driven away. She went to the fuel tank and opened the lid. Gasoline sloshed at the top; the tank absolutely full. She walked toward the wing strut, searching again for Doc. She could at least say a quick goodbye.

She saw movement out of the corner of her eye. Doc was running away from the building toward a row of hangars. He turned his head to look behind him. The man she'd seen leave the terminal just ahead of her was scurrying across the tarmac after him. Was it the same man who'd come after them at the university?

Damn it.

Had Doc been able to call for help? Were the police already on their way?

Whether Doc had called for help or not, trouble was fast on the heels of the old college professor.

CHAPTER 19

Morozov had driven to Kingman to begin his search and, after wandering around the hangars for half an hour, he'd spotted Dochauser leaving the terminal. He trotted after the physics teacher, who was clearly out of shape and out of breath. It wouldn't take much to catch the man, but Morozov had to be careful. Someone could notice them running and call for help.

Doc hustled across the tarmac toward a pair of hangars near a chain link fence. Beyond that, rows and rows of old airliners seemed to fill the flattened desert all the way to the mountains beyond. Morozov slowed to a walk, wanting to avoid attention. He let Doc gain a little ground, confident he could catch him at one of the hangars. He still had Doc's cell phone, which he'd taken from him at the lab. The man couldn't call for help. Maybe he was headed to the hangar in hopes of finding someone with a phone.

Morozov pulled his own phone from his pants pocket and dialed. "Carl, it's me. I'm at the Kingman airport," he took a breath, "and I found Dochauser in the terminal."

"Good," Carl said. "Because I've had no luck getting any leads where I'm at. Sounds like Dochauser got about as far north as I thought he might."

"Right. I'm following the guy now." Morozov moved closer to the hangar near the chain link fence. Dochauser had disappeared into the building. Its huge garage-style door was closed, but a smaller doorway stood on the side of the hangar.

"Hey, listen," Carl began, "I've seen a BOLO out for an airplane that might fit the description of the one you said Dochauser took off in."

"What?"

"A BOLO on an old yellow and red Aeronca. If it's the same plane, it's stolen."

Morozov stopped outside the hangar door. "Stolen? By who?"

"The BOLO doesn't say, of course. But it has the name of the owner and the tail number, and I've written them down."

"Well, well."

"So, if that's the plane, we're not the only ones looking for it now."

Morozov frowned. "Which complicates things."

"Means we have to move even faster."

"I've got Dochauser cornered, I think. I'm going into a hangar near some kind of parking lot for jumbo jets."

"The famous boneyard."

"I guess. How far are you from Kingman?"

"Maybe a half hour, I'd say."

"Get here as soon as you can and get to the far hangar. I'll get Dochauser and meet you here. Drive right up to it, okay? We'll need to get the guy into the trunk to get him out of here."

"Right. I'll call off the hounds on that airplane rental."

"Oh?"

"Won't need it now that you've got Dochauser cornered."

"Yeah. Talk to you later." Morozov put his phone back in his pocket and approached the side door. He turned the handle slowly and it opened into a cavernous space with two high-wing airplanes fit tightly inside, winged puzzle pieces angled together.

Morozov closed and latched the door behind him. Too bad Dochauser hadn't thought to lock it. His eyes adjusted slowly to the dim light inside and he pulled his Glock from its holster.

Boxes were stacked behind the tail of one of the planes. A workbench lined the opposite wall of the hangar, parts and tools hanging from a white pegboard. Two large toolboxes on wheels, one red, one blue, had been rolled to the center of the space. Two fifty-gallon drums anchored the far corner, but the planes and toolboxes blocked much of his view. He began a careful search of the perimeter, walking softly along the wall where he'd entered. He'd need to keep an eye on the door, in case Dochauser was smart enough to double back.

CHAPTER 20

Doc bent forward, his lungs heaving air. He really needed to get in better shape. No one seemed to be in the massive hangar, dark but for some ambient sunlight from panels near the roof. As his eyes adjusted, he saw two high-wing airplanes fit snugly between the walls. He hurried along the nearest side then along the back wall behind the planes to a pair of fifty-gallon drums. Boxes were stacked against the far corner, the smell of grease and metal in the air. He'd hoped to find help in here, someone, anyone with a phone, anyone who might hide him. He'd spotted Morozov just in time, as the man had entered the terminal. He'd slipped out the door toward the runways, but Morozov had seen him anyway.

The side door to the hangar banged open, the sound echoing against the concrete floor and aluminum walls. A shaft of light glared against one of the cockpit windows.

Doc tip-toed to the boxes and squatted low behind them, searching the hangar as he went. Morozov's legs appeared below the tail of one airplane, stepping slowly along the far wall, then disappeared behind a desk-sized toolbox on wheels. Doc looked for loose tools, parts, anything he could use as a weapon or a shield. He'd run into a metal cavern with no one to help him and nowhere to go.

Doc twisted away from the boxes and shuffled along the far wall and toward a workbench and a gigantic door nearly the size of the wall itself. The door opened onto the taxiway and allowed planes to move in and out of the hangar. The thing was huge and heavy, horizontal hinges in the middle to let it fold upward. He could see an electric motor used to raise and lower it. There must be a button to make it work. If he could get it started, he could roll under it and out into the open again.

Morozov bumped into something in the far corner.

Doc hurried a few more feet toward the hangar door, watching as he went.

"Dochauser!" The shout sounded like a trumpet inside a tin can.

Doc stopped along the bench, his mind flashing back to the gunshots in the lab, Belle falling dead to the ground.

"I'm not here to hurt you. I'm here to ask you some questions. That's all we want. We need the part that goes to the prototype and how to use it. That's all." Morozov stepped toward the boxes in the corner.

Doc slid closer to the hangar door, looking from there to the back of the space where he heard Morozov shuffling. Doc noticed a panel the size of a cell phone on the wall, one button green, one yellow, one red. He moved as fast as his leaden legs could take him, turning to the panel. In the low light, he could just read "open" above the green button, so he pushed it quickly.

Nothing happened.

Morozov reached the boxes in the corner and now had a clear line of sight to the hangar door. And to him.

Doc placed his hands on the workbench, his throat tight, his knees turned to dough.

Morozov hurried forward, pistol in hand.

Doc lifted his hands to his chest, his feet cemented to the floor, then pushed the green button again, wiggling it, shoving it in, willing it to work.

Morozov's lips rose in an angular grin that celebrated both victory and retribution.

CHAPTER 21

Chloe had to respect an old guy who could find this much trouble this quickly. And a sedentary physics professor at that. Doc had to be doing something right. Right?

She ran across the pavement, angling directly for the hangar where she'd seen Doc, then the other man, enter. The giant door in front could open to let airplanes maneuver in and out. Most hangars had only one other, normal-sized entrance and exit, the doorway the men had just used. Doc could end up cornered inside the large metal building.

A man in jean overalls left an adjacent hangar, walking toward the terminal. She tried to hide her agitation and slowed to a more casual pace. The man gave her a quick wave, which she returned. When his back was to her, she hurried again. A chain link fence connected to the far corner of the hangar then stretched away for hundreds of yards. Behind the fence lay the famous aircraft graveyard, huge, abandoned jets lined in rows, blue and red airline logos still painted on their tails.

She ran the last few yards to the side door and twisted

the handle. Locked.

A shuffle and a bang sounded from the far side of the hangar, so she sprinted across the front toward the corner where the chain link fence was attached.

The giant aircraft door began to rise, the mechanism on a slight delay.

She could see two pairs of feet entangled on the floor, then one of them stepped away from the other.

The door rose nearly two feet as she reached the end of the hangar. She dropped to her hands and knees and peered inside.

Morozov had worked fast. Silver duct tape wrapped around Doc's chest and arms, a partial mummification. More tape secured his waist against a wooden leg of the workbench. A strip of it plastered his mustache against his mouth and extended across his cheeks. His eyes went wide when he saw Chloe staring up at him.

Morozov hit the "stop" button on the massive door. He turned to look behind him, then crouched to the ground.

Eyes pale as winter ice stared directly at Chloe, inches away.

She jerked backward and rolled from the door, jumping to her feet, searching for a place to run. She spotted a slit in the chain link fence, right where it met the side of the hangar, and sprinted toward it.

Morozov scooted under the hangar door and onto the taxiway.

Chloe pulled the links apart and squeezed between

them, her shirt catching on sharp edges. Morozov stood and dashed forward. Her clothing caught again on the metal bramble, pinning her there. She was stuck halfway through, fingers fumbling against the barbs, peeling her shirt away one hook at a time, Morozov closing fast, when she finally jerked free and fell to the ground on the other side, scrabbling away as his clawing hands reached for her.

She'd entered the aircraft boneyard.

Morozov did not hesitate. He pulled the tear in the fence as wide as it would go and stepped through, twisting his torso to avoid the thorny edges.

Chloe turned and ran toward the retired behemoths, searching for places to hide.

CHAPTER 22

Crumbled tarmac spread out before her, lines of grass reclaiming the pavement in stretched-out rectangles and narrow lines. A flat desert topped the plateau and dark mountains loomed in the distance. Jumbo airliners and smaller jets spread across the boneyard, piles of scrap wings and parts stacked between them.

She ran forward, glancing left and right. A long row of Delta jetliners lined the pavement to her left, their tails still painted red and blue. Yards of open, empty space stretched between them. Ahead lay a huge jet painted solid yellow with red stripes, "DHL" stenciled on the fuselage.

Closer at hand was a string of passenger jets and cargo planes. The distance between one plane's nose and another's tail was about two car lengths. She'd best choose a good place to hide; if she kept running between these planes, she'd be easy to spot.

"Hey!" he yelled.

She ignored the man, loping beneath the nose of an old Leer jet and toward a fat-body cargo plane, dual tires still on the wheels. She sprinted toward the nose and around the front, where she found an open panel above the tires. She ducked below and searched for the man's legs beneath the fuselage.

He stopped, seeming to search for where she'd gone. When he began to walk in the direction opposite from her, she moved quietly to the open panel and lifted herself inside.

She listened for any sound of the man, but heard nothing. Her eyes adjusted to the semi-dark, and she began to crawl on hands and knees into the empty storage bay. An aluminum cavity yawned before her, a massive soda pop can. A stack of scrap metal was piled near the rear of the plane. She stood, slightly bent over, and walked gingerly toward the back.

The cargo plane seemed like a great place to hide. He'd have to check every one of a dozen airplanes that she could have ducked into.

Would Doc be alright? Could he get himself out of all that duct tape and call for help? Could she get out of here before the cops arrived?

Her shoes scraped a bit across the bottom, the sound of a bucket being scratched. Every six feet or so, metal ribs wound full circle inside the bay. She stepped over three separate ribs to reach a neat pile of metal parts.

Would the gunman give up the chase? If he did, he'd go back to get Doc, wouldn't he? Maybe she hadn't really helped him at all. Maybe she'd only made it worse for both of them.

She felt a large piece of sheet metal in the stack of parts and turned behind it. Light glowed where she'd climbed into the plane, a stab of chrome across the dull nickel floor. Suddenly, the chrome changed its shape, someone partially blocking the sun.

She knelt quickly toward the floor and behind the scrap metal, peeking through cracks in the pile. She fiddled with her necklace.

The man poked his head through the open hatch, glanced up and down, and crawled inside.

CHAPTER 23

Chloe's legs shook like they'd been dipped in ice water and exposed to the wind. Her vision flickered along the edges and narrowed to a funnel that focused only on the searching eyes of the man in the cargo bay.

He pulled a pistol from his holster and stepped toward the pile of scrap metal. She reached slowly to the floor, feeling for something, anything to grab, anything to throw at the man.

She was trapped.

How had he found her? Was he the same man who'd shot at them at the college? The one Doc called Morozov? Yes, it must be him.

If only she could dissolve into Doc's quantum particles, she could melt through the bottom of the cargo hold, nothing to it. But the laws of physics weren't going to bend just for her.

Her fingers found a loose screw and she tossed it high over Morozov's head. Tin on tin echoed in the chamber and the man turned to look behind him, pistol raised. She searched the stack for something larger and found a tube of aluminum the length of her forearm.

She had to get past the man. She braced herself.

While Morozov was turned, she jumped from behind the pile and ran toward him, the pole raised to strike. He twisted back toward her, pistol swinging forward, and she pounded the metal into his arm as hard as she could, lowered her shoulder into him, and drove past. She heard a heavy clatter, the sound of the gun striking the floor, and hopped over the aircraft's ribs, one, two, three, and to the open hatch, where she dove headfirst into the light.

Her left arm smashed into the ground, and she rolled twice to a rough stop. Gasping, she lifted herself from the dirt, still holding the metal tube, and limped toward the tail of the plane, behind the tires, back toward the row of jumbo jets.

She gained some rhythm as she went, speeding across the open ground, past a private jet and then under the tall wing of a 707. She angled more directly toward the chain link, counting the seconds passing, passing, and when she reached the fence, she nearly crashed into it, a metal post halting her momentum. She looked back toward the cargo plane, searching for Morozov, and finally saw him as he rounded the tires. She'd earned a decent lead ahead of him.

She stuck the metal tube into the opening in the fence and twisted, slipping past the barbed edges more easily than when she'd gone through the first time. The edge of the hangar was close at hand, the doorway still two feet off the ground. She rolled under and hopped up inside the hangar. Doc was still standing there, half mummified, trying to pull away from the work bench. His eyes widened and a muffled sound left his taped-up mouth.

Chloe found a box cutter on the tabletop and cut Doc away from the bench. She held him still and sliced close to his right arm, pulling it partially free from the tape wrapped around his chest, then did the same for his left arm. Then she dropped to the ground and cut the tape that held his legs together. She slid the razor back into the cutter and put it in her pocket.

"Doc, we gotta go!" She pushed the button to close the hangar door and pulled his arm to drag him forward, across the giant panel as it closed, then in front of the airplanes and toward the side door.

Doc mumbled something underneath the tape, but she ignored it, hurrying them to the exit. She unlocked the door and they each stepped through and into daylight again.

Doc's legs and arms were mostly free, but his chest was still restricted, and he shuffled across the pavement, a penguin fleeing a polar bear.

She glanced behind them and saw Morozov at the fence line, holding the arm she'd hit with the pole. No one else was out on the tarmac. The fuel truck had moved farther down the line. No one came out of the terminal, no one yelled at them or shouted for help.

She led Doc to the Aeronca, dropped the tube she'd used as a weapon, and pushed him inside. He'd reached the duct tape on his mouth, struggling to pull it aside.

She hurried to the other side, turned on the magnetos, gave it a pump of fuel, and spun to the front of the plane.

Morozov was almost through the break in the chain link fence.

She pulled the propeller downward, and the engine popped once, then stopped.

Morozov was running across the taxiway now, straight for them.

She pulled again. Nothing.

She dropped all her weight into the next pull and the engine sputtered to life, the prop finally spinning into a healthy idle.

Morozov was halfway across the field.

She tossed the chocks in the baggage bay and hopped into the pilot seat, not bothering to check anything this time, ramming the throttle full speed, praying that they could roll out quickly, faster, faster, she urged.

The Aeronca moved forward, the engine roaring now. She glanced behind them and saw Morozov pull the pistol from his holster.

CHAPTER 24

Chloe had no time to reach the proper runway. She turned the plane directly away from Morozov and aimed for open ground ahead of four high-wing airplanes that were tied down in a row.

Doc peeled the rest of the tape from his mouth and gulped cool air into his lungs. "We've got to get to the police."

She ignored him again, the engine at full power, the little plane jarring across bumps in the taxiway, rolling faster and faster toward the line of parked airplanes, their size growing at an alarming rate, closer and closer. The Aeronca hit 30 miles per hour, then 38, 42, suddenly rising a foot off the ground.

"We're gonna hit 'em, we're gonna hit 'em." Doc braced his hands on the dashboard.

She lifted the left wing, skimming mere inches above the parked airplanes, the engine a throaty roar as they lifted higher into the sky.

She levelled the wings and continued to climb above

the airport.

Doc's skin had turned oyster-gray, his eyes wide and locked onto hers.

"What?" she asked over the noise of the engine.

Doc shook his head then turned to look out his window.

Her hands shook for a moment, but she forced them under control and tried to take slow, regular breaths. She checked the instrument panel and turned gently to the north, putting Route 93 on the right side of the plane. She wasn't sure where they could stop at the end of the day, but it had to be remote, someplace Morozov wouldn't think to find them. Maybe someplace south of Las Vegas.

Doc turned back toward her. "We've got to get to the police."

Chloe put on her headset and pointed to the one beside Doc. He put on the passenger-side headset.

"We've got to get to the police," Doc repeated, still yelling a bit to overcome the sound of the engine.

She checked the altimeter and leveled the nose of the airplane. "I can't go to the police," she said.

His nose wrinkled like he'd smelled pickled cabbage, his question implicit.

"I have to…" she stopped. "I have a confession to make."

He nodded for her to continue.

"Well, a couple confessions."

"Yes?"

"I'm not 18 years old yet." She couldn't look him in the eye. "I'm running away from a foster home."

"What?"

"I really am going to my grandpa's place in Spokane. And this really is my instructor's airplane, but..."

Doc leaned toward her.

"My instructor didn't know I was going to borrow it."

"Shit."

"And..."

"There's more?"

She figured she may as well lay all her cards on the table. She was going to need his help, or at least his co-operation, if she was going to make it all the way to her grandfather.

"I don't actually have my pilot's license, just yet."

Doc's mouth fell open, his face drooping like wax in the sun.

She figured it was his turn to push her out of the airplane, but she hoped he was rational enough to wait until they landed.

CHAPTER 25

Chert vozŕmi. Damn it again. Morozov holstered his Glock and watched as the Aeronca rose just in time to clear a row of parked airplanes. He clenched his fists and turned a full circle, searching for anyone who might have seen them. A young man walked from behind a fuel truck, fifty yards away, wiping his hands on a cloth. He seemed uninterested in Morozov or the departing aircraft.

A blue sedan rolled through an open gate and toward the hangar at the end of the tarmac, the one nearest the chain link fence. Morozov shook the tension from his arms and walked across the lot, thinking how Ivan would be pissed, really pissed, then thinking maybe Ivan didn't need to know what had just happened.

Carl got out of the car, spotted him, and waited.

Morozov pointed back toward the terminal. "They just took off."

"Damn."

"Give me a minute." Morozov went through the side door of the hangar and to the workbench on the far end.

He unwrapped the remaining duct tape from the leg of the bench and checked for any other signs that he and Dochauser had been there. He wiped several surfaces clean of any fingerprints and carried the ball of tape back outside.

"What happened?" Carl asked.

"I had Dochauser. I had him in the hangar." He shook his head.

"He got away?"

"Yeah, and you won't believe this. The pilot of that stolen airplane..."

"...the Aeronca..."

"...is a teenage girl."

"She's the pilot?"

"That's what I said." Morozov threw the tangle of tape onto the back seat of the car.

"Some teenager helped him escape?"

"That's what I said." Morozov repeated, his words dripping with anger.

"I don't get it. What's the connection between them?" Carl asked.

"Hell if I know."

"Well, from the BOLO, we've got the tail number and the make of the airplane. That old thing can't go but maybe 90 miles an hour, tops. And I'd bet is has no modern nav equipment, either."

"So?" Morozov spread his hands.

"So, we can plot out how far they'll get on a tank of gas and when they might get there. And they'll be landing at small airports only, which narrows their options considerably."

"Oh."

"Which way did they go?"

Morozov pointed behind him.

"Still headed northwest. We'll assume they'll keep that heading, to start. Time to rent us something faster and that can stay in the air longer between re-fueling." Carl opened the driver side door.

Morozov climbed into the passenger seat. "Can we get something here?"

Carl slid in next to him and pulled an iPad from beside the seat. He tapped and swiped the screen for several moments, then a smile rose on his lips.

"Right here. We can get a Cessna or something at the shop on the other end of the terminal."

"Let's go."

CHAPTER 26

Doc seemed eerily silent, staring out his side window at the plateau below.

The sun glared through the windshield, harsh and low on the horizon. Soon enough, it would be behind the distant hills and Chloe was going to have to land. Flying at night was dangerous; lights on the ground and stars in the sky can disorient an inexperienced pilot. She'd done it only once so far with her instructor and it had put the fear of God into her. And finding a safe place to land in the dark—other than at a well-lit airport—would be impossible.

She searched for cultivated fields or dirt roads or just blank places on the landscape that were mostly flat. She'd hoped to find the little runway at Kidwell but now feared she'd missed it. The mighty Colorado River appeared suddenly beneath them, glistening wet. She eased the plane to the south, watching for smaller rivers or streams that emptied into the Colorado, someplace there might be an irrigated hay field.

The map showed State Route 95 running parallel to

the wide river, so she looked for the highway and dropped a few hundred feet closer to earth. The sun quickly disappeared, leaving the land in a ghostly afterglow.

Doc roused himself and shifted in his seat. "Looking for a place to land?"

"Yep." She spotted a dirt road some miles from the river and saw that it followed a stream. She dropped them a bit lower and angled toward a field of grass framed by trees and, presumably, a fence line. Barbed wire was yet another hazard for landing, but she didn't see any posts or power lines crossing the field, so she lined up for an approach.

At about 300 feet above the ground, she added power and flew the length of the field, looking closely for the best spot to land, making sure there were no tractors, ditches, or other hazards. She eased left, circled over the trees, and lined up again. They were soon lowering to the ground, easing downward until the grass seemed to reach up and touch the wheels and they jarred and bounced toward a grove of cottonwoods.

Chloe added enough power to take them closer to the trees then shut down the engine. They sat for a few moments, adjusting to the quiet, the air suddenly as still as dust floating in an attic.

"We have to move the plane. Would you help me?" she asked.

"Yeah," Doc slid from the cockpit and stretched his legs.

Chloe hopped out and walked to the tail, where she lifted it from the ground. "Just push on one of the struts, please."

Doc did as requested and she steered the Aeronca under the canopy of cottonwoods.

She set the tail back on the ground and wiped her hands on her pants. "Nice spot to camp."

"Camp? Can't we use your phone to call for someone?"

"My so-called foster mom took my phone."

Doc lowered his chin, his eyes a mix of disappointment and disbelief.

"Okay, look…social services put me in a foster home—temporarily." She raised her finger. "I call her Mascara Mary because she practically paints her face on every morning. She has three little foster kids, and she expects me to change their dirty diapers at all hours, wash their clothes, do the dishes. And her slug of a husband looks at me crossways and makes my skin crawl. Has me make him a gin and cranberry juice every night. Likes to touch my hands and calls me sweetheart."

Doc put his fists in his pockets.

"A couple of nights ago, I have this fight with Mary. She takes my phone and her husband grabs my wrist and starts taking off his belt—like he's gonna hit me with it, but he has this look in his eyes, too. Sick. I couldn't take any more of it. I got away from him and he tried to follow me into my room. I grabbed some stuff and went out the window. Spent the night at the airport terminal and took off the next morning."

"Oh, no. I'm so sorry to hear that. Thanks for telling me." Doc scuffed his shoe across the dirt. "I'm not sure what else to say."

"No need to say anything."

"But no more lies." He pointed a finger at her.

"No more lies," she agreed.

They stood in silence for several moments.

"Well, I don't have anything with me to camp." Doc spread his empty arms. "I'll freeze to death tonight."

"I have a sleeping bag. You can have that, and I'll wear my coat and sleep in the plane."

"Ugh."

"Well, it's the best we can do."

"No, no, it's far from the best." He walked closer to her. "Look, I appreciate all you've done for me, I really do, and I've tried to repay you by buying fuel and such, but I've got to get help from the police, or the FBI, the NSA, the CIA. Hell, I'll take it from the EPA."

"Doc, you're a really smart guy, I mean brilliant and all, but landing at another airport tonight could have been the death of you." She put her hands on her hips. "I mean, literally."

He nodded at the ground, acknowledging her point. "How the hell old are you, anyway?"

"How old do you think?"

"Hell, you looked eighteen until you said you weren't, but sometimes you sound like a 30-year-old."

"I don't know if I've been complemented or insulted."

"I don't know, either."

"I know I'm starving, though." She went to the plane and rooted through her pack.

"Of course, you are. You're a teenager." Doc leaned forward, hands on his knees, and began to chortle.

"What's so funny?"

"Nothing." He shook his head, the chuckle rolling faster, deeper in his gut. "This whole situation," he took a quick breath, "is goddamned hilarious." He laughed.

A nervous snicker escaped through her nose. "Well, we're here for the night. So, we may as well make the best of it."

"See what I mean?" He waved at her. "There's your 30-year-old."

"Yeah, whatever. At least we're safe from anyone who might want to shoot at us."

Just then, a pair of headlights popped over the horizon and moved quickly toward the Aeronca.

CHAPTER 27

FBI Special Agent Brad Johansen hung up his desk phone and checked the clock. Almost seven in the evening. He'd been in the office nearly twelve hours, canceled a lunch date, and missed his time at the gym. He'd gained a few pounds around his waist and lost a few hairs above his forehead since he'd started this job. But he loved it.

He'd spoken with a Deputy Yazzie twice today. One of his witnesses was a lineman—a fuel pump worker—at the Kingman airport, who was pretty sure the Aeronca had flown northwest, which meant it would soon cross into Nevada and what was likely a theft would become an interstate crime.

Johansen would take the matter from here. He'd thanked Yazzie, who could stand down, for now, at least.

He pulled up an aerial map of southern Nevada on his computer and stared at the screen. He'd authorize the usual field office and local law enforcement alerts. And the FAA, just in case a pilot or airport employee called the agency about anything suspicious.

His phone rang again, and he picked it up.

"Deputy Yazzie on the line."

"Yes, put him through."

"Agent Johansen, sorry to seem like a pest..." Yazzie began.

"No problem. What is it?"

"I just had another witness call me about the BOLO we circulated."

"Yes?"

"Well, it seems that someone from the FAA is going to airports in the area asking about the same Aeronca that we're looking for."

"The FAA?" Johansen sat up straighter.

"Yep. An FAA inspector was asking about the plane in Wickenburg, southwest of Kingman. I figured you guys would all coordinate, but the FAA already knows about this and is out in the area searching. You might want to give them a call."

"Yes, yes, deputy. Thank you for that. I will indeed be calling the FAA."

"No sweat. Talk with you again sometime."

"Wait, wait. This is damned strange, deputy."

"Oh?"

"Over land, the Air Force and the Civil Air Patrol conduct searches for missing airplanes. The FAA never puts people in the field to do that, especially not for general aviation planes like a little Aeronca. They go to airports for inspections, yes, but those are conducted to check for compliance with FAA regs. Even if they did conduct searches, how would they know so soon that the plane was missing, even before you guys with the county sheriff knew about it? And why didn't the FAA report it to you or the Civil Air Patrol or the FBI? This report sounds really odd."

"Our witness says the man showed him an FAA ID card."

"A photo ID?"

"I didn't ask."

They both stayed on the line, pondering the information.

"You think the FAA has screwed it up somehow?" Yazzie asked.

"Other than alerting pilots or other federal agencies, I don't see how the FAA would be involved at all. Not in conducting the search itself."

"So, who the hell was this supposed FAA guy?"

"I'm going to need the name and contact info for that witness, deputy."

CHAPTER 28

This must be what a deer in the headlights feels like, she thought, staring into the expanding lamps, part awe, part trepidation. The truck door opened, screeching on its hinges, and out popped someone in the shadows. He stepped in front of the pickup, a mere silhouette of a man, hands on his hips.

"Hello, there!"

At least he wasn't shooting at them.

"I saw you circling around," he spun his finger in the air, "and thought I'd better see if you needed help."

He stepped closer, the lights illuminating a diminutive figure, an elf of a man, white hair flowing nearly to his shoulders, crinkly beard spiraling from his jowls. "I'm Chester." He held his hand out to Doc, who shook it and introduced himself and Chloe. Chester the jester, she thought.

"What put you down in my little field this evening?" Chester asked.

"Nightfall." Chloe glanced at the north star, the first to appear in the darkened sky.

"Well, you folks need a place to stay for the night?"

Doc and Chloe looked at each other.

"Hey, I don't mind if you camp here but you're welcome at the house. Maude and I would love the company."

"I think we'd like that, too." Chloe watched Doc, waiting for his reaction.

"Sure, yes, thank you."

"You wouldn't be willing to sell us some gasoline, too, would you?" she asked. "Ten or twelve gallons?"

"I think I can scrounge up that much. It's not airplane gas, though."

"Same difference for the Aeronca. It runs on anything from 85 to100 octane, whether it's from an airport or a regular gas station."

Chloe grabbed her pack and they all climbed into a rust bucket on wheels and bounced across the field, through an open gate, and along a dirt road for maybe a mile. They stopped at a low-roofed clapboard house, a small crabapple tree in the front yard and flowerpots by the front door.

"Maude!" Chester yelled as they entered.

He pointed to the right, saying, "Bathroom there." Then he pointed to his left, saying "Living room there. Make yourself at home." He moved deeper into the house, toward a kitchen in the back.

Natural wood paneling gave the place a rustic feel, though it had a modern television and some sort of radio set in the corner. A wood stove rested on an inside wall, cut logs stacked on the floor next to it. Photos hung above a couch covered with two thin, gray blankets. One picture showed a young man atop a mountain crest, grinning from ear to ear. Another showed him rafting whitewater waves beneath sandstone cliffs. Others showed someone with a yellow puppy, all soft and fuzzy.

Chloe plopped onto the couch and stretched.

They'd gotten lucky.

"Maude!" Chester yelled again.

A golden retriever scurried into the room, tail wagging her entire back side, wet tongue lolling out, front legs prancing. Chloe sat forward and reached her hands toward the dog, which was all she needed to run full into Chole's arms, licking, huffing, rubbing her head against Chloe's knees.

"Sorry about that." Chester came into the room with two tall glasses of iced tea. "She's a lousy guard dog but great fun to have around."

"This is Maude?" Chloe had assumed that Maude was the man's wife.

"Yeah, just me and Maude out here in the hinterland." He set a drink next to Chloe.

Doc returned from the bathroom and sat on the couch opposite Chloe. Chester gave Doc the other drink and sat in a recliner next to the TV.

"That's an Aeronca, isn't it?" Chester asked.

The question surprised her. "You know your airplanes."

"N411Z." The tail number.

"Right." This guy was pretty observant.

"Very cool little airplane. A friend of mine had a Piper Cub, so I got to know some of the kinds of planes out there. Fun to fly."

"You're not a pilot yourself?"

"Whenever I had the time, I didn't have the money. Whenever I had the money, I didn't have the time." A relaxed smile lifted his beard, brown eyes squinting with goodwill.

"Yeah," Chloe glanced at Doc. "My grandpa taught me, basically, then I took formal lessons that he paid for." She felt the turquoise stone in the necklace he'd given her.

"Lucky girl."

"Yeah." She pictured her parents, gone for years now.

"What brings you to my little patch of the universe? If I'm not prying."

"Well…" How much should she say? "I'm headed to Spokane to see my grandpa. Doc, here, teaches physics at…"

"…Azteca College," Doc interjected.

"…and wanted a ride there, too, and decided to join me."

"Kind of a last-minute thing." Doc rubbed his hands together. "Always wanted to fly in a little airplane."

Doc was a terrible liar, she thought.

Chester looked at Chloe's daypack, then at the empty space at Doc's feet, but he didn't say anything about Doc's missing luggage. Chloe shifted in her seat. Maude turned her back and sat, inviting Chloe to stroke her ears.

"So, you are a student of his?" Chester waved

toward them.

Doc shook his head as Chloe said "Yeah," then they stared at each other.

"It might help you guys to get your stories straight." Chester sat back and crossed his arms, no longer smiling.

CHAPTER 29

"I still can't figure who the young girl is, the pilot." Morozov scratched above his ear.

"Maybe she's a student at the college, or another one of Dochauser's research assistants." Carl spread an aerial map on the bed in Morozov's hotel room. "Or just a pilot Dochauser knows."

"She's awfully young."

"Maybe she's a relative. A niece or something."

They'd leased a Cessna 172 at the airport, but a quickly approaching sunset made a search by air futile until tomorrow morning.

"Look here." Carl pointed to the map. "Assuming they stay out of big traffic airports, here's Kidwell, then Searchlight, then nothing for miles until maybe Jean, which is a little north, just under Vegas airspace. Farther out is Kingston Ranch, which is private, and Sky Ranch. They can't go much farther than that on one tank of gas."

"So, what's the plan?"

Carl shrugged. "I say we take a crisscross pattern

starting here," he touched the map, "then keep heading northwest and land at the four places closest to their route."

"Won't that eat up a lot of our time? Landing and taking off again?"

"Not really. Maybe thirty minutes each time. We won't have to refuel at every place, so we land, flash our FAA credentials, canvas the terminals and anyone we see near the hangars, then take off and hit the next one. It'll take time, sure, but our best bet is to find them on the ground."

"Where we can take care of the issue."

Carl nodded. "And most small airports have a courtesy car, an old clunker they loan for free to pilots who need to run into town or drive a short distance."

"Oh, that's perfect." Morozov's eyes narrowed. "We catch them, toss them in the loaner car, and deposit their bodies in the desert."

"Our best and our worst advantage will be finding witnesses who've seen Dochauser or his pilot. Those same witnesses could also see us dealing with the two of them."

"We'll need more firepower than just this." Morozov patted the Glock in his holster. "I've tried hitting that airplane one bullet at a time but at a distance, it's too fast and too small."

"I've made arrangements with Ivan to pick up a machine pistol for you tomorrow." A machine pistol was capable of fully automatic fire.

"And if we find them not at an airport, but in the air?"

"Then we shoot—disable the plane if we have to—

and force them to land. We'll follow close behind."

Morozov nodded. His patience with Dochauser had run out. The girl's involvement was new, but it gave them fresh leverage to get the quantum component. He imagined shooting the girl in the leg, then the shoulder, then, if need be, in the stomach, escalating as he went. Dochauser would almost certainly give up the attachment to the quantum module.

Ivan had made it clear how important the gadget was. Once they had it, and any information they could squeeze out of Dochauser, there was no more value in keeping him or the girl alive.

CHAPTER 30

"Look. I open my home to you, so I don't expect a pack of lies. You don't have to tell me what you don't want to, it's none of my business, but the least you can do is stick to the truth." Chester looked at each of them in turn.

Chloe stopped rubbing Maude's ears and the dog looked up at her, questioning why. She recalled her earlier thought and quickly revised it. Chester was no jester.

"You're right." Doc leaned forward. "I'm in a bit of trouble and Chloe helped me out, at the last minute. We didn't even know each other before then."

Chester uncrossed his arms and nodded. "Got it. And you really are a physics professor?"

"More on the research and development end, but, yes, I teach a couple of classes, too."

"Anything else you want to correct?" Chester asked.

"No, and you're right. We won't lie to you again. We just might not," Chloe paused, "give you all the gory details. Really, if you ever have to talk to the police, you're better off."

Chester raised a brow.

Doc spoke up. "I'm working on a revolutionary quantum computer that someone has been chasing us to get. Even shooting at us. He killed my lab partner."

Chester's eyes widened.

So much for keeping things quiet. "I guess we can tell you all about it, if you really want to know," Chloe said.

"Feds involved?" Chester asked.

"And a foreign spy, we think." Chloe glanced at Doc.

"Okay, okay." Chester raised his palms. "I believe you guys. I guess you're right. I don't need to know all the bloody details." He wiped his forehead.

"Well, you have the nub of it now anyway," Doc said.

Maude's tail thumped against the floor in a steady beat.

"So," Chester stood, "let's get us some supper."

Doc glanced at Chloe. A sigh left his chest like a deflating balloon.

Chloe resumed massaging Maude's ears and the dog leaned into it for more. She focused on the soft, amber fur, the black nose, tongue dripping sideways out of her mouth, and relaxed like she'd sunken into a feather bed. Dogs just had that effect on her. She found herself whispering to Maude about what a great dog she was, the two of them wrapped in a blanket of mutual admiration.

Later, a hint of tomato and oregano wafted from the kitchen. Chloe's stomach rumbled with anticipation. Chester brought three bowls on a tray, spoons in each, into the living room.

"Thank you." Doc took one.

"Thanks." Chloe took another. It looked like canned SpaghettiOs with crackers crumbled on top but at this point, she'd devour just about anything.

Maude slumped to the floor, content to lay on Chloe's feet, and they ate without speaking. Chester brought Chloe a second helping. When they finished, they each lay back in their seats and rested.

"I didn't realize how hungry I was 'till I smelled food." Doc patted his stomach. "Thank you, again."

Chester nodded. "I'd like to hear more about the physics you research, if that's not a secret or anything."

Doc set his bowl on the table next to him.

"I'm really interested in this black hole, dark matter, and dark energy stuff." Chester said.

Doc cleared his throat. "Well, dark matter is about 27 percent of the universe and dark energy is about 73 percent. Which means that only about 4 percent of the universe is made up of regular matter, like planets, moons, and stars."

"And us," Chester added.

"Right. We think that dark matter consists of weird particles that don't interact with regular matter, or even light. That's why they're invisible. But they have mass, and that mass exerts a gravitational pull, just like normal matter. That pull affects the velocities of stars and other phenomena in the universe, which verifies the existence of this dark matter."

"Then, what's dark energy?" Chester leaned

closer to Doc.

"Dark energy is even weirder. Researchers were trying to calculate how fast the universe was expanding, to see if it would spread out into oblivion or if gravity would eventually pull us all back in on ourselves in a massive 'Big Crunch.' Astronomers predicted either that the universe has been expanding at roughly the same rate or that its expansion has been slowing over time, as energy from the Big Bang dissipates."

Dochauser touched the fingers of his hands together, accentuating his points, the lecturer on a roll.

"They were shocked to find that the universe seems to be accelerating its expansion. All the mass and gravity in the cosmos ought to eventually pull us back into a Big Crunch. But it's not. So, we know there's some other force at work, and it's been called dark energy. But try as we have, we can't detect any of these dark energy particles or dark energy waves. We can't see them, touch them, feel them, but we see their effect. They are real, very real, all around us, but unknowable to us."

"Unknowable," Chester repeated.

"Plus, since the universe is expanding, that implies that dark energy should thin out over time, spread out somewhat with the universe. But we've recently discovered that it doesn't seem to do that at all. Instead, the strength of dark energy seems to remain the same, its effects seem to be a constant. How can that be?"

Doc swallowed a long drink then set his tea back on

the table. "That's sort of a summary, I guess." He shrugged.

"Amazing," Chloe said. "I really need to take one of your classes, Doc."

"Hey, I have something to read to you guys." Chester rose from his chair, went to another room, and returned with a small book.

"What's that?" Chloe moved her foot from under Maude and shook the feeling back into it.

"This is a description of the force behind our existence, behind the entire universe. Let me read it first and have you guess who said it." Chester kept the book cover hidden, flipped through a few well-worn pages, and began to speak: "Look, and it cannot be seen because it is beyond form. Listen, and it cannot be heard because it is beyond sound. Grasp, and it cannot be held because it is intangible. These three natures are indefinable and are joined into one…Stand before it and there is no beginning. Follow it and there is no end." He looked up from the book.

Doc scratched between his eyes. "Einstein? No. Carl Sagan? Michio Kaku?"

Chester looked at Chloe.

"No clue."

"It was written by a Chinese monk 2,500 years ago. Lao Tzu is what he's called, though that was a term of respect and probably not his real name. But he founded Taoism. The ancient Tao is the unseen, the unknown, and the source of all existence. The Tao is the breathing force of creation."

Chloe's eyes widened.

Doc leaned forward. "You're saying that the Tao is dark energy?"

"Or dark matter, or both. They are not truly knowable."

"Doc." Chloe turned toward him, her tone deeply serious. "You've been messing with the breathing force of creation."

"Well, you might be on the edges of it," Chester said.

"Yes," Doc agreed. "And we've nearly unlocked one of its greatest secrets."

CHAPTER 31

Chloe slept next to Maude, under some blankets and on top of an old sleeping bag, and Doc spent the night on the couch, snoring away. Long hours of flying, the stress from knowing she'd stolen the Aeronca and run away from the foster home, the uncertainty about where they would land tomorrow and the day after that, and the day after that—all of it was utterly exhausting. She'd slept like the proverbial log.

Maude yawned, stretched her back, and padded away into the kitchen. Sunlight seeped through cotton curtains, warming the room. Chloe kicked off her covers and slipped quietly into the bathroom. When she returned, she heard Chester clanging dishes and thought about helping him when Doc rose quickly from the cushions, confusion sweeping briefly across his face.

"Oh," he said.

"Morning," Chloe replied. "Bathroom's open." She pointed.

They ate at the kitchen table, a Formica top with gray

and pink "s" patterns, something from the 1960s. The cabinets were light blue. They'd been repainted over the years, chips showing white underneath. The stove was propane, two tanks under the burners. Chickens squawked in the back yard, loosely guarded, she guessed, by Maude. At least the dog wasn't out there wringing their necks.

Denver omelets, toast, and hot coffee buoyed her spirits and filled her belly. After second helpings of toast and jam, she laid her arm over the back of the chair and smiled.

The men finished eating and loaded dirty dishes into the sink. Chloe spread her maps onto the table, measured distances between waypoints, and made notes on the chart and on a small pad of paper.

"All set for the day?" Chester handed her two egg sandwiches.

"Oh, man, thank you again." She refolded her maps. "Yep. We asked about fuel last night. Can we still get about ten gallons from you?"

"Sure."

Doc pulled three twenty-dollar bills from his wallet and handed them to Chester. "It's the least we can do."

"The cans are around back."

"I'll go get them and put them in your truck, okay?" Doc said.

"Sure."

"You'll give us a ride back to the plane?"

"Of course."

Doc left out the back door.

Chester set a roll of black electrical tape next to Chloe's coffee. "You know, if you borrow this from me, you can change your tail numbers from a '1' and a '1' to an 'H.' Just add some tape in between the two numbers." He wore a sideways grin and winked.

"What?" Her muscles froze.

"Maybe even make the 'Z' on the end into an '8'."

Oops. Chester knew that they'd stolen the Aeronca and that they should change the tail number to avoid getting caught. Maybe he'd heard about the BOLO or maybe he was just that intuitive. He had a radio set next to his TV, maybe even a police scanner, and maybe he'd heard it there.

She thought for a moment and realized that his suggestion didn't require an answer. And she knew not to lie to the man. So, instead of a reply, she said, "You've been so nice to us. How can we thank you?"

Chester looked to the ceiling and said, clearly quoting, "The more a man does for others, the more he has."

"Do I already know who said that?" she asked.

A gentle smile spread across his lips.

CHAPTER 32

Chloe and Doc rumbled across the open field and into the smoothness of flight. They'd thanked Chester profusely and shook his hand, twice.

Chloe banked gently to the west and checked her notes. Route 95 should be dead ahead.

Doc seemed much more comfortable in the cockpit, smiling, watching the cottonwoods and open desert roll out beneath them. "Is that the highway?"

"Should be, yes."

"No traffic signs up here to tell you, huh?" he asked.

"Nope. But that's got to be it."

"Interesting man. Chester, I mean."

"Yeah, I really like that guy."

"Say, you haven't said much about your grandfather. What's he like?"

"I'll tell you but then it's your turn, right?"

"Sure."

She checked the instrument panel as they continued to climb. "He's been my rock. After mom and dad died, he kept me from spinning out. Took me camping and to his skeet shooting competitions. He got me focused on flying; taught me how, really. I got an instructor just to make it all proper and legal." She glanced at him, gauging his reaction.

He gave her an ironic smile.

"Anyway, well, what's to say? About six months after they passed, he took me to get a puppy from the shelter. Explained a few things to me."

Doc waited for more.

"How impermanent this world is but also how connected we all are, even after someone we love has passed to the next life. Entangled. Kinda like those quantum particles you like." She flashed him a quick smile. "We took a road trip north, into Colorado, up to Pike's Peak, Montezuma's Castle, Red Rocks. Rented one of those campers with the big paintings on the side. Helped me get my head out of my ass. Well," she shook her head, "still working on that one."

Doc grunted.

"The puppy was mostly black with a white chest. We named him Jeeves because he looked like a butler, you know. One time, he got away from us for a while and when he came back, he had a snoot full of porcupine quills, poor thing. We had to take him to a vet, who put him under and removed the quills." She shook her head. "He stopped chasing varmints after that. Dogs are angels sent down to keep us company, you know." She blinked some extra moisture from her eyes.

"Yeah. I haven't had a dog since I was a kid."

"You could use another one now."

"You're probably right."

"Grandpa was a Navy pilot. Showed me a few maneuvers," she winked. "He was still pretty young after he got out of the Navy and, after the service, he went to an academy and became a detective. He retired from that when my folks passed away."

"Sounds like an interesting guy."

She leveled the plane at 2,000 feet above ground and watched as they crossed over the highway. A line of low mountains rose ahead of them and she began another slow ascent. "Your turn."

"What do you want to know?"

"Whatever you feel like saying."

"I've busted my butt for more than a decade on the problem of quantum stability—what we need to make quantum computing a more valuable, working tool. I disagreed with Belle, my lab assistant, on lots of important aspects: what tests to conduct, what the results could mean, all of that. But dealing with different points of view helped us both, I think. I still can't…" his voice choked.

Chloe understood.

They lapsed into silence for a long while, passing between high points in the McCullough Mountains. They soon flew over a four-lane highway, Interstate 15, that led north into Las Vegas. A few miles beyond, the radio crackled to life, startling her.

"This is LAS. Aircraft on southern edge, please

ident 3440."

"What?" Doc asked.

She thought for a moment then switched the radio from intercom to broadcast mode. "LAS this is Aeronca November four," she omitted the rest of the tail number. No need to help the police find them.

"Aeronca November four, state your full tail number and ident 3440."

"Aeronca has no equipment to squawk. We're south of your airspace, aren't we?"

The Harry Reid Airport at Las Vegas went quiet for a moment and her heart rate accelerated. Finally, LAS said "Aeronca, you have entered LAS airspace."

"Aeronca here, our mistake. Turning south immediately." She banked them hard to the left.

Nearly two minutes passed.

"Roger that, Aeronca, we see you turning south. Have a nice day."

Chloe released a sigh. Doc pointed to the radio, and she switched back to intercom so they could speak just between themselves.

"What happened?"

"Seems I wandered into airspace I shouldn't have, but we're getting out now and they don't seem to care, as long as we stay away."

"They can see us?"

"Yeah, their radar sees us but since we don't have the equipment to broadcast out, they don't know what kind of plane we have or our tail number until we tell them. We're just a blip on the screen that shouldn't be there without their permission."

"I see."

"That's good for a rush, though." She tapped the compass and kept them moving south until they saw a body of water that she thought should be Mesquite Lake, then she aimed them northwest. "Let's not do that again."

CHAPTER 33

Carl throttled back and leveled the Cessna. Morozov watched as they passed the Colorado River and fiddled with the buttons on his shirt. "Where to, again?"

"We need to check out the Searchlight airport first."

The early sun spread shadows over every hump and ridge on the landscape, the desert surreal and desolate. Morozov squirmed in his seat, tight in the small cockpit, anxious to be done with it all.

Carl quickly pushed the left side of his headphones against his ear, listening intently.

"What?" Morozov tucked his feet beneath his seat.

"Shhh."

Morozov waited impatiently.

"Holy shit." Carl turned toward him, broad smile on his lips.

"What?"

"I think I just heard them. On the radio."

Morozov snapped to attention.

"LAS called a plane and asked it to identify itself and

its intentions. The pilot sounded like a woman, maybe the one flying Dochauser. She said they lacked the equipment to enter that airspace and turned south, to get out of it. She said they were Aeronca November four, N-4, but she didn't give the rest of the tail numbers."

"Sounds suspicious."

"Hell, yeah. That's them. It's gotta be. How many Aeroncas are in the air right now, heading northwest, without modern equipment?"

"Plus, a female pilot?"

"Right."

"Can we follow them?" Morozov asked.

"Not directly, but we'll catch up with them. We won't stop at Searchlight anymore." He shook his head. "Now, we know they're on the edge of LAS airspace, correcting their trajectory to the south, probably heading either to Kingston Ranch, which is private, or to Sky Ranch for a refuel. Those two are right next to each other; they won't take long to check. If not there, the farthest they could go would be Calvada Meadows. We're really close."

Morozov's lips formed a slender smile.

"When they get near an airport, they'll announce themselves to local traffic, though maybe without their tail number. Anyone doing that has got to be them."

"So, they announce right before landing? Then we'll know just where they're going to be."

"Hang on to your socks—we're heading straight to Sky Ranch." Carl shoved the throttle all the way in.

CHAPTER 34

"Did you really figure out how to solve the problem? The quantum computing problem?" she asked.

"Yes and no. We figured out how to improve on the modular approach, which is a big step forward, but..."

"Yeah?"

"Something's been bothering me. I think there's another way to go at the problem, but I just can't get there."

"Well, you've got some time to think up here, away from all the distractions in life." She waved at the horizon. "A little altitude is good for the brain."

"Not bad for the rest of me, either." Doc stared out the side window, a faint smile under his mustache. He hadn't shaved in days and a healthy beard was cropping up. But what the man needed most was a clean set of clothes and a toothbrush.

"I think we should stop at Calvada Meadows," she said, "near the town of Pahrump. It's a small airport and we can stretch our legs."

"Fine by me."

"Maybe borrow a courtesy car and go to town and get you some fresh clothes," she added.

"That bad, huh?" He wrinkled his nose.

"That bad." She grinned.

"Sure. I'll even buy lunch."

"We have egg sandwiches, remember?"

"We'll have them later, then."

She nodded and watched as they soared over the dry terrain. Sky Ranch appeared on their right, a sizeable town from the air, but she figured they had enough fuel to reach Calvada. At least, she hoped so. They were making good time, so maybe they had a tail wind this morning. The farther they were from Kingman, the better she felt. Those guys after Doc had no way to track them, and chasing them from the ground would be tough. Unless they'd rented a plane of their own. Still, she and Doc needed a break and more fuel, so Calvada it would be.

They flew on across the landscape, low mountains, flats, scattered roads and ranches along the way. A quilt of upper clouds diffused the desert sun. She watched the fuel gauge drop closer and closer to empty and a knot grew in her stomach. She kept them relatively high, in case she had to make another unscheduled landing.

A snow-capped mountain came slowly into view on their right. She checked her notes—it was most certainly Mount Charleston in the Spring Mountain Range. They needed to fly farther along the range before they turned north because Nellis Air Force Base conducted high speed maneuvers and training missions on the other side of the mountains. They would go around the range, on the western side, and avoid the restricted area marked on the map.

Eventually, Mount Charleston stopped growing larger in their windshield and seemed to slide along their right side. She searched the ground for Calvada and finally found the small strip ahead.

She relaxed a notch and angled directly toward the runway. She pulled back the power and lowered the plane. "Keep an eye out for a windsock."

Doc searched the ground, too. "I see one, but I can't tell if it's moving."

"Yeah, I see it now. Wind must be light." She switched the radio to broadcast and said, "Calvada traffic, Aeronca inbound for runway 15."

She turned into a left-hand flight pattern.

"Helo five miles north of Calvada, local maneuvers," someone announced.

"Aeronca on base for 15. Now on final for 15." Chloe banked the plane in a tight turn and lined up for landing.

Their tires released a quick squeak as they touched down. They taxied back toward the end of the runway, toward a self-service fuel pump and shack with a payphone attached to the outside wall. A chemical outhouse sat nearby. She reached the pumps and shut down the engine, staring at a fuel gauge on empty. She decided not to comment about it to Doc.

They both stepped outside, letting their ears adjust

to the quiet and their bones settle into the absence of vibration. The tarmac absorbed an early afternoon sun and released its heat back into the air in waves. Doc went to the pumps and inserted his credit card while Chloe refilled the fuel. The 15-gallon tank took 14.8 gallons. They each used the outhouse. Chloe stretched her legs and swung her arms to revive her circulation.

"I don't see any courtesy car here." Doc leaned against a shed near the pumps.

"There's a business card taped up for a taxi service. I could call them if you still want to find a place for lunch." A greasy, double-stack hamburger with fresh fries commandeered her imagination.

"I think we could both use a break."

"Looks pretty quiet here, pretty empty. I think we'd be okay to do that," she nodded.

The sound of an airplane droned in the distance, background noise. She dropped a quarter into the old payphone and dialed the number for the taxi service, but it rolled into a voicemail that didn't provide any information about hours of service or when she might call back to reach someone.

"I think we're out of luck here." She hung up the phone.

"So, it's egg sandwiches after all." Doc stretched his arms.

"I've got lots of protein and granola bars."

"Should we get back in the air?"

"Let's do that." She pulled out two snacks and handed one to Doc. "And have the sandwiches later."

They pushed the Aeronca clear of the fuel pumps. Doc settled into the passenger seat and Chloe started the plane then jumped in beside him. They put their headsets on, and she set them to "intercom" so they could speak to each other without broadcasting.

She spun the Aeronca toward the taxiway and rode slowly to the end of the runway. The radio scratched and someone announced: "Cessna on downwind for 15." Chloe stopped the plane and checked the instruments.

"We'll wait for this Cessna to land," she said.

A white and blue Cessna announced it was "on final" to land and passed over, only a couple hundred feet above them. The Cessna wobbled a bit, then landed and taxied off the active runway.

"Earlier, I heard a helicopter out there somewhere, so I better announce what we're doing," she told Doc. She switched the radio to broadcast mode and said: "Calvada traffic, Aeronca departing on 15."

She pushed the throttle forward and they were soon in the air again, banking toward the northern end of the Spring Mountains.

CHAPTER 35

"What about that one?" Morozov pointed to the yellow winged airplane on the taxiway. They hadn't found any leads at any of the other airports today, and the find excited him.

"Maybe," Carl said. "But like I said, yellow is a popular color. It's on lots of small planes, especially tail draggers. Could be anybody but keep an eye on it."

They lined up with runway 15 and dropped lower.

"I think it's an Aeronca," Carl said as they soared over it.

"Go around," Morozov said.

Carl ignored him, pulling the nose higher, setting the wheels down on the tarmac. "Not sure we had enough runway for that," he said, turning them onto the taxiway. "We were already more than half-way down the strip." He announced on the radio that he was clear and turned them toward the Aeronca.

"It's got the red stripe." Morozov pointed.

Their radio squawked: "Calvada traffic, Aeronca departing on 15."

"It's them!" Carl agreed. He sped the Cessna back toward the Aeronca, but the yellow plane rolled forward and was quickly in the air.

"We should refuel before we go after them," Carl said.

"No! We can get them now. Quickly!" Morozov tapped the dashboard.

"They probably refueled here, which means their tank is full. We've got maybe another hour of fuel, which really means only half an hour because we have to get back here before we run dry."

"But they're right there," Morozov pointed, "heading toward the mountains. We could lose them."

"Your choice." Carl nodded.

"Go for it." Morozov raised the machine pistol in the air in a show of confidence.

"Okay. I won't be announcing ourselves on the radio anymore." Carl throttled forward, turned onto the runway, and sped forward. They lost sight of the Aeronca as they took off but found it again once they were in the air.

"They can't see directly behind them." Carl looked at Morozov. "I'll get behind and above them, but then what?"

"What's the best way to force them onto the ground?"

"Let's get them, and us, over some flat terrain. I can fly over and past them and drop down in front of them. We can go twenty or thirty miles an hour faster than them, so they can't catch us, can't run into us," Carl said.

"Scare them into landing?"

"Yes."

"Why not tell them to land, over the radio?"

"Lots of potential listeners out there. We have to be careful what we say."

"Oh, yeah."

"I could line up next to them and you could point to the ground. Show them the gun."

"Or I could just shoot them."

"Don't you want them alive?" Carl asked. "Be careful to hit only the engine, not their flight controls. We want to force them to land, not to crash."

Morozov thought for a moment. "Right. Try your approach first. I'll motion them to land. If that doesn't work, I'll send them some warning shots."

"Yeah, well, be damned sure you don't hit anything on our plane with that thing or we'll all be in deep shit."

CHAPTER 36

Special Agent Johansen had talked to Yazzie's witness and now had a general description of the two men claiming to be FAA inspectors. One wore a dark dress jacket, was average weight and height and looked fit. Light skin, brown hair, probably blue eyes. The other was dark-haired and was either growing a beard or just needed a shave. His first name was Carl. The witness couldn't remember their last names, but of course they could be bogus anyway. Both men were white, probably in their thirties.

He called the Las Vegas tower control, Nellis Air Force Base, Flight Service Station, and a whole series of FAA contacts that each of those places suggested. Finally, he seemed to have found the right official and was told that no one from the FAA was involved in any active search of any missing aircraft. He confirmed the name of the owner of the Aeronca and its tail number.

He reviewed the air map of southern Nevada, made notes about each airport, and called the county sheriffs with jurisdiction over Searchlight, Kidwell, Jean, and Calvada Meadows. He also talked with the municipal police in Boulder City and Pahrump. He'd decided not to call the Civil Air Patrol, at least not for now. The Aeronca was reported missing not because the pilot was thought to be lost or because the plane had made an emergency landing.

Yazzie may have already spoken with the owner, one Peter Burgess, but Johansen thought he ought to circle back and do it again. But Peter had no idea who would have taken his airplane. He didn't suspect any of his three students or anyone else he knew. Johansen took the names of the students and decided to touch base again with Deputy Yazzie.

"Yes?" Yazzie answered the phone himself.

"Agent Johansen here again. I've alerted law enforcement in all the surrounding airports, just so you know, but listen, I just got off the phone with the owner of that Aeronca."

"Peter?"

"Yeah. He has three students right now. Have you spoken to them?"

"No."

"I thought maybe your office could contact them to see if they had any ideas. Maybe they've seen or heard something that could help."

"Sure. Good idea."

"The names are Chloe Rochelle, Robert D'Angelo, and Gina Coyle."

"Got it. Hey, uh…"

"Yeah?" Johansen tapped a pen on his notepad.

"That first name rings a bell, I just can't…"

"…sure…"

"…wait."

Yazzie could be heard sliding and tossing papers across a desk. "Hey! Here it is. Chloe Rochelle is the subject of an Amber Alert."

"What? She's a child?"

"Sixteen years old. Foster home run away."

"Hell, Yazzie, that's gotta be her! She's stolen her flight instructor's airplane!" At least they knew she hadn't been abducted. Or had she? The woman who worked the desk at the Kingman airport terminal said a middle-aged man paid to refuel the Aeronca. Who was he? What was his connection to the girl? Was he flying with her, as her captor?

"Hell, yes, that makes sense," Yazzie's voice rose.

"Do the foster parents know where she might be going?"

"It's not in the materials we have, but I sure as shit need to talk to them," Yazzie said. "And to the social worker."

"Send me the link to that Amber Alert?"

"Of course."

"Keep me posted. And great work."

CHAPTER 37

Chloe flew them north, toward the tip of the Spring Mountains, rising gently as they went. She and Doc ate protein bars and washed them down with water. They eased west of Desert Rock to avoid restricted airspace. They'd fly without clear landmarks for a while then look for Highway 95, which they could follow to the northwest.

She adjusted her heading and leveled out at about 1,500 feet above the ground, settling in for the flight.

"Shit," she yelped as a high-winged airplane soared ahead of them, only a hundred feet above, and dropped directly in their path. Electricity seemed to shoot through her veins, clamping against her lungs, stealing her breath.

"Hell!" Doc yelled, hands above his head in a futile defensive move.

"Shit, shit, shit!" Chloe dove the Aeronca to their right, dropping as she went.

"What the hell?" Doc put a hand to his chest.

"What does this jerk think he's doing?" Chloe gasped. She leveled the wings so she could see the other plane, a white Cessna with a blue stripe on its side.

The Cessna slowed, coming alongside the Aeronca.

Chloe's palms began to sweat, her voice trembling. "This guy's a maniac." She turned away from the other plane again, circling back toward Calvada, but then she lost sight of the Cessna. It was behind them.

She'd dropped 200 feet but kept steady at the lower altitude, afraid to climb for fear the other plane would try that crazy maneuver again.

"What a shithead!" she yelled into the cockpit then switched to broadcast mode and yelled it again. This time, the shithead could hear her.

The Cessna appeared again, slightly ahead and above her, lowering to fly alongside.

Then she saw the passenger. Doc had said his name was Morozov. The one who'd shot at her and Doc back at the college. The one who'd nearly killed her in the air-craft boneyard.

Her hands began to shake.

Morozov pointed down to the ground, again and again, an exaggerated message for her to land. Then he raised a gun of some sort.

These people were absolutely nuts.

"Do as they say, Chloe, do as they say," Doc was pleading. "They want me, not you, just do as they say."

Her mind swirled in confusion, muscles tensed, the plane jerking up, down, left, right, erratic. She had to break out of this spastic, panicked state. She thought of something her grandfather said: never let someone else do your thinking for you. She knew that was how bullies worked. She couldn't let fear corral her into self-defeat. It was the only clear thought in her head.

Doc's fingers were trembling, his face the color of wet sand. He'd seen Morozov kill his friend, his lab partner and now they were here, after him.

How could this happen? Just when they were starting to feel free from it all, safe high in the air above the Nevada desert. How had these people managed to find them?

"Land us, take us down." His voice shuddered.

It was the fear on his face that made up her mind.

She darted directly toward the Cessna, a swallow toward the hawk, dipping below it by mere feet, zipping under and to the other side and out toward the mountains again, dropping toward the ground at a hundred miles an hour.

CHAPTER 38

Chloe spoke into the radio: "Mayday, mayday, Aeronca N411Z is under attack by a white Cessna with a blue stripe, just north of Calvada, mayday, mayday."

Weak static rasped in her ears.

She repeated the mayday call.

The Cessna certainly heard them but did not respond. Morozov was literally maintaining radio silence.

More static, something from a great distance away.

No one had heard her, not even the helicopter they'd heard briefly on the radio back at Calvada. Either the chopper had landed and shut down, or now they were too far away to make contact.

They sped downward again, a roller coaster drop that lifted them from their seats. Doc's hands were on the dashboard, knuckles tensed, his eyes locked and ghostly.

She leveled out 500 feet above the ground, gravity now shoving them deep in their seats, stomachs flattened against their spines. Blunt foothills rose up quickly to meet them, sentinels for peaks that towered thousands of feet above.

The Cessna was faster at level flight and would catch them soon. But Chloe was used to flying low, cresting over hills, dipping into valleys, skimming the desert floor. And the dive was a sprint that should put them ahead. For now.

Rocks and sand and sagebrush blurred beneath them. Stony outcrops stood ragged on upward slopes, bands of crimson pin-striped across the polished surface. She flew beneath the hardened ridge, following the desert floor into an arroyo that took them into the mountain folds.

Doc groaned a kind of slow, worried pain, his face ashen.

Chloe banked to their left, dipping the long wing toward the ground. They were soon between rounded hills, funneling toward a high canyon carved from the mountain rocks. She stayed low, speeding as fast as the old Aeronca would take them. The terrain lifted suddenly, cedars and bushes appearing on the slope, and she followed its contour upward, her wheels barely twenty feet above the trees. The arroyo bent again, this time to their right, and she followed as the drainage narrowed.

Ahead lay a pointed hillock, covered in pines and brush, with leaves that had turned yellow in the autumn sun. She banked left a bit then tugged hard on the yoke, slowing as they rose, struggling against the pull of the earth, the engine straining to keep them in flight. She turned right a bit, taking them in a switchback motion up the rugged hill and the little plane slowed even more, tugging, tugging them sluggishly toward the crest when they broke free, just above the hilltop.

She leveled their ascent, easing the strain on the engine, speeding faster again, but they were caged in now, ridges of impenetrable stone rising around them. She circled above the hillock, gaining altitude, looking for the Cessna, but she couldn't see it.

They spiraled slowly upward into another turn, searching for a pass, a saddle, anything to get over the mountains and to the other side. She saw a crack, a low spot along the ridge, and aimed the nose of the plane there, pulling them higher as she went.

Granite cliffs towered around them, hemming them in, blocking the sun and swelling fast. She aimed for the dip in the rim and tugged hard on the yoke again, watching her speed, holding, holding just short of a deadly stall.

"God, no," Doc blurted.

CHAPTER 39

Chloe ignored him, keeping the Aeronca on the razor edge of flight, closing fast on the rocky terrain, feeling each second pass—one-two, one-two—jaws of rock biting at their tires, stone ramparts rising above the nose of the airplane. They sped straight for the blackened bluffs, a massive stockade, and in one last moment of mad impossibility, they topped the rim and were suddenly high above a shadowed valley that dropped into the horizon.

She could feel herself breathe again.

She lowered the nose of the Aeronca, speeding down a narrow gorge, sliding the controls to keep them below the rim, curving, yawing with each bend in the canyon walls.

She looked at Doc. He swallowed hard and stared back at her, crooking an eyebrow.

They stayed as low as they could, banking toward the cliffs as the canyon grew wider. Ahead lay desert again, flat like a dry lakebed, dotted with cacti and sage. She turned farther right, keeping to the far edge of the gorge. When they reached the rock wall, she banked hard left, pirouetting toward the open flat, and lined up for landing. The Aeronca bounced hard against the baked sand but quickly rolled to a stop. She powered up again, taking them into a stand of brush at the base of the canyon. She spun them around, dust blowing like a storm, then she quickly stopped and shut down the engine.

They each took a cool, deep drink of air.

Then Chloe was out the door, pulling the plane, Doc still inside. She tucked the tail into the brush as carefully as she could then pulled branches off, collecting them in her arms.

Doc rolled out the door and onto the ground, his legs limp and nearly useless. He leaned against the tire on his side of the airplane and retched into the sand.

Chloe tossed branches atop the plane, hoping the yellow wings would blend with the autumn leaves. She stacked more branches across the windshield to keep it from glaring in the sun.

Doc slowly lifted himself from the ground and hobbled a few feet away.

Chloe pulled the boxcutter from her pocket, the one she'd gotten to release Doc at the hangar, and she cut more switches, placing them along the fuselage and over the black tires. She looked above them for any sign of the Cessna.

"What the hell?" Doc said, his breath ragged.

Chloe shrugged.

"At first, I thought we were going to die." He walked closer to her and sat on rock. "Then I was afraid we were not going to die, that the torture would never stop."

"Sorry about that. I'm pretty queasy myself. But I figured it was our only chance—stay below the horizon and duck over the mountains."

"Did it work? Have you seen them?"

"So far, it worked." She cut more brush and kept adding it to the wings.

"Damn, that was some flying." He wiped his mouth with his sleeve.

"So, do I fly like a teenager or a 30-year-old?" She grinned.

"Like a wild-eyed, drunken teenager." He nodded. "No doubt about it."

She laughed and stood next to him, utterly exhausted.

The sound of an airplane engine rumbled over the mountain top.

CHAPTER 40

Chloe watched and listened as a high-winged plane soared across the mountains, thousands of feet above them. Though it was too far to see it clearly, it had the distinct sound of a Cessna.

She steadied herself, staring at the dot in the sky.

Doc wobbled next to her.

The plane circled north of them then began to fly back over the peaks. In minutes, the sound of its engine faded away.

Her legs lost their strength and she plopped into the dirt next to Doc. "They're gone."

"Thank god."

She lay back and stared into the empty sky.

"I can't do that ever again," Doc mumbled. "Never again."

The thought of it all, the release of stress, the feel of solid earth beneath her made her laugh.

"What about this is funny?" he asked.

"You. Me. All of it."

They rested for quite a while, reliving their flight over ragged slopes and the sharpened spears of bristlecone pine.

"Well, what now?" Doc asked.

"You're asking me?" She closed her eyes. "I'm the teenager here."

"You're not allowed to just switch that on and off, you know."

"Why not?"

They looked at each other and broke out in chuckles.

"I guess we're stuck here now." Doc had become serious again.

"We're safe here." She rose up on one elbow. "Remember, I've got camping gear, food, and water. We can share."

"Oh?"

"I have a sleeping bag, and you can have it. I can sleep in my winter coat."

Doc rested his head in his hands. "What a mess I've gotten you into."

"Hey, we're okay now. But I'm starving."

"There's that teenager again."

"I'm eating that egg sandwich now. I have a small camp stove and ramen noodles we can have later."

"Have my sandwich, too, if you want it. I'm not going to be eating any time soon."

"Thanks, I will."

Chloe stood and emptied the Aeronca of her gear: a palm-sized stove, plastic mug, and sleeping bag. She carried them to a spot about fifty feet from the plane, at the base of a boulder, and set up camp. Then she settled into a spot on the ground and ate both egg sandwiches and washed them down with warm, bottled water.

Doc eventually began to move, wandering around the bottom of the arroyo and ending up across from her and the little stove. She made him a cup of noodles, which he ate with a kind of slow reverence, the final meal of a condemned man. She gathered driftwood from the dry stream bed and stacked it for a fire later.

They'd landed on the northeastern side of the Spring Mountains and were already in shadow. The sky warmed to an orange glow along the ridges above them, the deep black of space seeping into the night sky. The Cessna would not try to find them until morning. She and Doc would have to decide their best plan for tomorrow.

Their chase through the canyons had become a game of cat and mouse.

CHAPTER 41

The soulful wail of a lone coyote echoed up the arroyo. Doc huddled closer to the small fire.

Chloe took a flashlight, boxcutter, and the black electrical tape that Chester had "loaned" her. She went to the Aeronca and aimed the light on the side of the plane. Chester had had a great idea. She stared at it for a while, calculating what she needed to do. Carefully slicing the tape, she laid four strips horizontally between the "1" and the "1," converting it to an "H." She stepped back and checked her work.

Very good.

She moved to the "Z" and cut three strips, placing them diagonally on the letter so it looked like a flattened "8." Then she carved pieces with rounded sides and added them to the tops and bottoms of the letter, smoothing its appearance until she was satisfied.

Then she repeated the process on the other side of the fuselage.

She made a final check with the flashlight and returned to the fire.

"Feeling any better?" she asked Doc.

"I think my head's been in a blender."

"Here." She rummaged through her pack. "Aspirin."

"Thank god."

Chloe unrolled her sleeping bag and handed it to Doc, who removed his shoes, slipped inside, and slid it up to his waist. She handed him another granola bar.

"How will you stay warm?"

She'd pulled a sweater and a winter coat from the Aeronca. "I brought a heavy coat for the colder weather in Spokane."

"Good thing you did."

"What do you want to do tomorrow?" she asked.

He stayed quiet for a moment, watching flames curl through the dry driftwood. "My body has had enough, really. I'm sore in places I didn't know I had, my stomach aches, my head aches…"

She stirred the fire with a stick, flecks of red-hot ash spiraling into space.

"You saved me—and us—again today. That flying was crazy, but it worked. You're a hell of a pilot. I just don't know how much more I can take. I'm thinking you should drop me at the next place with a phone. I'll call 9-1-1 and get myself into protective custody."

"My grandpa can help us. Like I said, he's a retired detective. He's smart and tough."

"You know, Chloe, now that I know you've stolen

the Aeronca and run away from a foster home, I could be charged as an accessory. I'm the so-called adult in this equation."

"Shit."

"Hey, I'm not saying I agree with that. But the police could see it that way. And listen, I'll give you my credit card, to help you pay for gas…"

"…you think that's what I want?"

"…no, I…"

"Hell, Doc, I have money." She straightened her back, pride filling her lungs. "I've saved up for months."

"But aviation gas is what—six or seven dollars a gallon? You're welcome to use my card. Let's make sure you have enough to get to your grandfather's place."

"That's not why I want you around, you know." She turned her back to him.

"Chloe, I didn't mean to insult you. You've helped me so much I just want to repay you for some of it."

"By leaving me?" She'd heard the desperation in her words, the low whine, and regretted them as soon as she'd said them. She kept her face turned away, angry at him, angry at herself for being so tired, so suddenly needy, feeling all of it at once. She felt the necklace under her sweater. Tears dripped from her cheeks. "For a professor, you can be so totally, god-awful stupid."

CHAPTER 42

When they'd lost track of the Aeronca, Morozov and Carl flew on to Pahrump, Nevada, where they'd taken a taxi to a hotel for the night. The next morning, before sunup, they returned to the airport. Carl was outside, refueling the Cessna under halogen lights and doing his pre-flight check. Morozov wandered the empty terminal, shuffling along the carpet, examining photos of famous aircraft along the walls. They planned to be in the air and close to the mountains by sunrise. If Doc's pilot used their aircraft lights as required, they would be easy to spot. Even without their lights on, the early sun would cast long shadows that ought to make them easier to find. Carl figured that Doc would get back onto his northwest course, so he'd mapped a route that would probably intercept him.

Carl came back into the terminal. "Let's hit the head then get in the air."

Morozov nodded. They turned back toward the men's room when the main doors opened wide and a deputy sheriff strode in, adjusting his utility belt as he walked.

The man's belly hung forward, his uniform stretched at the waist. His face seemed freshly scrubbed, but his eyelids drooped like he'd just rolled out of bed. His right hand was on the grip of his pistol, his left hand on his belt, both elbows poking outward and ready to move.

"Mornin'." The deputy's tepid smile didn't reach his eyes.

"Good morning, officer." Carl stopped.

Morozov slid to Carl's side.

"Flying this morning?"

"Yeah." Carl sounded friendly, relaxed. He pointed behind him. "Just fueled up."

"Where you guys headed?"

"Sulfur Springs."

The deputy nodded, his eyes checking the empty room. "Bud here yet?"

"The manager? Met him yesterday but haven't seen him yet this morning." Carl glanced at the customer countertop, a coffee maker, cups, and microwave behind it.

"Right." The deputy squinted at Morozov, some hint of suspicion in his voice. "Your names?"

"I'm Carl Curtis." He pointed at Morozov. "This is my pal, Bobby Morozov."

Morozov tried to smile. Nobody ever called him "Bobby."

"Who's the pilot?"

"I am." Carl raised a finger.

"Well, I'm looking for a missing Aeronca."

"Missing?" Carl wrinkled his nose.

"You guys seen one around here?"

Carl looked to the ceiling, pretending to ponder the question. "No, I don't think so. Missing?"

"Yeah, doesn't happen very often, that's for sure." The deputy stepped closer. "You look familiar to me somehow," he said to Morozov.

"I can't imagine why."

"You seen an Aeronca around here?"

"Deputy, I'm not a pilot. I assume an Aeronca is a type of airplane, but I wouldn't know one if it hit me on the head."

"Yeah." The deputy sounded disappointed and shifted his gaze to the countertop.

Morozov slid his hand beneath his jacket, fingers on the butt of his hidden pistol. Carl sucked on his teeth and made a barely perceptible shake of his head. But Morozov knew the deputy could pull his gun in a flash.

"You guys aren't with the FAA, are you?"

"No," Carl said, some surprise in his voice.

The pilot had an easy style and a quick mind, Morozov thought. Showing their fake FAA papers to the deputy could become problematic really fast; a quick call to the feds and they'd be toast.

"Seen anyone from the FAA on your trip?"

"No." Carl glanced at Morozov. "Why?"

"We're coordinating with them, is all. You up to date on all your equipment? Radio? Navigation, all of that?"

Morozov wrapped his fingers around his gun, keeping them out of view.

"Yes, sir." Carl stepped closer to Morozov, ready to block his arm.

"Good. We'd ask that if you see that Aeronca, you call the flight service station and report it."

"Of course, officer. What color is it?"

"Yellow with a red stripe."

"Got it. Will do, officer, no problem."

"Well, then, have a safe flight." The deputy put his arms down by his side and turned away.

Morozov backed his hand from his holster and took a step toward the door to the runway.

CHAPTER 43

She seemed to be sitting on a couch in her grandfather's house, sounds of a chainsaw outside the door, when a wall of books began falling into her lap, one by one, piling high but not hurting her at all, until something pulled her from her dreams and into a ball of hat, coat, and mittens, curled up by a burned-out campfire. Across the way, Doc snored deep within the sleeping bag like a troll with sinus problems. Warm-shaded sepia filtered through bushes and between scattered rocks, painting the sand with shadows.

Yikes. The sun was already up. She'd overslept.

She rolled onto her back and allowed herself some time to wake more slowly. They'd missed the opportunity to take off before dawn, so there was no longer a rush.

A high-pitched beat of pistons reached across the quiet air, soaring to the north. She couldn't see the airplane yet, but it had to be the Cessna. Out before dawn. Maybe oversleeping would turn out to be a good thing.

She checked to make sure the fire was not smoking then took a long drink of water. May as well sit here for a while, listening to Doc snore in blissful ignorance.

She finally spotted the Cessna, a tiny dot circling several miles north, then again farther east, over the desert. They were searching in the wrong spot, she realized, one deep canyon away from her and Doc. The engine faded to a meager beat, and she lost sight of the plane. She stood and hopped up and down, warming herself, then went to the Aeronca and gathered her map and notes. She returned to the makeshift camp and sat in the dust, spreading the map on the ground.

Doc continued to saw trees in his sleep.

She ran her finger across one of two potential routes they'd need to fly next.

That is, if there was a "they" anymore. Doc said he wanted to be deposited at the next airport with services. She'd miss the old bastard. She realized that her reaction last night was born of her own desire for company, nothing Doc had done wrong. In fact, he really had helped her. She didn't have a credit card, so she needed airports with a terminal, a fuel depot manned with people. Self-serve kiosks seemed to be common at the smaller airports but were of no help to her.

The sound of the Cessna had faded away completely.

Doc stirred in the sleeping bag, a caterpillar squirming to break free. A tangled head of hair, left cheek red and misshapen, popped from the bag. No butterfly here, she smiled.

He grumbled his way through the zipper and ran off

to relieve his bladder. When he returned, he'd combed his hair somewhat and straightened his clothes. He sat by the ashes and stared into them.

"You okay?" she asked.

"Stiff as a board."

She handed him two aspirins and a water bottle.

"About last night," he began.

"It's okay. We'll head out this morning and find a good spot to drop you off."

He clicked his tongue. "I've changed my mind."

"Oh?"

"I'd like to meet that grandfather of yours. If you'll still have me as a passenger."

"What changed since last night?" She leaned toward him.

"I thought a lot about it after we talked. Honestly, you've kept us safe since I ran away from that lunatic at the college. I need help from federal authorities, don't get me wrong. But I'd rather we get our stories straight and both go to them, together."

"Maybe with grandpa along for the ride?"

"You said he was retired police?"

"Detective." She nodded. "After he retired from the Navy. He'll know how to help us both."

"Right."

"Are you really sure? I mean..." she glanced at her shoes, "...sometimes I'm not so sure I can really do this, you know?"

"Chloe," Doc looked her in the eye. "I have a feeling there's nothing you can't do, once you put your mind to it."

Her cheeks grew warm. "Well…"

"Then, let's call that a plan. Just, no more roller coaster flights."

She tensed her brow. "Hey, no promises."

He groaned.

"Continental breakfast?" She grinned, lifting a granola bar.

CHAPTER 44

Yazzie parked in the lot behind a stout, brick building with the words social Services painted on the door and went inside.

He'd taken Route 95/60 to the Phoenix outer belt, then Interstate 10 west, then south to find the small town where Chloe Rochelle lived. Special Agent Johansen was closer but had to appear before a grand jury that week in another case, so Yazzie had volunteered to talk with Mrs. Koel, Chloe's social worker. The sheriff had called some of his old contacts, who'd said Koel was a "long-termer," one of the few social workers who'd lasted more than twenty years, now ready to retire. Old school, according to the sheriff's source.

"I'm looking for Mrs. Koel." Yazzie straightened his tie.

"Go on in, deputy. The conference room is around the corner, and she'll be right in."

"Thank you." A faux wood table centered the room, its surface scratched, edges chipped. The walls were plastered with children's artwork: coloring book figures with greens, blues, pinks, all outside the lines. Hobbit-sized houses and plastic kitchenettes lined the far wall. A first aid kit hung where only an adult could reach it.

"Yes, good morning." Koel entered, coffee mug in hand.

"Good morning. Thanks for your time today." Yazzie took a seat at the table.

"You want to talk about Chloe Rochelle." She sat across from him, all business, a compact woman in her early sixties, he'd guess, short-cropped gray hair, brown eyes pinched in mild pain, like her shoes were too tight. Maybe they were. She wore a white blouse and tan pants, her only jewelry a wedding ring and a simple turquoise necklace.

"Yes, ma'am. There's an Amber Alert out on Chloe—"

"I issued it…"

"…and we'd like to get a little more information."

"You're from up in Kingman?"

"Yes, ma'am."

"You found her up there?"

"No, we're still looking."

She huffed.

"We think she may have stolen an airplane."

Koel's eyes widened for a second and she shook her head. "That girl…"

"What can you tell me about her?"

"She's a real piece of work, let me tell you." Koel placed her weathered hands on the table, fingers interlocked. "She's brash, rude, crude, resistant to her foster parents, rebellious at school, and totally irresponsible. And a sneaky little vixen."

Yazzie stiffened.

"Well, it's true," Koel continued. "She's completely unfocused. I've tried to get her into church or sports or after-school activities. We—me and the foster parents—agreed that she needs to delay this flying nonsense. It's just not safe, you know. Until her grades get back up. It's not that she can't do well in school. I suspect she's quite bright. But she's been working evenings at a diner down the road, lying to her foster parents about where she was, doing odd jobs around town. God only knows what she's doing with her money."

"Well..."

"Drugs. That's what it always is. Drugs."

"Actually, we think she's been paying a flight instructor."

Koel straightened her back. "Oh. Oh my god, she's been warned about that!"

"She's been banned from flying?"

Koel squeezed her fingers against themselves, lips clamped. "Absolutely. She has to get her grades up first and even then, well, it's just not safe."

"She has to get her grades up but then if she does, she's still not allowed to fly?"

"That's right, deputy. I completely agree with the foster parents about this."

Yazzie thought for a moment. Contrary to Koel's assessment, Chloe seemed rather well focused. But the social worker was standing squarely in her path. "We're interested in where she might go, Mrs. Koel, now that she's out of the area. And in an airplane."

Koel pursed her lips, a blend of frustration and distaste.

"Does she have any friends or family out of the area? Anyone she might run to for help?"

She blew a quick sigh. "A grandfather in Spokane. The girl's parents died when she was younger, and the grandfather moved down here to care for her. But then he had a stroke when he was on a trip back to his own home in Spokane, so we had to place Chloe here. This is not the first foster home she's run away from."

"I see. And is the grandfather still alive?"

"Yes. He's asked to have Chloe sent up to Spokane. I guess he's in physical therapy and all that, but he's close to ninety and I don't think he can handle a live-wire teenage girl anymore."

"So, he's recovering up there?"

"We believe so."

"But he's not eligible to have custody returned to him?"

"You think a ninety-year-old stroke victim can handle that heathen?" Her left brow rose, a dark comma above her eye.

"Hmm. Well, I'll need the grandfather's name and contact information, if you would. She may well be headed there."

"Of course, deputy."

CHAPTER 45

Carl and Morozov landed in Sulfur Springs, a little burg northeast of Beatty, Nevada, the Gateway to Death Valley. Carl refueled then borrowed a courtesy car to go into town for sandwiches and candy bars.

The day before had been frustrating, to say the least. Carl couldn't stop talking about how low the Aeronca had flown, disappearing behind the walls of a side canyon, barely skimming over the rim. He was amazed they hadn't exploded against the rocky gorge. He'd had a glimpse as the plane topped the mountains, but by then they were too far away to catch it. Carl had to turn back to Calvada for fuel, and when they'd landed it was dusk, so they'd gone into town to spend the night.

This morning, they'd flown in circles over the area and found nothing but rocks and brush. If the Aeronca had landed, they couldn't imagine where. Maybe the pilot with Doc had kept going, circled back to the northwest. Or maybe they'd landed last night and left before sunup this morning. Who knew?

Damn it.

Carl pulled back in through the gate and parked by the small terminal. "Let's get going." He tossed a wrapped sandwich to Morozov.

"Where to?"

"I want to fly back to Beatty, make sure they didn't land there, then circle back to Sulfur Springs and around this area."

"How long will that take?"

"Not sure. Maybe two hours."

"If you're still going to be near here, why don't you let me stay on the ground in case they land here."

Carl frowned. "Better if we stay together."

"But if you start in a wide circle and then narrow in, you'll be close to Sulfur Springs when you're done, and you can pick me up. In case they fly in while you're west of here or someplace."

"Hmm."

"We can stay in touch by cell phone, right?"

"You might have to shout at me over the engine noise."

"If you really need to follow them in the air, call me and I'll rent a car and meet you at the next place--wherever you think they're going."

"That could work."

"I need to check in with Ivan anyway. I'll find a spot where I can watch the fuel pumps. If they stop here, they'll refuel for sure, won't they?"

"Yes, for sure."

"Then I'll be in a good position to catch them. So, how about it?"

Carl reached into his pocket. "Here's some small binoculars for you. Found them at the convenience store. You may as well use them here on the ground."

"Perfect. I can sit near the terminal and watch for them. And I can ask around, find out if anyone's seen them."

Carl nodded. "See you in a couple of hours, then. If either of us see them, call."

Morozov sat at a picnic table under a boxelder tree, about thirty yards from the terminal. He popped a few pumpkin seeds in his mouth and watched Carl do his pre-flight check. Ivan was going to chew him out for losing track of Dochauser. Or worse. But he'd had three messages from the man, so he had to call him. He spit the shells into the dirt and ground the seeds with his molars, reviewing his options but finding no new ones. He swallowed and dialed.

"Morozov." Ivan's voice ground like boots on gravel. "Speak."

Morozov reviewed recent events, trying to sound hopeful but falling flat. The Cessna roared at full throttle, sped down the narrow runway, and lifted off. "Carl's back in the air again, doing another search pattern. They can't have gone far."

"You know that I have sources everywhere."

"Yes…"

"Including law enforcement."

What was Ivan getting at?

"We have a new lead. It seems that the young pilot has a grandfather in Spokane. As a runaway, that's the most likely place for her to go."

"Oh!"

"I will text the man's name and address to you. Find the nearest airport and either cut off Doc and the girl or beat them to Spokane and wait for them."

"Brilliant, Ivan. Sir."

"Of course."

"We should be on our way in less than thirty minutes."

"Keep me posted, Morozov, and don't ignore my messages."

"Never, sir, it's just that we've been in the air."

"Your phone works just fine there, too."

"Yes, sir."

"Tell me when you see them along the way or when you arrive in Spokane." Ivan ended the call.

He wondered what sources Ivan had with the police; the man had tentacles everywhere. But those sources had just saved them the time and aggravation of more aimless searching.

Carl had explained that a giant swath of restricted airspace lay just north of Las Vegas. Doc was generally going north but would have to choose between heading east or heading west of the restricted space. That or be escorted to the ground by the U.S. Air Force.

In case Dochauser had gone west, it was prudent to search this area around Sulfur Springs. But if they didn't find them, Carl could pick an intercept course north of the restricted airspace, then keep going all the way to Spokane.

They could beat the old Aeronca around the military airspace and plot which places Dochauser might have to stop for fuel. There were only a few options along the remote mountains and deserts. And if that didn't work, they could get to the grandfather's place, maybe grab a hostage, and wait. Morozov's mouth rose in a lop-sided grin.

Time to call Carl.

Time to plan a fresh ambush.

CHAPTER 46

Sunlight stabbed sideways through the cockpit, glaring in Doc's eyes until they settled on their course. Chloe raised her left wing, searching for any sign of other aircraft, then repeated the process on her right. The morning sky was empty, ocean blue above the copper hills and dusty flats.

They flew directly west until she spotted Highway 95, then followed it past restricted air space. She'd read about the infamous Homey Field and Groom Lake, north of them. Waterless, Groom Lake was a large salt field used by the air force for experimental aircraft and weapons testing. Best known as Area 51, the region was famous for intense federal secrecy and alleged alien activities. The airport identifier was KXTA—some joked that it was the abbreviation for "extra-terrestrial." If they could only get close enough, maybe they could beam themselves directly to Spokane.

In addition to Area 51, other sections north of Las Vegas were MOA, military operation areas, and highly restricted airspace. Chloe had to decide whether to go west or east of the region. She'd decided to go west, past Desert

Rock and toward the airport at Sulfur Springs. She hoped the Cessna chasing them would go east, toward Lake Mead and the airport at Mesquite, but her chances were no better than even.

She took them first to Beatty, a small, neat field on the edge of Death Valley. They flew low to the ground, checking the airport for any sign of a white Cessna with a blue stripe. Seven planes were tied down at Beatty, none of them Cessnas. She checked her fuel and decided they could easily reach Sulfur Springs, a small town northeast of there.

The radio crackled and a Cessna announced its departure from Sulfur Springs. Her stomach tensed.

"What?" Doc asked over the intercom.

"A Cessna at Sulfur Springs just took off."

"Morozov?"

"No way to tell. They're plenty of Cessnas around."

"If he just took off, maybe he's leaving the area," Doc said. "Maybe that's a good thing."

"True. We'll stay low and head on in. We need to refuel."

They heard no other radio communication from the Cessna pilot or anyone else. When they reached Sulfur Springs, she flew over the field, searching for Morozov's plane. Seeing no obvious trouble, Chloe lined up for a landing and rolled gently to a fuel pump on the southern end of the runway. She shut down the engine and they sat for a moment, adjusting to life on land. She pulled her hair into a ponytail and tucked it under her shirt. Doc ran his fingers through his hair, to no real effect.

"I see an old Chevy over there." Chloe pointed to one side of the terminal. "Most little places have courtesy cars, keys in the ignition. It's an honor system and you're welcome to take it for short trips to town. We need some supplies. Maybe you can even find a clothing store."

"Or an RV campground, where I could get a shower."

"Better yet." She grinned.

They slid out of the plane and closed the doors.

"You want to go first?" Doc asked. "I can watch the plane 'till you get back."

"I don't have a driver's license."

His brows rose, chin dropped, and a look passed between them. "You're kidding." A moment later, a smile split his face, a sunbeam burst through the clouds, and laughter rolled from his belly.

"Well," she kicked the pavement with her foot, a guilty smile on her lips.

"Okay, then, I'll take the car into town. What about you?"

"I want to borrow their computer, if they have one. I need a better idea about the weather that's ahead of us."

"Want some food?"

She tilted her head down and looked at him under her brow.

"Sorry. Stupid question. I'll bring us something."

"See you in, say, an hour?"

"Two at the most."

Doc walked to the courtesy car while Chloe refilled the tank with one of his credit cards. Then she pushed the Aeronca to a parking spot for planes and tied it down, securing the wings to hooks anchored in the pavement.

She grabbed her daypack and strolled to the terminal. Big glass double doors faced the taxiway, and a side entrance faced the fuel pump. Inside, a large room waited for weary travelers. A faux leather couch faced the glass doors. A coffee table full of old flying magazines littered the top. Dust motes floated in the air, stale and quiet. Restrooms were down a hallway to the right and, beyond them, an office with an open door. She went to the office, which was as empty and stale as the main room. Taped to the door was the password for an old computer, which sat on a desk. She closed the door behind her and turned on the computer, waited for it to warm up, then typed in the code. Weather sites appeared on the screen, so she began searching for forecasts in areas north of Sulfur Springs. She found a flight planning program and used that to chart a path toward her grandfather, measuring distances, plotting options, and making notes along the way.

A time-worn, landline telephone, boxy and baby blue, sat next to the computer and she stared at it for a while, wondering whether to make a call. She had purposely kept her grandfather in the dark about her trip. Her foster parents had taken her cell phone and Doc had lost his. She could use the phone now, though she might have to call grandfather "collect," the old-fashioned way.

Or she could wait until she was closer to home. She didn't want him to worry or get in trouble for what she was doing. The less he knew about it the better, at least until the last minute. Maybe she wouldn't have to call him at all. He had twenty acres south of Spokane and she was pretty sure she could land there, if she could find it from the air, and surprise the hell out of him.

Then they could talk about all of it and figure out what to do next, how to make sure Mrs. Koel or the other social workers never separated the two of them again. She smiled at the thought. And get some sort of federal protection for Doc.

After a few moments, she decided. Best to wait for now.

CHAPTER 47

Morozov unwrapped his sandwich and settled in for an early lunch. He decided to eat something before he called Carl with the news about Spokane. They had some time to spare, and he could use a break from the cramped Cessna. Flying with Carl required rising before the sun and flying for hours before a rest. Noon seemed to be much later in the day than it really was, but he'd learned that the air was often smoother in the morning than the afternoon. Better to fly early. By three o'clock, though, he was ready for a nap. Hell, he could take one now.

A yellow plane floated quietly toward the runway, the sound of its engine so low he almost missed it. It glided gently to the ground, landing with a squeak of its tires. He watched as it taxied to the fuel pump.

Yellow with a red stripe!

Was it an Aeronca? How could he tell?

He put the binoculars to his eyes. A woman exited the plane, her build familiar to him, but her hair seemed to be cropped short at the neckline. The teenager he'd seen piloting the Aeronca had much longer hair. A passenger exited the far side, but he couldn't see him very well. He set down the binoculars and dialed Carl.

"Hey, I've got a yellow and red airplane down here. A tail dragger as you call them."

"Yeah?" Carl shouted.

"How do I tell if it's an Aeronca?"

"There are lots of yellow airplanes around. It could be an Aeronca or a Cub, or a Super Cub, or a homebuilt."

"So, should I check it out?"

"Check the tail number. Can you see it?"

"Yeah."

"That will tell you for sure. You won't have to guess. What is it?"

He lifted the binoculars again. "N4H8."

"It's not them. They're N411Z, remember?"

"The N4 matches..."

"All private planes in North America start their tail letters with the 'N'."

"Oh. Damn it."

"Sorry."

"Any luck in the air?"

"Nothing. I'm over Beatty now, so I'll be another hour or so."

"Maybe I'll take a nap."

"Whatever."

"Ivan says hi."

"Oh? Is he pissed?"

"Oh, yeah. But he found out the girl—the pilot—has a grandfather in Spokane. She's a foster care runaway, so the cops think they're headed there."

"Shit, man, that's huge. If we don't find them in this area, that means they may have taken the eastern route around the military air space. But we can head north from here and catch up with them."

"Or meet them in Spokane."

"Right."

"I'm still going to go check out that airplane, maybe chat up the people flying it. Use those FAA credentials. Maybe they've seen something."

"Yeah, you may as well. I'll speed up my search and see you in a bit."

"You bet."

CHAPTER 48

Morozov checked inside the terminal, but it was as empty as a church on Monday. A hallway near the restrooms led to what looked like an office door, but it was closed. No one home. Where had the pilot and passenger gone? The yellow plane was tied down, so maybe they lived near here. Maybe they'd gone home or into town for a visit. He popped a few pumpkin seeds in his mouth and watched the quiet airstrip through the front doorway.

He shrugged and walked back outside to the shaded picnic table to wait.

****

Doc had hit the jackpot. Sulfur Springs had a "re-peat" store full of used clothing, clean pants, fresh shirts, even new underwear, still in its packages. He grabbed a plastic bucket and added what he liked, including a wide-brimmed hat and a forest green fleece jacket with yellow stripes on the collar and wrists. He found toothbrushes and paste, combs, nail clippers, bars of soap, and straight razors for shaving. He asked the clerk about campgrounds and was told the Sleeping Stones was a mile south of town.

He paid the campground ten bucks to use their showers, which had shampoo and liquid soap dispensers and clean towels. He luxuriated under hot water, scrubbing, rinsing, washing again, until all the dust and grime he'd accumulated had finally swirled and flushed down the drain.

He put on a fresh, button-up shirt with blue and gold stripes and a comfortable pair of jeans. He transferred his wallet, keys, and cash to his new pants. He reached inside his old, blue jacket and lifted the modular component that fit on the prototype quantum processor. He held it in his hands for a moment, staring at its unusual shape and the prongs that would connect it to the processor, the gadget that could revolutionize quantum computing.

And get him and Chloe shot.

He slid the component into the pocket of his new green fleece and put it on. When he finished dressing, he stuffed his old slacks, shirt, and jacket into a nearby trash can. He brushed his teeth, shaved his days-old beard, and trimmed his mustache, no longer the errant whiskers of an old sea lion.

He felt ten years younger. And suddenly very hungry.

Doc rode back into the small town and stopped at a gas station. He filled the tank on the courtesy car, his way of repaying the anonymous favor. The station had a well-stocked convenience store inside and, in the corner, an

ATM. Something about the kiosk got him thinking about the use of his credit card for fuel. Could Morozov track his purchases? He'd heard it was easy, if you knew how to hack a computer system. If Morozov had ties to the Russian FSB, he might have someone to help him do that. Was he over-thinking it? What if he got cash from the ATM and bought a pre-paid credit card with it? If his purchases could be tracked, the trail would end here. In the future, Chloe could use the pre-paid card for fuel and no one could track it.

He used the ATM and bought a $750 pre-paid card. He went back to the shelves and picked up several wrapped sandwiches, bottles of iced tea, and even a pint of whiskey. Just in case.

He drove up the small plateau to the airport, enjoying the simple act of driving again. He pulled into the same parking space where the car had been parked earlier, left the keys in the ignition, and grabbed his bag of supplies. His feet crunched over fresh pumpkin seed shells. As he reached the side door of the airport terminal, Chloe popped through, pack on her shoulder.

"Doc! Is that you?"

He smiled and spun around, touching his hat with his fingers, a mock display of modelling perfection. "And you'll be happy to know I have lots of food." He lifted his bag in the air.

"Perfect. I'm ready if you are."

"Let's hit it."

"You're in a good mood now."

"Amazing what a shower and a shave can do."

They strode across the tarmac to the Aeronca. Doc and Chloe placed their bags in the back and Doc helped her untie the wings from the ground anchors. She placed a pair of blocks on the left wheel, set the magnetos and throttle, and moved to the propeller. Doc buckled in and put his hands in his lap, a bubble of optimism and fresh energy.

Someone was walking toward them from a picnic table on the other side of the terminal, someone too far away to see clearly, but still vaguely familiar.

The air left his lungs. Could it be?

Chloe pulled the propeller down and the pistons clunked twice but did not ignite.

His skin began to tingle.

She yanked again, falling to the ground, and this time the engine popped into life. She tossed the blocks behind her seat and climbed into the cockpit. Doc quickly elbowed her and pointed to the man who was coming across the tarmac.

Chloe cast a glance out the window and shoved in the throttle. The little engine roared, pulling them farther away from the terminal, spinning them toward the runway. She kept her eyes ahead, intently focused on her take-off.

Doc turned and saw the man stopped on the open pavement; binoculars raised to his eyes.

In moments, they were sailing smoothly into the desert air, wondering whether they'd just been discovered.

CHAPTER 49

Chloe didn't hear any radio traffic but searched the sky in case. She leveled the plane at about 500 feet above the ground.

"Here," she pointed at the yoke, "take this."

Doc sat up straight, his eyes wide. "What?"

"Take the yoke while I look at the map."

"Didn't you do that already?"

"Yeah, before we thought that man on the taxiway might have been the one chasing us."

Doc put his fingers gingerly on the yoke. Chloe released her grip and the yoke moved quickly toward the dash, the Aeronca suddenly nosing downward.

Chloe grabbed it again. "Here, hold it like this."

Doc tried again, feeling the plane level out. His eyes darted from the windshield to the yoke, and outside again, his hands making micro-adjustments, trying to keep the Aeronca from diving into the ground.

"Here." Chloe took control again. "Keep your hands on the yoke and feel what I am doing." She pushed it in, and they dropped, pulled it back and they rose, turned left, then right, then leveled out. "See, you don't have to correct every tiny movement, just go with the flow a little bit."

He nodded and she reached behind them and into her daypack. She pulled out the aerial map and folded a section of it in front of her.

The plane began to dip, so she pulled back gently on the yoke, reminding him to pay attention.

"I set a course for Tonopah, Nevada, the next place I'd like to stop for a rest and gas."

"Yes?"

"But if that guy really was Morozov, that's where they'll try to find us next. It's the next logical stop." She studied the map some more. "Here, Walker Lake and the Hawthorne airport is northwest of Tonopah. We can get there, top off the gas, then fly east to a sky park ranch. It's about 130 miles each leg, but we stay north of Tonopah."

"Sounds like a good idea."

She checked the heading for Hawthorne and replaced the map. When she retook the yoke, Doc relaxed into his seat.

"We'll keep the mountains on our left until we cross what should be Highway 6, then follow 95 north around Excelsior Mountains and then on to Hawthorne. I'd say, we'll get there in less than two hours."

The radio squelched and a Cessna announced its approach to Sulfur Springs. Chloe and Doc looked at each other.

"We're already off the direct path to Tonopah," she said. "If that's them, by the time they're in the air again, we'll be too far away to find."

"Said the rabbit to the fox." Doc turned to stare outside his window.

CHAPTER 50

"Like I said, Carl, I'm really not sure it was them. The man resembled Dochauser, and it was a yellow tail dragger airplane, but the tail number didn't match. I started toward them, to try the FAA routine, but they left before I could get to them."

"Okay, okay." He patted the air with his hands. "Which way did they go?"

"That way," Morozov pointed.

"Makes sense. Tonopah is that direction. It used to be a WWII bomber training base. We're still hemmed in by military airspace until we get there. It's the next good stop for anyone going that direction. I really think if they were between Beatty and Sulfur Springs, I would have seen them on my search."

"So, we're on to Tonopah?"

"Right."

"If we don't find them there?"

"Let's cross that bridge when we come to it." Carl started the Cessna and rolled to the end of the runway. He went through his "run-up" routine, checking the tail, ailerons, fuel mixture, and more, then took them back into the air, north toward Tonopah.

****

An hour and three-quarters into the air, they rounded the mountains below Hawthorne airport and followed the road until they spotted the runway. Chloe announced them only as an "Aeronca," which no one questioned, and they lined up for landing.

A gust of air blew her left wing upward, a nasty blast. She dipped the wing into the crosswind and pushed the rudder to the right to keep them straight on course for the runway. The air calmed, so she leveled the wings and touched down with a smooth squeak of the wheels when suddenly the gusts returned, spinning the tail of the Aeronca left, aiming them crossways on the runway and directly toward a row of hangars, rotating them past the buildings and back toward the way they'd come, a centrifuge spinning them out of control as they skid down the tarmac. She shoved the rudder pedals hard right, but their momentum twisted them in their seats, pinned them against their seat belts, and spun them nearly full circle off the pavement and into the lumpy grass, jarring to a stop.

"Shit." She stared out the window, collecting her thoughts.

"The hell?"

"Sorry. Ground loop." She flushed with embarrassment.

"What?"

"Happens sometimes. When a cross wind hits the tail, it can spin these tail draggers around right as you're landing."

Doc released his grip on the dash. If it hadn't been metal, she was sure there would be handprints there.

The engine idled as they sat. No one spoke to them on the radio; no one came out to see if they were all right. She revved the engine and pulled them back onto the tarmac and to a three-sided shed that housed the fuel pumps.

"Well, we'll try not to do that again," she quipped.

After a forty-minute break and refueling, they lifted off without incident and climbed toward the east. The winds were blowing in that direction, so they'd gain some time on the next leg of the trip.

"We go northeast, over the Monitor Mountain Range," Chloe said over the intercom. "We're going to want to find a pass through there if we can. It looks like there's one on the north end of the mountains, just past the high peak, which is about 10,800 feet, between that one and another peak about 9,900 feet high. That will take us into a long valley, then over Park Mountain Range, which is a little less rugged than Monitor Range. Then we're in an even wider valley with what looks like a sky park or ranch on the map, though I'm sure there will be other ranches, too."

They were flying over the Great Basin National Park, a huge desert area created by rain shadows of the Sierra Nevada Mountains on the west and the Rocky Mountains on the east, natural barriers that restricted rainfall. In a true "basin," precipitation cannot flow to the Atlantic or to the Pacific, staying instead as fresh-water lakes, evaporating in large salt flats, or absorbing into the soil. She'd read that the basin had several distinct climates, including those with harsh salt flats, rolling steppes, and alpine forests, and unique animal species like the kit fox and kangaroo rat.

"We're aiming for the sky park?"

"Yep."

Mountains rose quickly from the flat desert floor, taking them to an alpine climate marked by bald rock faces, high lakes, and forests of bristlecone pine and willows shedding their golden coats. They found the mountain pass that appeared on the map and crossed the Monitor Range, peaks rising eerily above them and within a hundred yards of either wing, funneling them eastward.

Ahead lay the Park Mountains, and they headed straight for them, climbing as they went. Both ranges ran north and south, parallel to each other, appearing like gigantic blankets rumpled into the heights.

Chloe dropped them a few hundred feet after crossing the second range. A huge valley opened before them, a riparian area right below them, dotted with willow, choke cherry, and cottonwood.

"Keep an eye out for a large ranch with a nice runway," she said.

They flew another twenty minutes, the air becoming

bumpy, tossing them up, left, down, right, Chloe adjusting as they went. Doc seemed to be getting a little more used to the vagaries of flying in a small aircraft, but still looked a little green around the gills.

A hay field came into view on her left, but it seemed too early to be the sky park they were looking for, and there was no runway. A string of trees meandered on one side of the field, no doubt a stream providing the water for both. Another field appeared east of that, and she could see animals there, cows or horses most likely. They were probably fifty miles from the sky park and, hopefully, a shower and comfortable bed for the night.

Clang, clang, clang, clang!

"What's that?" Doc said.

The noise stopped as suddenly as it started.

"I don't know," she said.

Clang, clang, clang!

"Shit, what's happening?" Doc's voice grew louder.

"I don't know, I don't know." She checked the instruments on the dash, but they all appeared to be normal. The metallic banging had stopped again.

"What do we do?" He asked.

"It's quiet now. Maybe we can make it to the ranch, just take it easy." She slowed their speed and lifted the nose, the clanging still at bay but when she dropped the nose, the clattering began again.

"Is it the engine?" Doc's hands gripped the dashboard.

Clang, clang!

"Damn it, we're going to have to go down," she said, banking toward the open field.

"Oh, sweet mercy," Doc pronounced, eyes wide, teeth grinding on teeth.

She pulled the power back and lined up along the winding trees, keeping a slow descent.

Clang, clang, clang, clang!

She worked the rudder pedals, adjusting for rough currents, aiming, lining up with the field, losing her approach and finding it again, fighting a cross wind that threatened to toss them sideways into the trees. A fence appeared below them and they cleared it quickly, just barely, the air settling a little, letting her steer toward the open grass.

Clang, clang, clang…

The battering, banging, crash of metal-on-metal was constant now, tearing at their eardrums, choking all other sounds, an alarm that rattled their eyelids, their toenails, the fillings in their molars, and even the brittle bones of the old Aeronca.

CHAPTER 51

She shut down the engine as soon as their wheels touched the grass and the terrible racket finally died away. They bounced over the uneven field and rolled to a stop alongside a row of trees.

"Whew." Chloe wiped her brow with her hand.

Doc opened his door and lowered himself to the ground.

They waited there, motionless, grateful for the stillness and quiet. Chloe left the plane and stretched out on the grass. Animal shapes seemed closer than they had been, and she realized that several horses were moving casually in their direction, curious to see the interlopers.

"You okay?" she asked.

"Barely," Doc whimpered.

She pulled the plane closer to the trees and placed chocks by the front wheel to keep the plane from moving forward or backward. She tied the rear wheel to a tree trunk about the size of her arm. The last thing they needed was for the plane to leave the ground or even flip upside down if the winds continued to gust.

A steady clomp-clomp vibrated the ground. She stood slowly. A man with long hair came toward them on the back of a spotted gray horse, bobbing with each stride.

"We have company," Doc said, pulling himself up with the wing strut, brushing off his jeans.

"I think we're the company," Chloe whispered as the man came closer.

"Hey, there, you guys all right?" His hair was the color of snow, his skin an autumn wheat. His voice was deep and smooth, the sound of a man three times his size. He pulled his horse to a stop in front of the propeller. "What's going on?"

"Hi, I'm Chloe and that's my friend Doc," she pointed. "We're going cross country and our engine started making a terrible noise so we put down at the closest place we could."

The man's horse snorted.

"I'm so sorry," she continued. "We didn't have a choice, really. I've got to figure out what the problem is."

"That's all right." He smiled a corn-cob row of teeth, white against his leathered skin. "I'm Alfred but you can call me Al, like the song."

"What song?" Chloe asked. Doc, though, smiled at the reference.

"What do you need? Tools? Parts?"

"I won't know until I get under the cowling. But it's too hot now. I'd get burned poking around under the hood." She nodded toward the engine.

"What can I do to help?" Al asked.

"Let us camp here for the night?" Chloe said.

Al's horse stomped the dirt. "I can do better than that. You're welcome to stay at my place. Nothing fancy, but I have two couches in the front room."

Doc gave Chloe a quick nod.

"We'd be grateful, Al."

"Can you guys ride?" he asked.

"Ride?" Doc wrinkled his nose.

Al slid from the saddle and handed the reigns to Doc. "Here, you take Gray, my old faithful. Chloe and I can take one of the others."

"Can't we just walk?"

"If you like. It's about a two-mile hop to the house." Al pointed behind him. "Here, let me help you up."

Al lifted Doc's left leg into the stirrup and told him to grab the horn. "Now, I'll push, and you pull your other leg over the top."

Al shoved Doc's behind with both hands. Doc's leg swung over the saddle and his rear plopped hard into the leather seat. Doc wore a look like he'd reached a terrifying perch, his legs straddling a beast that could belch thunder.

Chloe chuckled.

CHAPTER 52

Special Agent Johansen stared out the conference room window in the high-rise offices of the Phoenix Field Office of the FBI, trying to get his mind refocused on the stolen Aeronca and runaway teenage pilot. He rose and wandered along a row of desks in the central office area, pulled, not so subconsciously, toward the desk of one Special Agent Marilyn Pyne. She looked up as he approached, her smile fluttering Johansen's stomach.

"What's up?" She sat back from her computer screen, brown eyes glistening, her desk layered with stacks of incident reports.

"Not much." He touched the side of her desk. "Just getting some air. Maybe some fresh ideas." He sat in a chair next to the clutter.

She scratched above her eyes. "I'm just going through the Phoenix area local crime reports. It's outside our jurisdiction but it helps to know what's going on in our neighborhood."

"Yeah." He reached for a pile and spread it farther

apart, glancing at the subject lines and photos.

"The homicide unit's got a murder on the Azteca campus." She pulled the report. "Belle Smith, lab assistant to a research professor who's gone missing."

"Huh." He sat back. "Are we watching that one for any special reason?"

"Yeah, at NSA request."

"NSA? National security's involved?"

"Apparently. This lab assistant and her mentor were working on a physics project for the development of quantum computers. There's some prototype component that's gone missing. NSA has been monitoring their progress."

Johansen wrinkled his nose, the question implicit.

"Well," she sighed, "quantum computation has national security implications because the first nation to leap ahead with it will have huge advantages…" she searched the papers on her desk, "…in medical advancements, but of more interest to the NSA is the ability of a quantum computer to crack codes. Here it is," she lifted a page, "'all existing levels of encryption and computer security, including military computing security.' And the kinds of developments a quantum computer could advance could change the nature of warfare, the types, and sophistication of weaponry."

"Really."

"Oh, yeah. Weapons and defense systems we haven't even dreamed of could be developed with quantum computing. CIA and NSA have been watching the leading research about this all around the world."

"And we've got one of those researchers right here in Phoenix?"

"A little town, really a suburb, west of here, at Azteca College. And like I said, the victim's mentor, the lead researcher, is missing. He's wanted for questioning."

"Who is this mentor?"

"Uh," she pulled a page from the stack on her desk. "Dochauser is his last name."

"So, he murdered his lab assistant and ran off with some kind of prototype?"

"That's one theory."

"Do they have any leads?"

"The college has a pilot and aeronautical program of some sort, so they have a little airstrip there and a few airplanes."

"Wait. What?"

"A witness was too far away for any useful descriptions, but he saw a man, average height, a little portly, jump into an old plane and take off shortly after the murder. Could be this Dochauser professor. Someone else seemed to be chasing him, but that guy could have been Dochauser, too. Or it could be totally unrelated. Anyway, both of them are long gone."

Johansen straightened. "What kind of airplane?"

"I don't know, a little one, I guess." She looked through the papers. "Yellow was all the witness could say. Oh, and that it was a high-wing 'tail dragger,' he called it.

The third wheel on a plane can be at the front, under the engine, or at the rear, under the tail."

Johansen was already rushing toward his desk.

CHAPTER 53

Chloe stuffed her map into the daypack and tied Doc's plastic bag to the outside. Al caught a sorrel and held it for her. She hadn't ridden a horse since she's gone into foster care, but she remembered the basics. She slid onto the bare back of the mare, then spun so she lined up with the horse's backbone and sat up. She clamped her thighs to the mare's stomach, wrapped her hand in the mane, and waited while Al caught another horse.

Doc had the reins in his hands but looked completely out of place.

Al moved behind Doc and Chloe, clicking his tongue until all three of them were heading down a narrow trail along a line of willows.

Doc shifted with each step, out of sync with the horse for several yards before he seemed to get the hang of it. They rode without speaking, a mile or so along the pasture, then crossed an irrigation ditch and through the trees to another, dryer field. After a while, they crossed an empty ditch and up a short rise to a gravel road that led to a white, ranch-style home shielded by giant cottonwoods.

The sun had dropped low on the horizon, shadows reaching across the valley. They stopped to dismount. Al patted his horse on the rump, and it wandered off. Chloe slid down, and her mare followed the other horse.

Doc slid his left foot out of the stirrup, clung to the saddle horn, and slid his other leg over the horse's rump. He plopped onto the ground, knees a bit wobbly, but seemed proud of himself. Al took the reins and led Doc's horse toward a barn to the side of the house.

"Go on in." He pointed to the front door. "Make yourself at home."

"Thank you." Doc glanced at Chloe and headed for the house.

The living room was large and open, two brown couches facing each other, a coffee table between them. Built-in bookshelves guarded a wide entry into the kitchen. Photos of Al, a woman she assumed was his wife, horses, and colts peppered the other walls. A television and rack of movie DVDs sat in the corner.

Chloe got herself and Doc a glass of water.

Al returned with a smile, a large dog in tow that looked to be part German Shepard, part Labrador, and part something else. The dog seemed nonplussed at first, then moved from Doc to Chloe and back again, tail wagging, harvesting ear rubs from each of them.

"Meet Wally." Al pointed to the four-footed blur of fur.

Chloe and Doc introduced themselves to Wally as if he were part human. The way he looked at them, maybe he was. They gave Al a bit more background about what they were doing, flying the Aeronca to Spokane, omitting references to deceased lab partners, teenage runaways, or Russian spies.

A retired behavioral psychologist, Al had worked for Los Angeles County, the City of Las Vegas, and as a private practitioner counseling employees, police officers, and college students. His wife of fifty-five years had died two years ago.

"How are you gonna get your airplane repaired way out here? Is there someone I can call for you?" Al's eyes were a unique shade of green, at least indoors. Outside, they'd looked brown.

"I'd like to take a look at it first thing tomorrow," she said. "I have some basic tools with me, if I can figure it out."

"Damn thing about gave me a heart attack." Doc touched his chest. "Made an awful racket."

"I suspect something came loose and was hitting the propeller, but I'll have to check."

"Yikes," Doc said.

"You're welcome to stay here for the night. Two couches as you can see."

"We really appreciate it," Doc said.

"I see you have a TV." Chloe rubbed Wally's ears.

"Satellite only, yes," Al nodded.

"Do you have a weather channel I could watch? We

could leave the sound off."

"Sure." Al turned on the set and found the channel. "Now let's get you some food."

CHAPTER 54

Yazzie picked up the phone. "Yes, Agent Johansen?"

"Hey, listen. You figured out that the Amber Alert for Chloe matched up with the stolen airplane."

"Right."

"Well, I think I've just made another connection. The murder of Belle Smith, the lab assistant at Azteca College?"

"Yes?"

"A man fleeing the scene was probably a quantum physicist at the college named Dochauser, and he got into an airplane that fits the description of the one the teenager stole."

"Wait. Why would a physicist jump into a stolen airplane?"

"Another man might have been chasing him. That, or he had arranged for the airplane as a getaway, for after he shot Belle Smith."

"Why shoot Smith?"

"Good question. But now we have another big connection—Richard Dochauser and Chloe Rochelle."

"Great work, Johansen!"

"Thanks."

"But why would the two of them be connected? And what was Dochauser doing to get himself in this kind of trouble, whatever it is?"

"Yeah, that's another thing. It seems that Dochauser has developed the newest breakthrough in quantum computing. A breakthrough that's worth millions and even has the NSA nervous as hell."

"The NSA's involved?"

"Yes, sir. This is now a matter of national security."

Yazzie let the news sink in. "You think these events—Dochauser flying away and maybe being chased—is part of that? This new computer chip?"

"I think it's some kind of quantum computing equipment, more than just a chip, but yes."

"Holy crap."

"Yeah."

"Are other countries trying to get the quantum chip or whatever it is? China? Russia?"

"My next call is to the NSA or the CIA to find out."

Yazzie leaned back in his chair and stared at the blank ceiling.

"You still on the line?" Johansen said.

"Yes, yes. Again, great work, agent! And thanks for the update."

"Keep me advised, too?" Johansen said.

"Of course."

Yazzie hung up the phone and slowly rubbed his brow. This was now the hottest case of his career. He wondered if he had time to do what he was thinking. He had some calls to make.

CHAPTER 55

"The weather looks like it will hold another couple of days." Chloe waved at the TV. They'd eaten chicken patties, mashed potatoes, and green beans while watching depictions of cold fronts and wet storms wriggling across the country. Wally lay snoring in the corner, not once begging for food.

"What kind of dog is he?" Doc asked.

"The good kind." Al smiled.

"Right." Chloe agreed.

"You're a professor, you said earlier?" Al asked Doc.

"Quantum physics. More of a researcher, but I teach a couple of classes, too."

"What's your research about?"

Doc and Chloe shared a look and Doc shrugged. "Quantum computing is the wave of the future." He set his empty plate on the coffee table. "But it's hard to get sub-atomic particles to hold still long enough to use them for computation. Right now, some developers have managed to keep them in special chambers at close to absolute zero—that's minus 460 degrees Fahrenheit. That sustains a limited number of particles with a limited computational power, but we're looking for something larger and more practical."

"Why use quantum particles?" Al asked.

"Their ability to be in two places at the same time. Have you heard of Schrödinger's paradox? Schrödinger's cat?"

Al shook his head.

"It illustrates how the laws of physics differ at the subatomic level and has added to the multi-verse theory— that there are many existing simultaneously, like the theoretical cat that can be both dead and alive at the same time."

"Why a cat?" Al asked.

"Doesn't matter what it is, it's just an illustration. Assume that quantum particles in one state allow the cat to live, and in another state cause the cat to die. And they're in both states at once. If you extend that circumstance, the cat itself exists in both states at the same time. When we open a box it's in, we disturb the particles and the quantum state collapses into one path or the other, and the cat is either dead or alive, but it's no longer both. Our whole world is built on quantum particles that can both exist and not exist at the same time, at least until they are disturbed. So…" he spread his hands.

"Our world is one of many possibilities?" Chloe said.

"Our world co-exists with many, infinite, others," Doc nodded. "At least, that's the theory."

Wally stood and wandered to Al, who scratched behind his ears. He'd trained his human well.

"Because of this, quantum particles can test all of the

solutions to a problem instantly and simultaneously. Problems that are way too big for current computers to solve become a piece of cake."

Chloe turned off the TV. "You said a couple days ago, Doc, that plants use quantum processing of some sort for photosynthesis, right?"

"Yes."

"And of course, plants do that at room temperatures."

"Right."

"So, I've been thinking about this…"

"When?" He smiled. "While we've been flying?"

"Well, sure. Why can't you design something that works the same way? Maybe use the leaves of plants themselves, to get the little neutrinos moving in the right direction."

"This is the 30-year-old Chloe speaking." Doc grinned.

"She's got something there," Al said. "Plants are amazing creatures, you know."

Chloe and Doc shared a glance.

Al raised a finger. "Plant cells have been shown to act with intelligence. In fact, intelligent behavior has been found in single cells and bacteria, which use bioelectrical information and signaling."

"You're well informed," Doc said.

"Fascinating subject. Retirement hobby of mine."

"Bioelectric signaling?" Chloe asked.

Doc nodded. "All life forms function with electrical systems, sometimes called bioelectricity. For example, our human brains transfer information through synapses using electrical signals. Our muscles respond to electrical signals, too, which is why pacemakers can regulate heart beats when they need to."

"Cell structure and chemical makeup allows that to work, right?" Al said.

"So why not take a closer look at plants?" she asked.

"Right." Doc stared quietly at some distant image, to a place where thoughts, like shadows, are seen.

"The natural world is amazing," Chloe said.

"And we get to learn about it from the inside." Al's eyes lit up. "As a part of the system itself, we're seeing it from the inside."

"Oh, yeah," she said.

CHAPTER 56

Chloe slept hard and long overnight, probably making Doc endure some snoring for a change. They'd woken to the smell of bacon, a luxury she hadn't expected. After a wonderful breakfast, they'd each showered while Al saddled three horses. He'd agreed to sell them five gallons of gas, enough to top off the fuel tank.

Assuming Chloe could get them in the air.

Al helped Doc into the saddle, the procedure a little like hands lifting a sack of potatoes.

Al rode Gray, his favorite mare, the pair of them comfortable partners. He placed the fuel on the saddle in front of him.

They were about to begin the short trek to the Aeronca when a spiral of dust appeared on the road.

"Oh, he's early." Al pointed.

"Who?" Doc asked.

"The sheriff."

Chloe's stomach clenched. "Sheriff?"

"Well, a deputy. I'm a possible witness to a theft at

the hardware store in Ely about three weeks ago. A deputy wanted to see me in person to record an interview, but I thought he wouldn't be here 'till noon."

Her muscles relaxed for a moment, then tensed again. "We really should go now. If we wait, we could lose the cool morning air."

"Assuming we can get the plane fixed," Doc said.

"Right. But we need to try. We should go now." She pressed her lips together and narrowed her eyes at Doc, signaling that they should hurry on.

"Oh, yes, we should go to the plane now," Doc agreed. His horse stepped forward and he grabbed the saddle horn for balance.

"All right." Al pushed Gray next to Chloe's horse. "I'd better stay back. Good luck to you." He handed the container of gas to Chloe. She wedged it in front of her.

"Thank you, so much!" She said. "We wish you the best in everything!"

"Thanks, folks, you, too. Hope you get that little airplane fixed. Leave the horses in the field, they'll be okay tied up for an hour or two. Wrap their reins in a bush or a tree and I'll get out there after the deputy is done taking my statement."

"Yes, thank you very much." Doc said.

Chloe touched her heels to her horse and they began moving down the road. Al slapped Doc's horse on the rear, and the mare hurried to catch up with Chloe, bouncing Doc like one of those vibrating massage chairs.

She could hear Al give a quick laugh.

The swirl of dust had grown much larger now, nearly motionless in the still air, a fine sign for flying. The deputy's jeep rumbled at the base of the rising powder, a dot growing steadily in size.

Chloe clicked her tongue and jabbed her heels again and her horse began an easy trot. They were soon at the trail below the road and crossed the ditch. The dry field stretched before them, and they kept a steady pace until the path crossed another irrigation ditch and turned into the trees. She pulled gently on the reins and twisted in her stirrups, checking behind them. Doc looked like a white-collar desk jockey atop a wild horse, his cheeks pale. A prisoner in the saddle.

But no one was following them.

They soon reached the Aeronca, still tied down and in place. They dismounted, Doc sliding off a little more gracefully than the last time. They wrapped the reins around branches of a chokecherry bush and walked to the airplane.

Chloe lifted the cowling that protected the engine and reached inside, checking, tugging at wires and parts. Her instructor had insisted she have a basic knowledge of how the engine and its systems work.

"Ah, ha." She lifted a metal tube, about two fingers around and five inches long.

"What is that?"

"A heat exchanger tube. It looks like the screw that holds it in place has sheared off."

"What does that mean? Does it need to be replaced?"

"Eventually. But it looks like it was sliding into the base of the prop, making that awful racket."

"So, we're stuck here until we can get it fixed?"

"Oh, no. We don't need it. It sends engine heat to the cockpit, but we're plenty warm enough, especially when the sun is out. I haven't used any cabin heat the whole trip."

"You're telling me we don't need that pipe at all? The plane will fly without it?"

"Yep."

"You're sure?"

"I'm sure. It just came loose and clanked against the prop. We take it out, no more clanking."

"Shit." He held his palm to his forehead, eyes pinched in a measure of disbelief.

CHAPTER 57

Chloe untied the tail and removed the chocks and they both pushed the Aeronca a few yards farther away from the horses. She filled the fuel tank to the brim and put the gas can next to the chokecherry bush. She did a slow, thorough check of the engine, ailerons, tires, and tail, noting again the bullet hole in the fuselage. She stared at the wounded fabric for a moment then placed two pieces of electrical tape over it, pressing carefully around the edges. At least no one looking at it would know that a bullet hole was underneath. Her alteration of the tail numbers seemed to be holding just fine.

The field was empty and relatively flat, though there were plenty of bumps and dips to rattle them on take-off. She walked the field toward the east, searching for the best route, then returned to the plane.

"Ready?" she asked.

"No." Doc slid into the passenger seat, closed the door, and slid open the window.

Chloe placed the chocks in front of the wheel again,

set the ignition and throttle, and pulled the propeller into a quick start. Then she removed the chocks and hopped inside. She adjusted the throttle, did a final check, and glanced at Doc.

He grimaced.

They rolled slowly at first, rising and dropping with bumps in the terrain but as the plane accelerated, the gentle swells quickly turned to jarring bangs and drops, jerking them right and left, concussing them down the field until finally the wheels lifted from the earth and they smoothed into airy flight.

Nothing was clanging under the cowling.

Doc released a long breath of air.

She took them away from Al's house, away from any curious deputies, north and into the empty desert between the hills. They flew for almost two hours before they reached Battle Mountain, where they took a needed break and refueled. Landing and taking off on pavement was a luxury she was learning to appreciate. They were both nervous about encountering Morozov or other problems, but they took turns watching and the stop went off without a hitch.

North of Battle Mountain lay a giant square on the aerial map showing another military operations area. However, the restrictions appeared to begin 500 feet above ground level, so they flew below that until they reached Owyhee for another break. They found no pilot's lounge, no restrooms, no fuel, no people anywhere around. Near the Nevada border with Idaho, the place had the look and feel of Death Valley.

They flew north from Owyhee along flat, empty country, then over a ridge and into busier airspace closer to Boise.

"There's a string of airports up ahead and although they're all likely spots for people to try to find us, there are also too many for them to be everywhere."

"Hide in the crowd?" Doc asked.

"That's the idea. Not that we can wait much longer for fuel," she pointed at the gas gauge.

She announced herself only as "Aeronca" and entered the pattern to land at Caldwell. She'd been monitoring the radio traffic on their way in, which was busy with helicopters, which made her nervous. You knew an airplane's general route and trajectory, but helicopters turned on a dime and rose or dropped in near-vertical patterns. But she landed without incident and taxied to a self-serve fuel pump, where she filled the tank. They'd been flying on fumes.

They tied down the plane in the designated area and ate at a little café attached to the terminal. The smell of hamburgers and onions and French fries made her ravenous. She ate two full burgers while Doc stole some of her fries and drank coffee.

"Are you up for another hour and a half of flying this afternoon?" She wiped her mouth with a napkin.

"If you're done eating, sure." He smiled.

"Well, for now I am."

"Where would we go next?"

"There's a little airport—more my speed—called Jo-seph State, across the border into Oregon. It looks like they have a small terminal, which usually means restrooms, and places to camp overnight. And fuel, of course."

"How are we doing? I mean, how's our progress to Spokane?"

"Today's been a great day." She reached into her day-pack and spread her map on the table. "Looks like Spokane is about 130 miles from Joseph State. So, if we get there this afternoon, we'll only have about a two-hour flight tomor-row morning to Spokane."

"Wow. That close." He rubbed his chin. "Guess I'd better brace myself for a talk with the feds."

"Like I said before, grandpa's a retired detective. I'll bet he's got good contacts there. He can hand you off to them right away."

"You'll tell him?"

"Yeah, it's time for me to call him. I'll use the phone at the terminal here, before we leave for Joseph State."

Doc grunted.

Time for one more leg of the trip and one last night of open-air camping.

CHAPTER 58

Johansen checked for NSA contacts in the Spokane area but found none close by. He settled for the Colorado office, which referred him to an agent near Phoenix. He called the woman on a secured line.

"Agent Taylor?"

"Speaking. Agent Johansen?"

He explained who he was, his role in a possible interstate kidnapping, and what he knew about the Phoenix murder investigation. He drew the connection between Dochauser, his quantum computing research, and the runaway pilot.

"I must say, I'm impressed with your work," she said. "But how or why would Dochauser get connected with a teenager in a stolen airplane?"

"That's one for the books, as they say. We have no idea."

"Still, you've pulled more of it together than we have. We've been working with the college on Dochauser's research for some time now—it's one of the things we do to protect national security—and we just learned about his lab assistant's apparent murder. And that Dochauser is missing. We had no idea where he'd gone, and you've already tracked him to a likely destination near Spokane."

"Yes."

"But here's what we know that you don't. The murder investigation found the lab assistant's calendar entries for the day that she was shot. It shows an early morning meeting with a Mr. Morozov."

"Yes?"

"Well, for years now, Morozov has been suspected as a spy for the FSB, the new security arm of Russia. His 'cover,' if you will, is as a reporter for a popular science magazine. He does, in fact, work that job as a legitimate reporter, but he contacts the FSB whenever he hears about cutting edge research that the Kremlin would be interested in. Sometimes, he digs deeper. He's been paid to steal research reports and even lab samples in the past. We suspect that's what he was up to in this case, that the lab assistant told him about some new breakthrough, and he tried to get ahold of it."

"So, Dochauser didn't kill his assistant. Morozov did."

"That's our working theory. There's no motive for Dochauser to shoot her, yet he's missing."

"You'll share that with the Phoenix murder investigators?" Agent Johansen asked.

"I meet with their team later today."

Johansen paused. "What will the NSA do with the information that Dochauser is going to Spokane?"

"You said a witness said someone might have been chasing Dochauser when he got into that little airplane?"

"That's not highly reliable. The witness did not say he was sure about that and couldn't confirm that it was Dochauser who got into the plane."

"Yes. My point is that if someone was chasing Dochauser, and they'd just shot his lab partner, that someone is almost certainly Morozov."

"So, they're all headed to Spokane."

"Seems likely. And Agent Johansen…"

"Yes?"

"Morozov is an extremely dangerous man and likely under some stress. His Russian contact is a spy known as Ivan, and he's probably told Morozov to capture or kill Dochauser. Ivan promotes himself as 'Ivan the Terrible,' a name he likes to live up to. In the past, he's tortured to get information. If he's helping Morozov, then Morozov has money, intelligence reports from Ivan's network, and probably muscle to help with the chase and capture."

"A shitstorm is descending on Spokane?"

"You got it."

"Assuming, of course, that Dochauser and this teenage pilot manage to get that far."

CHAPTER 59

Deputy Yazzie hung up the phone. Agent Johansen had updated him again, this time confirming that Russian agents were after the quantum component that Dochauser had developed, even naming one of the Russian operatives—someone named Morozov.

He called an old informant who'd moved to Phoenix, who led him to another contact, who led him to another. He was anxious to see what he could find out about Morozov and what he eventually learned surprised him. In the search for Dochauser, the Russians were throwing money around like rice at a wedding.

Yazzie called a friend at the Kingman airport and was soon connected with a private charter service there. A twin-engine King Air and its pilot were available right away. With a cruise speed of over 200 miles per hour, a straight flight to Spokane could be done in a few hours. He told the pilot the children's services program would pay for the flight, though he doubted it. There were cheaper ways to return Chloe to Mohave County, but his teeth were deep into it now.

He searched for a satellite image of the home of Chloe's grandfather and found one that was only two months old. The ranch-style house sat on a large lot in the country, surrounded on three sides by empty pastures. Plenty of room for a small airplane to land.

He'd tell the sheriff that he was taking a couple of personal days off. Better to ask for forgiveness than permission.

That computer chip, or whatever it was, had to be worth millions.

CHAPTER 60

Chloe hated leaving voicemails for her grandpa, but that's what she did. Two calls to him had gone unanswered.

She left the terminal and walked toward the Aeronca, where Doc said he'd be waiting. She turned the corner of the building and suddenly planted her feet on the pavement, momentum swinging her forward at the waist. Next to Doc stood a security guard scrolling through his cell phone, then chatting with Doc, then working on the phone again.

Why would he be talking to Doc?

Her chest tightened as she resumed walking toward them, her mind preparing to challenge the man's authority if he tried to stop them. A baton was tucked into his belt, but she didn't see a gun.

"Oh, my pilot's here," Doc said a little too loudly. "We've got to head out."

"Where to?" The guard was middle-aged, a paunch to his gut, brown hair, sunglasses, deeply tanned.

"Oh, I think to Owyhee," Doc said, pointing south.

"Not much there."

Chloe reached the two men. "All set?" she said to Doc.

"Beautiful old Aeronca." The guard nodded toward the plane. "1940s?"

"Forty-six." Chloe put her pack behind the pilot seat and quickly untied the wings from the ground anchors. Doc moved to the passenger side, got in the plane, and shut the door.

"Just admiring the old girl." The guard waved toward the altered letters on the fuselage but said nothing about them being suspicious.

"Yeah, thanks. Gotta go. Late already." Chloe set the magnetos and throttle, tossed the chocks in front of the wheel and went to the prop.

The guard stepped back.

She spun the propeller once, then again, and the engine chugged in a slow idle. She replaced the chocks in the luggage area and hopped into the plane.

"Have a safe flight!" The guard turned and walked toward the terminal.

They put on their headsets and Chloe gunned the engine, taking them onto the nearest taxiway.

"What did that guy want?" she asked.

"Just gabbing about the airplane. But he made me nervous."

"Hell, yes." She did her run-up, announced her intentions on the radio, and aimed for the runway. "Nice thinking to tell him we were going south when we're really going north."

"Thanks."

"We'll start south, in case he's watching, and circle back."

"Good."

"We'll be in Joseph State soon enough. This next leg of the trip isn't as congested as it is around Boise, but there's still about three other places we could stop."

"So even if they know to look for us going north, the odds are in our favor?"

"No, but they're better than nothing."

****

Morozov's phone buzzed. It was Ivan.

"Yes, sir?"

"Where are you now?" Ivan asked.

"Nampa, Idaho. Between Boise and Caldwell, I'm told." Morozov heard Ivan rustling papers in the background.

"Good. We just had a report from a contact at Caldwell. I'll send you a photo now."

Morozov waited a few moments then opened his text. There stood Dochauser in front of a yellow and red tail dragger. "That's him!"

"My contact said they told him they were going south. Is that possible?" Ivan asked.

"No, that's not right. Based on what you told us

earlier, they're headed for Spokane," Morozov said. "Besides, like us, they just came from the south. Why would they go back?"

"Yes, I think they were lying," Ivan said. "Our information that they are headed for Spokane is solid."

Morozov motioned for Carl to stand closer so he could hear them. "I agree."

"Then, go and get them."

Morozov enlarged the photo. "Ivan, it looks like they've changed their tail number."

Carl side-eyed him. "Really?"

Morozov pointed to the image.

"Clever," he said, an equal mix of surprise and sarcasm.

"You've got the new number, then?" Ivan asked.

"Yep. It's clear in the photo you sent."

Carl leaned closer to the phone. "There's a bunch of places to stop in southern Idaho but from here north to Spokane, it's more limited. Having the new tail number makes a huge difference. We'll head up to Spokane now, and search backward from there, north to south as they approach."

"Now I have to pay good money to the man who sent me this photograph, Morozov. So, make it worth my while. You know what I mean?"

"Time to bring you the goods," Morozov said.

"Time to quit talking about it." Ivan hung up.

CHAPTER 61

They flew west then followed Interstate 84 north until it veered away from the Snake River, part of the boundary between Idaho and Oregon. They climbed to about 7,000 feet and stayed with the river until they reached the southern edge of Hell's Canyon, nearly 8,000 feet top to bottom, the deepest gorge in North America. Chloe took them northwest from there until they spotted a road to follow and kept on track, flying above the mountains.

"Keep an eye out for Wallowa Lake." She pointed. "On the northern end is the town of Joseph and the little airport is there."

Pine-covered mountains rose on their left, part of the Eagle Cap Wilderness and Wallowa Mountain Range known as the Alps of Oregon. Chiseled peaks rose above the timberline, gray granite laid bare to the sun. Fingers of snow gripped the deep crevasses. Fir trees lined the valleys, ponds glistening in the afternoon light. They watched as the landscape seemed to roll beneath them, the earth spinning as they hovered above.

Chloe adjusted their heading again and they came upon an elongated body of water in the distance. As they grew closer, she became certain it was Wallowa Lake. Mirrored specks along the shore were the rooftops and windows of man-made buildings. The town was named after Chief Joseph of the Nez Perce, for whom this valley was home. Her grandpa had told her the story. The Tribe resisted its illegal removal, eventually fleeing toward Canada for asylum and to join a band of Lakota led by Sitting Bull. Eight hundred men, women, and children evaded and fought off the U.S. Army over 1,170 miles of rugged terrain before finally surrendering, just 40 miles below the Canadian border.

The land had lifted mightily since they'd left the Snake River, Sacajawea Peak rising 9,838 feet to their left, the town about 4,888 feet above sea level. They flew along the shore of the lake and announced their arrival on the radio. A Cherokee was in the pattern, practicing landings and take-offs. Chloe dropped low and crossed the airstrip mid-field, checking the windsock and searching for any plane resembling the white and blue Cessna that had been chasing them. She could see several outbuildings and hangars and maybe a dozen airplanes, none of them matching Morozov's Cessna.

"Look okay?" Doc asked.

"Yep." Chloe followed the Cherokee in for a landing and then took them off the runway and to the fuel pumps. She shut down the engine, the propeller shuddering to a stop.

"What a beautiful spot," Doc said.

They stepped out of the Aeronca and stretched their arms and legs. Chloe refilled their fuel and Doc paid with the pre-paid credit card.

"That trailer must be the terminal." Doc pointed. "I'm going to hit the head."

Chloe pulled the Aeronca to a spot on the tarmac marked for parking planes. She tied down the wings and tail and went to the tiny terminal. Behind was a level field of lush grass and picnic tables with raised bar-b-que grills. A sign nearby read: Public Camping – 3 night limit.

Doc came out of the trailer. "Restrooms inside." He pointed. "Nobody else there."

At nearly 5,000 feet, the September air was cool and clear. The sun lay its head on blanketed mountains, beams of light glaring into the pale sky.

"Why don't we camp here for the night?" Chloe said.

"Works for me. I might sleep on the couch inside the trailer, though. It'll be a bit cold tonight."

"Right."

Dusk fell quickly in the shadow of the mountains. They returned to the Aeronca and brought their gear to one of the picnic tables, setting up the pup tent for Chloe and arranging the stove and food for supper. She set a pot of water to boil on her little stove, instant noodles on the menu.

As they sat at the table, headlights approached along the road to the airport, four vehicles close behind each other, their yellowed lamps sweeping across the grassy field.

CHAPTER 62

A dozen or more young boys ran from the cars and vans, now parked by the trailer that served as the airport terminal, talking, boasting, shoving collegially, as energetic sprouts will do. Four adults barked orders to the boys, who eventually coalesced into some kind of rough formation and marched across the field with tents, poles, coolers, and sleeping bags in their arms.

The boys ignored Chloe and Doc, who sat waiting for their noodles to cool. The first man to walk by them waved and came closer.

"Hey, there. So sorry to invade your peace here." He held out his hand and they all shook. "I'm Ted, and this is our local scout troop." Ted looked like a friendly father type in his mid-thirties, brown hair in need of a trim. "Well," he added, "we hope to make it an official troop someday."

"Very good." Doc said politely.

"We'll stay on the far end of the campgrounds and leave you folks alone, but if you want to join us around the campfire later, you're welcome to."

"Thank you." Chloe said.

"Are you pilots?" Ted asked.

Doc looked at Chloe. "She is."

"Cool. George over there is going to give the boys lessons and rides in the morning. I hope we won't be too much of a disruption for you."

"No, no." Doc smiled. "You enjoy yourselves."

"Come by for the fire," Ted said over his shoulder. He followed the last of the group to a spot about forty yards away.

"We're going to hear them all night." Chloe said.

"You will. I'll be on the couch inside."

They sat at the picnic table in silence. Stars had begun popping across the sky, countless numbers of them, just bare pinpricks of light. "Sure makes you feel small down here, doesn't it?" She stared into the limitless black.

"Yes. A little lonely sometimes, too?" he asked.

"Yeah."

Doc cleared his throat. "You know, the four most active elements in the whole universe, everywhere," he swung his arm in an arc, "are hydrogen, oxygen, carbon, and nitrogen."

"Uh-huh." She sensed a chemistry lesson coming and prepared to tune it out.

"And those are the very same elements that each of us are made of."

"Oh." She spotted a falling comet, a line of light streaking across the black until it disappeared. He had her interest after all. "So, we're all the very same stuff. Just, arranged a little differently."

"You're a bright student, you know."

"I wish I could take your courses, Doc." It struck her that physicists like him, though fact-intensive scientists, could actually be pretty philosophical. In their own way. Not that Doc would ever admit it.

"The 30-year-old Chloe could enroll right now." He smiled.

"Maybe I will."

Doc put his hands in his pockets.

"You're a bit of a surprise, you know that, Doc?"

He released a deep, belly laugh. "Not nearly as much as you are, my friend."

They ate protein bars for dessert, eavesdropping on the chatter that drifted their way. Chloe slipped on her winter coat and Doc wrapped his arms around his chest.

"Cold? Want to check out their fire for while?" Chloe asked.

"Yes."

They crossed the grass to the boys' camp. Tents had been set up in a semi-circle. Folding chairs ringed a crackling fire inside a metal ring that was anchored to the ground. Ted welcomed them, making all the boys announce their names by way of introductions. He offered Doc and Chloe a pair of empty seats and they sat by the flames and warmed their hands. One of the male leaders seemed much younger than the others and pulled up a chair next to Chloe.

"Want some marshmallows?" His smile glistened in the flickering light.

"Sure." Her toes felt a tingle. "I'm Chloe."

"I'm David." He shook her hand then found a metal poke, slid two marshmallows onto the end, and gave it to her.

"You're a pilot?" he asked.

"Yes."

"I've always wanted to get my license. My uncle has a Super Cub and is going to take the boys for a few short flights tomorrow. You seem really young to be a pilot. Are you in high school?"

"Yes."

"Wow. Me too. I'm starting my senior year."

"Oh? What classes do you like the most?"

Doc nudged her shoulder and she turned to look at him, a little annoyed. "Yes?"

He winked and whispered, "I'm just enjoying the teenaged Chloe for a change."

"What?"

"I knew she was in there, somewhere." He cast a glance at her and grinned.

She huffed and turned back to David.

Doc stood and casually stepped away from the fire. "I'm calling it a night."

CHAPTER 63

A pearly glow lay on the horizon, daylight waking from its slumber. Stars melted into the morning sky. Doc rustled something behind her, probably rummaging for food.

"Hey, about last night—that David was a pretty good-looking guy," Doc said with a false nonchalance.

"Drop it," she said, her expression deadpan.

He unwrapped a protein bar for breakfast. "I'm just saying I noticed that. Did you notice that?"

"You want to fly with me today or not?"

He laughed.

A cool breeze stole the heat from her skin, the mountain sky clear as spring water. The scouts hadn't yet stirred from their tents. She was anxious to get back in the air. Spokane was finally within reach.

They repacked the gear into the Aeronca and Chloe started the plane with a practiced pull on the propeller. Doc snugged his seatbelt tight, a smile on his lips. He was ready to conclude their trip, too.

They rumbled across the taxi and were soon in the air,

climbing to 2,500 feet above the ground. They flew straight north, a little east of Enterprise Municipal Airport, then along a small peak and a ridge on their right. She checked her map again while Doc kept the plane straight and level. He seemed to enjoy it today.

Ahead, the Grande Ronde sparkled in the sun, a ribbon of green clinging to the edges of the meandering river. She heard some minor radio traffic from the Lewiston airport but continued to stay west of the controlled airspace. She pointed to two mountains on their left. "I think that farthest one's Diamond Peak."

Doc borrowed the aerial map from her, examining the unusual markings for flight vectors, airspace, and radio frequencies. Smooth, morning air seemed to float them across the landscape, dry desert giving way to another band of trees, some of them evergreens, some in coats of autumn gold.

They flew for a little over an hour, straight north and into Washington. They eventually passed Lewiston on their right, Moscow, a university town to the east, and on toward Pullman, another college town. Below stretched the huge Palouse Prairie, formed from topsoil windblown into the basin eons ago. Unbroken swaths of amber covered the gentle hills, spikes of wheat waving in the breeze like ripples on a quiet sea. She'd read that the Appaloosa, a Palouse horse, known for its spotted rumps and mellow nature, was first bred here by the Nez Perce.

They crossed Dry Seed Ranch and then a larger river,

which Doc pronounced to be the Snake.

"Beginning in Yellowstone National Park, the Snake flows south," Chloe explained, "then west across southern Idaho before it turns north through Hells Canyon along the Idaho panhandle. It turns west again, eventually emptying into the Columbia River and on to the Pacific."

Doc watched the horizon.

Chloe noticed that they'd dropped a few hundred feet, so she nosed the Aeronca upward, but it seemed sluggish, unwilling to climb.

Odd.

She adjusted the throttle and checked the magnetos that send an electrical charge to the spark plugs, but nothing changed. She tried again to gain altitude, and though the pistons were firing smoothly, they seemed to be losing power.

"What's up? Any problem?" Doc asked.

"Not sure. We seem to have slowly lost some horsepower. No big deal, except…"

"Except?"

"Well, we can't seem to get enough power to climb."

"Can't we just stay level?"

"In theory." She checked the map. "But whatever is causing the loss of power could cause us to start dropping. Maybe we can get to the next waystation, but if we can't climb…"

"What?"

She checked her instruments again. "We're losing altitude, Doc."

"No! Are we out of fuel?"

"No, no, we'd notice that right away."

"You sound like you speak from experience."

"Well…" She shrugged her shoulders, recalling why she had to land at Azteca College, where Doc had joined her on this journey.

"And you're sure we can't just stay level, and get to Spokane that way?"

"Yeah, I'm sure. It's a slow descent, but we're gonna have to land and see what the problem is."

"We're so close."

"I agree with you, Doc, but if we don't have enough power, we don't have enough power. Help me look for a good place. We can probably fly a few more miles before we need to land."

"Probably?"

They dropped to about 1,000 feet above the ground, weaving as they went, Chloe searching for landing spots. Hills and ridges swept away from the tree line into patches of desert sage. A ribbon of trees wound ahead of them, watered by a stream. Along the edge ran a narrow two-track, a rough dirt road worn by trucks or four-wheelers.

They'd dropped another 500 feet.

"There." She pointed. "Looks like it might be fairly clear."

"Oh." Doc had gripped the dashboard again.

"Straight, too." Well, sort of.

She banked toward the tracks, dropping to 300 feet, and lined up with the makeshift runway. Trees on their left, dry brush on their right, the ground came up quickly to meet them.

Doc's fingers had a solid grip on the dash.

CHAPTER 64

She throttled back and settled into a glide for the final yards before touchdown. The plane bounced against the dry dirt, launching them several feet into the air, then landed hard, tires jarring over back country lumps and dips, vibrating the old bird until Chloe braked to a stop. The engine responded weakly but with enough power to pull them under the shade of a few lodgepole pines. She shut down the engine and wiped a line of sweat from her brow.

"What now?"

"Stretch your legs for a while and I'll see what I can figure out."

"Don't burn yourself. That engine's still hot."

"Right." Chloe slid out of the plane.

Doc pulled a bottle of water from behind the seat and wiggled out the door.

Using a rag from under her seat, she lifted the cowling and looked inside. Wires in place, no oil leaks, no more loose heater pipes, no more loose anything. The outside of the engine looked fine.

Which meant the problem was on the inside.

A white pickup truck rumbled down the road, coming their direction. Chloe and Doc walked to the front of the plane and waited.

The passenger hopped out almost before the truck had stopped, rifle in hand. The driver stayed in his seat.

"What's going on here?" The man was in his early twenties, sweat-stained T-shirt, thick black beard, eyes hidden behind mirrored sunglasses.

"Had to land. Engine trouble." Chloe pointed at the Aeronca.

"Wow." The man lowered his glasses to look them over, his blue eyes bloodshot, lids droopy like he was half asleep. "What kind of plane is that?"

"An Aeronca."

"Hey, Ray," the man yelled at the driver. "Let's see if we can get a ride."

"It's not running right," Chloe said, backing toward the engine.

"It's like a crop duster or something," the man said to Ray. "And what's your name?" He turned to Chloe, pushing the sunglasses back onto his face.

She glanced at Doc. Something was wrong with this guy, but she couldn't tell what. "I'm Chloe."

The man took a step toward her, and Doc took a step to intercept him. He stopped and stared at Doc for a moment. "I'm Lee." His thumb touched his chest.

"Nice to meet you guys," Doc said. "Do you have a

phone we could use?"

"No." Ray opened his door and spoke over the hood of the truck. "No phone service out here." His face angled unnaturally, bullfrog-eyes bulging like wet marbles.

"No phone service here," Lee repeated, fondling the rifle barrel.

"Okay, well, thanks anyway." Doc nodded. "We'll just be a few minutes then on our way, right?" He looked at Chloe.

"Right."

"Just a minor engine thing," Doc added.

"Hey…" Lee began. "You guys got any kickers? Oxy?"

"What?" Doc said.

"China white, jackpot?" Lee asked, moving closer.

"No, no we don't." Chloe stepped forward. "We just had some engine trouble and we'll be on our way in no time."

Lee leered at her.

Dust rose above and behind their pickup, another vehicle rumbling down the uneven road, straight toward them.

CHAPTER 65

A green pickup with a Washington Department of Fish and Wildlife seal on the hood pulled up next to the white truck.

Ray returned to his seat and closed his door. Lee wandered a moment, then wobbled back to their truck and slid the rifle inside.

A woman with a single long braid got out of the Fish and Wildlife truck and stood by the front bumper, hands on her hips; an angry grandma with a stiff backbone. She reached for a radio on her belt, removed it, and seemed ready to call someone.

Ray nodded to her and slowly reversed the truck. He turned the wheel, pulling his pickup behind the green one, then put it in drive and spun away, kicking up dust as he went.

The three of them watched the white pickup disappear through the trees.

The woman slid the radio back into its holster and walked stiffly toward Chloe and Doc. An older lady with a slight build, she wore cargo pants, a blue flannel shirt, and a no-nonsense expression.

"What's going on here?" she asked. Though the truck looked official, she was not wearing any kind of uniform or badge. Was she a warden? Would she call for help? Would she call the police? Check Chloe's I.D. and question her?

"We had to land." Chloe pointed behind her. "Engine trouble."

"I'm Trish. Who are you?"

They introduced themselves and explained that they were on their way to Spokane when their engine lost power.

Trish's arms relaxed and her expression softened. "I see. Not drug runners, then?"

Doc looked like she'd hurt his feelings. "Of course not."

"Glad to hear it, because those guys are." She nodded her head in the direction Ray and Lee had gone.

"He asked if we had any kickers," Chloe said.

"Oxy. Opioids," Trish said. "This is a corridor for them, flying drugs in and out of this whole area, supplying Spokane, Pullman, Lewiston. They have several landing strips they use."

"They thought we were flying in drugs?" Doc asked.

"Probably. Wanted to know if you were homing in on their territory."

"Glad you came along when you did, warden," Doc said.

She laughed. "I'm no warden. I'm researching stream beds for Fish and Wildlife, cataloging dead pools where fish hang out in hot summer weather. I borrowed the truck, but I'm just a part-time contractor."

"Still glad you stopped by."

"Can I help you?"

"Well," Doc turned to Chloe.

"I just need to check the engine, but if I can't get it fixed here, is there a phone we could borrow?"

"No cell service here, but I can radio out."

"Let's not do that just yet." Chloe raised her palms. "At least until I can take a look."

"Need any tools?"

"I don't think so. I have a tool kit in back of the plane," Chloe said.

"I'm camped about a half mile back." Trish turned to look there. "If you end up needing anything or needing to spend the night, I'd like the company. I've got a camp stove and food, too. You're welcome to join me."

"Thanks. If we need to, we'll definitely find you," Doc smiled.

Trish nodded and went back to her truck, then pulled onto the two-track and drove slowly away.

"You can fix this. Right?" Doc turned back to Chloe.

"We'll see."

"Try to do so before the next batch of drug runners come along."

CHAPTER 66

Chloe pulled the tools from the storage compartment and waited for the engine to cool. Doc found a grassy spot and lay down for a nap.

After a suitable time, she put her head under the cowling, touching wires and parts, gently tugging on them. Nothing seemed to be loose or broken, again, telling her the problem must be inside the machine.

Not a good sign.

She stared at the metal fins on the air-cooled engine, designed to wick heat away from the cylinders. Two spark plugs for each piston, designed to keep the old girl running even if one of them failed. She wished she had paid more attention when her instructor discussed the mechanics of the Aeronca, but she did remember him telling her about cleaning the plugs. He'd done that once before one of their flights. Right? He was putting the last one back in place when she'd arrived for her lesson. He'd said something about keeping them clean.

A gust of cold air came out of the mountains.

She found the tool that fit the spark plugs, made a note of which plug she was starting with, and wrenched it off.

It looked fine to her. She scraped a little carbon off the gap where the spark explodes and replaced it. The next one seemed to be all right, too.

But the ones on the third cylinder were coated in black soot, a build-up of excess carbon that could rob the spark of its energy. She found a small blade in the tool kit and carefully scratched and blew it clean. She repeated the process on the other plug and again on the plugs on the fourth cylinder, which also were dirty. Maybe it's something that needs to be done every so often on these engines. Or maybe the fuel mixture is a tad too rich. Or maybe it's not the problem at all.

Clouds blocked the sun, cooling the air. A swirl of snow danced across the wings and spun into the distance, pulling her eyes upward. Pewter skies slid across the tree-tops, harbingers of winter.

"Storm moving in," Doc said as he searched the Aeronca for his green fleece jacket.

"Yeah."

"Any luck?"

"Won't know till we start 'er up."

"Now? It's getting cold fast." Doc zipped his coat.

"Well…" She stepped back from the engine, wiping her hands on a rag from the toolbox.

"Maybe we ought to find Trish's camp. See if she can help us keep warm."

"Yeah, maybe." Chloe put the tools away, closed the cowling, and put on her coat. "We shouldn't fly in this weather anyway."

"Besides, we're not in such a big rush now. We've lost that Morozov guy. He doesn't know we're heading to Spokane."

"Right. Help me push the plane toward that tree."

They moved the Aeronca closer to a fir. Chloe tied the rear wheel to the trunk and put the chocks on the front. They carried their camping gear from the plane and walked along the two-track toward the woods. After about a half mile, they saw Trish's pickup parked in a clearing sheltered by a stand of pine. Water rumbled over rocks a few yards away.

Trish greeted them as they approached her camp. Chloe set up her tent by the truck and stuffed her sleeping bag inside. Trish had readied a fire nearby and offered to let Chloe share her tent for the night. Doc could stay in Chloe's.

Heavy clouds dropped closer to the ground, shrinking their world, dimming the light. Trish lit a two-burner propane stove and heated cans of chili. She told Chloe to set up the camp chairs, and they were soon sitting with hot bowls of food, their universe suddenly much more optimistic. She and Doc had skipped lunch and now she was ravenous. She didn't hesitate to ask for a second helping.

"You're a life saver," Doc told Trish.

They cleaned up after supper and moved their chairs

closer to the fire ring. Trish lit the kindling and soon had a snapping little blaze that warmed their cheeks and hands.

"Tell us more about the work you're doing out here," Doc said.

Trish explained that she was counting and measuring pools in the nearby stream, an inventory of safe havens for fish. Trout need cold water, so they seek deep eddies in the summer to avoid the heat. In some places, volunteers might even dig holes or deepen them to improve the habitat, so her work was part of all that.

"We've damaged the environment in ways we don't even know about yet," Trish said. "This is just a little part of a bigger effort to protect it all."

Chloe explained that Doc was a physicist researching quantum particles. "Doc says," she waved her chin at him, "that we are all made up of the four most active elements of the universe: hydrogen, oxygen, carbon, and nitrogen."

"Fascinating. But I'm not completely surprised," Trish said.

"Hmm?"

"My grandmother used to say that four is a sacred number." She looked at Chloe from under her brow, a minor lesson being imparted.

"Why is it sacred?" she asked.

"Because the Creator has woven it into the design. There are four cardinal points, you know, four directions on the compass. Four seasons. Four stages of life – infancy, youth, middle age, and old age. Four primary dimensions

– height, width, depth, and time. Well, so said my grandmother, but I think she was on to something. Now, you tell me that life is made from the four most active ingredients in the universe. It fits."

A light fog crept down from the treetops.

Doc scratched his chin. "The Greeks said there are four elements in the world. Earth, wind, fire," he pointed to the flames in front of them, "and water."

"So, the old rock group was missing one." Trish smirked.

Doc grinned, but Chloe missed the reference.

"Four, huh?" Chloe said. "There are four forces of flight, too. Thrust, lift, drag and gravity. They say the FAA is responsible for the drag," she grinned.

"My grandmother said the circle is special, too. It's a basic shape, has a fundamental balance—its walls are equal distance from the center—and it's common all over the natural world. We see it everywhere. The stars and planets, of course, the earth itself. Wheels. Bird's nests. Fish eggs. Fire rings." Trish pointed to the flames.

"Propellers," Chloe added.

"Atoms," Doc said.

The fog dropped lower.

"She'd say it's a shape heavily favored by the Creator. It's baked into the universe itself, a shape that's influenced by underlying patterns we can't see," Trish said.

"Dark energy?" Doc mused.

"The unknown, breathing force of creation," Choe

said, thinking of the words Chester had used.

"Maybe." Trish nodded.

Doc stared into the silver mist, the kind where thoughts, like ghosts, can swirl. Flames crackled and leapt from the branches, fingers begging for unseen fuel. Hot mother coals pulsed below, micro-suns combusting in the cosmos. A dusting of snow lay on the ground beyond their little camp and despite the jittering flames, Chloe felt cold. And tired.

Trish shifted in her seat. "What's the plan for tomorrow?"

"Assuming the weather clears, we'll start the plane and see how she runs. If it was dirty spark plugs, what I did this afternoon should solve the problem. If not, we'll have to hike out of here to get help—an airplane mechanic, maybe—and see if they'd come back here with us."

"Pullman is probably the closest town." Trish pulled a ski cap onto her head. "Maybe I can help you get to the main road."

"Thank you again." Doc rubbed his hands together.

"What about those drug guys?" Chloe asked.

"Those guys were just dead heads. Or whatever they're called nowadays. The ones in charge don't touch their own product—too smart for that. And they have money. They tend to drive those hummer things. Those wide, four-wheel drive things that look like a jeep mated with a tank."

"Yes," Doc said, "I know what you mean."

"I'm going to have to get some sleep." Chloe rose.

"Me, too." Doc put his hands in his pockets.

"I'll stay a bit and put out the fire." Trish stirred the flames with a stick.

"Who knows what chaos tomorrow will bring?" Chloe stepped toward Trish's tent.

Doc stood, using his professor's voice. "Life is but a field of chaos, with isolated patterns in between."

CHAPTER 67

Chloe woke inside Trish's tent, the smell of coffee gently prodding her out of her sleeping bag. They ate bagels and yogurt from little plastic cups. The air had warmed, sunshine filtering through the pine boughs, snow steaming from the ground. The storm had moved eastward.

"I need to head to the stream north of here," Trish said. "But what I can do is circle back in the afternoon. If you're still here, you can ride with me into town for help."

"Perfect." Chloe sipped her coffee. "That will give me time to check the engine this morning."

"If you're gone, I'll assume you made it off all right and wish you the best."

"Again, Trish, you've been a life saver." Doc collected empty containers and stuffed them in a trash bag.

Trish poured water on the expired fire and stirred it with a stick, making sure there were no warm embers. Doc and Chloe packed up her camp chairs and stove, then helped roll up her tent. Chloe took her own tent down and put their gear by the side of the truck.

"Thanks for helping." Trish gave them a quick salute. "Best of luck to you guys."

Doc and Chloe waved as she drove slowly between the trees and back onto the dirt road, its surface slick with a thin layer of mud. They carried their gear down the road in the opposite direction and loaded it into the Aeronca. Chloe untied the tail, returned the chocks behind their seats, and waved at Doc to help her push the plane away from the pines.

"I'm gonna walk the road," Chloe said, heading farther away from last night's camp, back toward the stretch where they'd landed. Sunlight had warmed the open field sooner than it had reached their camp, and what little snow had fallen the previous night had all steamed away. Although there were a couple of slick spots, they were thin and most of the road was dry. She walked the full distance she thought was needed for take-off. The tree line began about fifty yards farther down.

She returned to the Aeronca. Doc was sitting inside. She placed the chocks by the wheel again and looked back beyond their camp, something pulling her attention.

An engine whined somewhere behind the trees. Had Trish returned?

A brown hummer appeared from the brush, its wide profile squatting like a sumo wrestler, lumbering over ruts in the road.

Then it stopped.

The men inside were looking at her. She reached in

and set the magnetos and throttle to start.

"Buckle up, Doc." She ran to the propeller and spun it down, the pistons clunking, clop-clop. She pulled again and one cylinder fired, pop, but the others failed, the propeller jerking to a stop.

The hummer began driving toward them.

She ran to the cockpit and shoved the throttle, in-out, in-out.

The hummer was bouncing quickly now, ninety yards away.

She hurried to the prop and spun it again, then again, then again.

Damn it. Maybe her work on the plugs had made it worse.

She could see the driver and passenger more clearly now, their vehicle sixty yards away, gaining speed as the road flattened.

She grabbed the edge of the propeller again and dropped with it to the ground, this time with all her weight, and the engine came to life, puttering leisurely, belying the urgency. She jumped into the cockpit, Doc now pointing to the approaching hummer, his breath fast and shallow.

"I know, I know." She wiggled the throttle and the pistons pounded into action, but they weren't moving. She opened her door, reached to the ground, and lifted the chocks from the wheel, tossing them behind her.

The plane lurched forward, onto the dirt road, the hummer now only twenty yards away. She straightened the plane, keeping the main wheels in the shallow ruts, letting the Aeronca gather speed.

They were soon twenty-five, thirty miles an hour, vibrating like a point five earthquake, jarring over lumps and dips, now forty-two, forty-five, fifty miles an hour, straight at the line of pine trees, and finally they lifted from the ground, flight slick as grease on a floor. She held it there, not climbing too quickly, trees expanding in front of them, a wall of darkened green, faster, faster, and then she lifted them sharply upward, wheels grazing the treetops.

Doc had both hands on the frame above the dash, eyes wide, cheeks bloodless.

She banked hard left, away from the rising mountain, back toward the open field.

The hummer had stopped, two men standing beside it. She veered right, toward the edge of the field and levelled her wings, pulling them higher.

Light flashed at the end of one man's arm, the sounds of his gun drowned by the engine. She dropped her right wing, spinning them past the field and over the forest.

"Shitheads," she shouted.

Doc looked at her, the question on his face.

"Those shitheads shot at us!"

They were out of range now, buzzing the trees well beyond where the hummer sat.

"Why would they do that?" Doc turned toward her.

"Because they're shitheads." She checked the instruments and lifted them higher. They had full power again.

"But really, why would they shoot at us?" Doc asked.

"Because the world is full of chaos with isolated patterns in between."

CHAPTER 68

Chloe pulled a deep, clean breath and buckled her seat belt. How many safety procedures had she skipped to get away from the men in the hummer?

Doc relaxed into his seat, watching out his window. She climbed to nearly 2,000 feet above the ground and levelled out again, turning gently north. After a bit, she reached into her pack behind the seat and pulled a bag of snack bars onto her lap.

Today, their journey would end.

"We're finally getting to Spokane," she said, gritting her teeth. "Come hell or high water, we're getting there to-day." She touched her necklace to her chest.

"Not soon enough for me." He looked at one of the protein bars. "If I have to eat another one of these things, I'll choke."

They passed a series of small towns, some of them little more than intersections between acres and acres of bronze wheat. Spokane Mountain, a mere shadow in the haze, was a welcome sight. Still, without GPS, their exact location was uncertain.

"I'm getting a little nervous, Doc," Chloe said over the intercom.

"You?"

"Yeah. I mean, I have to find grandpa's place from the air, after all this time I've been away. Now that we're in the area, I'm not sure I'll recognize roads or rooftops. I haven't been here for years, when my parents were still alive."

"Let me know how I can help."

"And I'm excited to find him but I'm nervous, too, because I wasn't able to talk to him on the phone. He didn't answer, so I just left a message that we were on our way."

"I guess we're here on a wing," Doc pointed above them, "and a prayer."

"You can say that again."

"But we can land somewhere and find a phone, call him again. Or find out where we are exactly and get directions to his place."

"Right." She scanned the hills beneath them, searching for something familiar. A crescent of smog appeared in the distance, likely downtown Spokane. Her grandfather lived south of there. They had to be close.

"Wait!" Doc shouted.

Chloe jumped a little. "What?"

"I have it! I think I have it!"

"What?"

"A way to corral the qubits in a temperature-neutral environment."

"What?"

"It's... I'll tell you more later." He jabbed his finger in the air, some kind of computational method.

"Fine by me, Doc." A long sigh escaped her lungs.

The engine droned on, Doc still deep in his own thoughts.

Chloe dropped to about 1,500 feet above the ground, but that didn't seem to help her find anything she recognized. She checked to her right and left, then eased toward a road ahead and nosed the Aeronca level again.

A white Cessna with a blue stripe suddenly appeared on their left, no prior announcement, no radio warning, only a few yards away, dangerously close in flight.

CHAPTER 69

"Whoa!" Chloe yelled, yanking them hard right, away from the Cessna.

Doc grabbed the metal brace above the dash. "Whaa?"

Her heart pounded, blood thronging behind her eyes. "They found us!"

"How?" Doc twisted in his seat to see. "Did they know we're going to Spokane?"

She levelled her wings then pulled hard on the yoke, throttle full, raising the nose of the plane to the sky, slowing, climbing into the air.

The Cessna matched her maneuver, appearing again to her left, rising with them, beating them in the climb.

The radio squealed. "Set her down the first place you see."

They watched the Cessna rising above them on the same course. The passenger—Morozov—pointed to the ground, another order for them to land. A pour of molten lava seemed to sear through her stomach.

They weren't going to let Chloe land at an airport or

anywhere else she might get help. A bullet in her engine would force her to glide to a landing.

"Hold on," she said to Doc, turning and shoving the yoke all the way in, diving toward and beneath the Cessna. The little plane gathered momentum, shooting them down at over a hundred miles an hour, a speed even the Cessna could not quickly match.

The maneuver had worked in the canyons. Right?

Doc had both hands on the dash, eyes wide, elbows locked.

She pivoted farther left, hoping to put more distance between the two aircraft, then began to level out. She had to. They were only 700 feet above the ground now, close to the low altitude used on final approach for landing.

Wheat fields had yielded to more frequent homes and country roads, pastures in between them. She could land on one, but what then? The Cessna could land, too, right behind them.

She searched desperately for something familiar, any landmark she could use to gauge her location, but it all seemed foreign now. She kept on a course she hoped would keep the Cessna behind them.

A kidney-shaped pond came into view, a ranch house and outbuildings just beyond. Cows wandered near the water, the ground a muddy mess, and Chloe and Doc were past the scene as fast as they'd come upon it, speeding ninety miles an hour.

Telephone wires whizzed beneath them, then gravel

roads and ditches, trucks and driveways. She turned a bit to the right and began an ascent—she shouldn't stay this low for too long.

"What do we do?" Doc yelled.

"Keep going, keep looking," she said, glancing at the instruments and the sky in front of them.

"Can we radio for help?" he asked.

She nodded. "Keep looking for them!"

"Yes."

She pressed the broadcast button. "Aeronca…" What tail number should she use?

"Careful…" a voice came over the radio.

"There!" Doc pointed to their left.

The Cessna had caught up with them already, matching their flight path, hovering slightly ahead and above them.

"Stop this!" she yelled over the radio at them, working to keep the Aeronca steady, glancing at the dash, the altimeter telling her they were only 800 feet above the ground.

Not enough for another deep dive.

"Chloe!" Doc shouted, pointing at the Cessna again.

The passenger door cracked open, fighting against the wind, a stubby-barreled machine pistol aimed directly at them.

CHAPTER 70

Chloe grinded her teeth and clenched her hands on the yoke, focused on the base of Spokane Mountain to help steady her aim. She lifted the nose and yanked the ailerons full to the right, dropping that wing toward the ground, down, down, twisting the plane into a corkscrew roll, the earth suddenly above them. Doc thrust his hands to the ceiling, gravity inverting, lifting them against their seatbelts as they spun upside down, hair lifting from their shoulders, packs and gear behind them shifting and clunking against the cabin ceiling.

Doc moaned.

She touched the rudder pedals, yawing them into the roll, then against it as the horizon began to spin toward normal, their weight shoving them hard, first sideways, then directly into their seats again.

The mountain rose quickly above them, which meant they were diving, so she pulled harder on the yoke, slowing and leveling them out.

Doc's hair still pointed upward, his eyes round,

cheeks like ripe tomatoes, a man whose nerves had just been given an electrical charge.

She pulled a deep breath, checking her instruments. They'd dropped to 600 feet above the ground.

"Don't you ever pull that shit on me again," Doc yelled.

"Kept us from getting shot," she said.

He put his hand to his chest. "Holy mother."

She lifted each wing, looking above and ahead of them for the Cessna. For the moment, their radical maneuver seemed to have shaken them away from it.

"We're going to have to land," she said, searching below them for a level field. A round pond zipped past them on their left, shielded by a patch of trees. Something about its shape was familiar to her. She turned gently alongside the trees, nosing up as she went.

A large field of winter wheat appeared about a mile away, green sprouts rising from the soil, its rectangular shape bordered by tall pines. She could see no obvious fences or ditches running through the field. Power lines were a safe distance away.

It was time to make a decision and this one would do just fine.

"We're going to land over there," she pointed.

"Yes, please." Doc wiped the sweat from his palms and gripped the frame above the dash again.

"Please don't throw up," she said. "Not yet, anyway," she whispered afterward.

"No promises."

She banked gently, lining up an approach to land, and as she levelled her wings again, the Cessna appeared on their left, above and ahead of them. Before she could think, Morozov had shoved his door open with his foot, keeping the gun barrel down.

They were only 500 feet above the ground when the Cessna dropped even closer, near enough for her to see the man's crazy eyes, glinting like arrowheads. He braced against his seatbelt and lifted the machine pistol straight at them.

CHAPTER 71

Brrurrrup!

A blast of bullets clunked into the fuselage behind her.

Brrurrrup!…Brrurrrup!

Chloe pulled them into a steep climb, shoving them into their seats, the horizon suddenly out of sight, the windshield filled with bare, blue sky. They rose slowly, slowly, nearly stalling the wings. The Cessna sped ahead of them but at an angle where, at least for the moment, Morozov could no longer hit them.

She dropped the nose, avoiding the dangerous stall, accelerating toward the earth again, descending to 250 feet above the ground.

The wheat field sped below them, there and gone, so she lifted the Aeronca and turned left, preparing to try again for an approach, searching for the Cessna as she went.

She lifted her wing again and there it was—the Cessna in a tight turn away from them. But she knew they would come in behind and above the Aeronca again, positioned for another try.

She banked hard to the right, a move that would delay the Cessna, and circled back toward the wheat field. Morozov's plane disappeared from view. They flew in relative quiet for several moments, climbing to about 400 feet.

"Where the hell are they?" Doc asked.

"Behind us, probably climbing to keep above us, too."

"Can we land now?"

"Soon as I get lined up."

"Can't they tell we're landing? There's no more reason to shoot at us—we're landing like they want."

"They can't be sure of that. We like to fly low, you know."

"We?"

They passed the field on a parallel course. She kept her altitude steady and lifted her right wing, searching again for any other aircraft. Seeing none, she lowered the wing and banked right again, moving perpendicular to the elongated field, then lining up with it.

The Cessna dropped suddenly into sight on their left, ahead of them by only twenty yards, a desperate move. Morozov shoved his door open again and took aim at the engine of the Aeronca.

Brrurrrup!

Jaaang! The wail of shearing metal pealed on high, the devil's own cymbals, shuddering the propeller, quaking the little plane. Chloe banked hard to the left and behind the Cessna, dodging more bullets.

Brrurrrup!

Slugs shredded the tail of the Cessna, pieces exploding into the air—Morozov's aim had followed the Aeronca as it went behind him. He'd accidentally shot his own airplane.

The gun fell silent.

The Cessna wobbled, pitching up and down, veering away.

Chloe banked to the right and yawed to the left, keeping them aimed at the field but slowing their speed dramatically, dropping them rapidly toward the ground. The engine screeched like a wounded cat, power dropping.

"Shit," Doc closed his eyes.

She leveled the wings and straightened the rudder, lowering below the treetops.

Their wheels smacked against the ground.

They rolled across the soft earth, slowing fast, tail high, nose to the ground, momentum tugging them against their seatbelts until finally the plane seemed to relax, nose up again, tail back down where it should be. They rolled to a stop.

The engine had seized, the propeller no longer spinning. She turned off the magnetos, resting her head on the yoke, trying to breathe.

CHAPTER 72

Doc slid to the ground like he'd been poured from a pitcher of goo and clung to the tire, his eyes sunken, hair spiked in places, blended in others. Chloe stepped out of the Aeronca and stood in the dust, leaning against one of the struts under the wing. She knew she must be breathing, but her lungs, eardrums, fingers had all numbed, shocked into some kind of narcotic state.

After several moments, she began to feel her toes again. She ran her hands over the fuselage, walking toward the tail of the plane. Bullet holes spread randomly through the fabric, pieces hanging literally by a few threads. How they'd not severed the cables that connected the yoke with the tail and horizontal seemed like a minor miracle. If they had, she would have lost all control, and they certainly would have died in a crash.

Crash. The word buzzed in her ears like an irate rattlesnake.

What had happened to the Cessna? She'd seen parts of its tail disintegrate under a storm of bullets.

She walked unsteadily around the rudder of the Aeronca, bullet holes there, too. The horizontal, though, was well intact, undamaged compared to the rest of the plane. She rounded the tail and saw Doc more clearly, now sitting atop the black tire, rubbing his forehead.

"How are you?" She walked toward him, feeling her way along the fuselage.

"Ugh."

Fifty yards behind Doc, in front of the Aeronca, lay the white Cessna, the right wing angled toward the sky, its belly exposed. The tires had punctured, the front wheel and undercarriage twisted back. The propeller had frozen, its blades bent inward. The earth around the plane had been plowed up, loosened and scattered behind where the Cessna had come to rest. The passenger door was hanging open on its hinges.

Had Morozov or the pilot survived? She could see neither of them from this distance.

The Cessna, though ruined, had landed instead of crashed; another minor miracle considering how Morozov had shot up its tail. Should she go to see if they needed help?

Doc turned to see what she was gawking at.

"Ha!" He spun back toward her. "Got what they deserve."

"We'd better go get some help." She moved to the struts and rested on one of them. "They might still be alive inside."

"As long as Morozov doesn't start shooting at us."

"Well, at least it wasn't my social worker." Chloe tried to smile, but her cheeks hurt. "That woman's a real bitch." She chuckled at the weak joke.

"So, I've heard," Doc said.

"Well." She looked across the field.

"Somebody should have seen us, or heard us," Doc said.

"You got that right." Morozov's voice seemed to slide down her back like a sheet of ice.

Chloe turned toward him. Doc looked up at the man and groaned.

Morozov pointed his machine pistol at them. "Time to get what I came for."

Doc dropped his head into his hands.

"What?" Chloe asked, though of course she knew.

"The prototype. We have all of it except the piece you took at the college." A thin line of blood creased the side of his face, sweat and dirt and grime ground into his skin, but his eyes brimmed with wild energy, a dangerous, butane blue.

Doc lifted his head and unzipped a pocket in his fleece jacket.

"No, don't do that." Chloe reached as if to stop him. Was he buying time?

Morozov stepped closer, bracing the pistol against his hip.

Chloe stopped moving.

Doc raised one hand in the air, slowly using the other to pull the modular component from his pocket. "You have to attach it the correct way." His voice was hoarse and defeated.

"Tell me." Morozov tightened his eyes.

"You'll let us go?" Doc asked. "Her, at least?" He pointed to Chloe.

A mad, pinched smile wrinkled his lips. "Of course."

It was clear that Doc did not believe the man, either, but what could they do?

She felt as if she were treading water, her toes reaching for the bottom when none was there, and time seemed to drop beneath her.

After all they'd been through, they had lost.

CHAPTER 73

Doc lifted the component. "See this side, here? Where the corner is sort of shaved off?"

"Show me." Morozov motioned with his fingers.

Doc struggled a bit to stand, bracing against the strut to get his legs straightened. He stayed in place, reaching his hand toward Morozov.

Morozov took three quick steps toward Doc, grabbed the component, and took one long step backward. He examined the strange-looking thing, part memory board, part hard-wired transistors, Frankensteined together.

"See the cut-off corner?" Doc said.

Morozov turned the component in his hand.

"That goes on the right side when you attach it to the top of the prototype. Otherwise, well, you'll fry the thing."

Morozov smirked and placed the unit into his pants pocket.

"Shot up your own airplane, huh?" Anger burned in Chloe's chest, white-hot. She was going to get her own shots in—before he did.

Morozov looked at her.

"You can't hit the side of a barn with that thing, can you?" She pointed at him.

His eyes narrowed.

"You're just some petty thug, you know that?"

He took a step back and raised his gun.

"Chloe, don't," Doc pleaded.

"Pretty stupid, too, you know. Is your pilot dead? You killed your own pilot?" She sneered at him.

"Chloe!"

"Look who's talking about stupid." He aimed the gun to fire.

Boooom!

Morozov's torso shuddered, his eyes suddenly round, mouth slouching open, arms and pistol dropping to his side and his muscles fell limp, marionette strings sliced razor-clean, and he collapsed to the ground.

CHAPTER 74

A wiry man with a Chiefs baseball hat lowered a double-barreled shotgun, his lips a tight crook across his face. White hair touched his shirt collar, mud spattered across his boots and jeans.

"Grandpa?" she whispered, then a smile broke across her like an exploding sun, and she ran to the man, arms outstretched.

She hugged her grandpa like a two-year old: tightly, warmly, mumbling incoherently at first, awash with relief and joy and a deep sense that she'd finally reached her home. She sobbed openly, tears washing her cheeks, feet bobbing her up and down with delight.

The old man embraced her with one arm, the other still holding his shotgun.

"Grandpa, I wanted to call you, but Mascara Mary, that awful foster mom, took my cell phone and the social worker said I couldn't live with you anymore, and..." her breath heaved in and out. Doc would say that she sounded like the teenaged Chloe now, but she didn't care.

"Slow down," he said.

"But that witch is gonna find me and she's gonna try to keep us apart again…"

"I'm better now. I've been working hard at it. My rehab's nearly finished."

"Ohhh." She began to sob again.

"Chloe, dear, it's all right. But what the hell is going on here?" He pointed to Morozov and to the holes in the Aeronca.

She sniffled and gasped and slowly got her breathing under control. "Yeah." She turned toward Morozov, who lay motionless. "That man was trying to kill us."

"Us?"

She stepped back so he could see Doc. "This is my good friend, Mr. Dochauser."

Doc gave a weary salute.

Morozov awoke, moaning and twisting on the ground.

Her grandpa handed her the shotgun and leaned carefully toward the ground, grunting a bit at the movement. He picked up Morozov's machine pistol and slowly straightened. "I only shot the son of a gun with salt pellets. He'll be in a world of pain for a while, but he'll live."

"Oh."

"Hey, Chloe," Doc said. "Where's," he pointed at Morozov, "you know?"

"His partner!" She turned toward the Cessna but saw no one.

A man in a suit jacket was running across the field,

hand-held badge raised above his head.

"Is the pilot...dead?" Doc asked.

"FBI! Everyone stay where you are!" the man yelled.

Morozov tried to roll onto his back but screeched in pain at the effort.

"Special Agent Johansen," the man announced, trotting close to the Aeronca and where Chloe, her grandpa, and Doc stood. Morozov had stopped trying to move, his eyes closed tightly, breathing labored.

"Sam Rochelle," her grandpa said to Johansen. "Retired detective. I took this," he lifted the machine pistol a bit, "from him." He pointed to Morozov. "The suspect was ready to shoot my granddaughter, and I won't stand for that. So, I shot him full of salt pellets."

Chloe raised the shotgun, showing the agent.

Johansen's brow rose. "You're Chloe Rochelle?"

"You know who I am?"

"Been chasing you across the country."

"This is Mr. Dochauser." Chloe pointed.

"And the man on the ground must be Mr. Morozov," Johansen said. "The one who's been working for the Russians."

"Yes," Doc said. "That man killed Belle, my friend and lab assistant."

"We know."

They stood for a moment, a breeze rustling the autumn leaves.

A man with a deputy's uniform stepped slowly from

behind the tail of the Aeronca, pistol pointed toward the ground. "Mohave County Sheriff's office here."

Johansen spun toward the deputy. "Who are you?"

"Deputy Yazzie. I assume you're Agent Johansen?"

Johansen relaxed. "Yes."

"Hell of a chase these two put us through." Yazzie nodded toward Doc and Chloe.

"This is Chloe's grandfather," Johansen said to Yazzie and pointed.

Yazzie nodded.

Johansen looked at Chloe. "This is the deputy who helped us find you." His eyes narrowed and turned back to Yazzie. "But why did you come all the way to Spokane?"

"We have an order to return her to the child services department."

"Oh, right," Johansen said. "But we'll need to question her first."

"Of course." Yazzie moved closer to Johansen, slipping his pistol into its holster. He reached his hand toward the agent, who holstered his gun, too. The men shook hands.

Chloe's grandfather laid Morozov's machine pistol in the grass at his feet. Chloe kept her grandfather's shotgun aimed at the ground.

"You must be Dochauser," Yazzie said. "The physicist."

"Yep."

"And this guy," he pointed to Morozov, "was trying to steal some computer chip or something?"

"He has it," Doc pointed.

Yazzie moved quickly to Morozov and searched his jacket. "This?" He held up the component.

"That's it." Doc stood and reached toward Yazzie.

"Evidence," Yazzie said, pocketing the flat component.

"I'll take that," Johansen said.

"Nope." Yazzie swung around, pulling his pistol as he went.

CHAPTER 75

Johansen took a half step back and raised the palms of his hands. "Hey!"

"This theft was in Arizona. FBI or not, this is my jurisdiction." Yazzie turned squarely toward Johansen.

"You've got your gun on a federal agent, Yazzie. You don't want to do that. It's a federal crime, you know that." Johansen slid another half step away.

"I've busted my ass for this and it's evidence in our case."

Chloe held her breath.

Her grandpa looked at her, drawing her attention, and mouthed the word "pull." His eyes went from hers to the shotgun and back again.

She blinked an acknowledgement. He wanted her to shoot Yazzie when the time was right. The double-barreled shotgun had one shell left to fire.

"Bullshit!" Her grandfather stepped toward Yazzie, getting his attention. "You're not here to take evidence back home."

"Shut up and hand me that pistol." Yazzie pointed at the machine pistol on the ground, the one her grandpa had taken from Morozov.

"You're an inside man." Grandpa shook a finger at Yazzie, scolding him. "You work for the same guys Morozov does. You work for the Russians."

Yazzie's face reddened. He turned the pistol toward her grandpa.

"How else did Morozov know where to find Chloe? You knew, as a deputy. You knew Chloe would fly here, to me. The FBI knew." He pointed at Johansen. "So, somebody had to tell Morozov and that was you. Wasn't it?"

Yazzie backed away.

"What did they do? Offer you money?" he said, contempt in his voice. He moved sideways, putting Yazzie between him and Agent Johansen. And in clear view of Chloe.

"Not just money." Yazzie's eyes narrowed, and he stopped, standing his ground this time. "Two million dollars cash. Tax free."

"Yeah, now what? You're gonna pull the heist of the century or something? Pull a fast one?" He stared into Yazzie's eyes, holding them for a moment.

Yazzie broke his gaze, turned toward Johansen, and raised the pistol to fire.

Chloe dropped to one knee, lifting the heavy shotgun to her shoulder, and squeezed the trigger.

Boom!

The pistol flew from Yazzie's hand and he tumbled

backward into the grass, rolling to a stop.

Johansen pulled his pistol and ran to Yazzie, who lay unconscious.

Chloe stayed on the ground, her knees turned to sponge.

Johansen touched Yazzie's neck and said, "He's got a pulse."

Grandpa came to her and lifted the gun from her hands. He pointed to her shoulder. "That's gonna bruise up nicely tonight."

Doc appeared above her and offered his hand. "Is there nothing you can't do, my friend?" He smiled.

CHAPTER 76

Sirens filled the air as police vehicles turned a corner and sped away from the trees and across the bumpy field toward the broken Aeronca.

Grandpa lifted Morozov's machine pistol from the ground and walked to Yazzie. He held the pistol at the ready and nodded at Johansen.

Johansen went to Morozov and shook him until his eyelids opened a crack. "Morozov, listen to me. You'll be put to death for treason unless you help me right now."

Morozov moaned as he turned toward the agent.

"Tell me now, before the federal government and the States of Arizona, Nevada, and Washington all come down on you: who are you working for What's his name?"

"Go to hell."

"Your pilot is most certainly dead. If you tell me now, we'll cut a deal, but this is your one and only chance."

Morozov raised his head, searching for Carl, it seemed.

"We'll tell everyone that your pilot told us before he died. We'll tell everyone that you kept your mouth shut."

"No."

Three tan pickups with sheriff stars on their hoods skidded to stops thirty yards away. The sheriff and two deputies hurried out of their vehicles, hands on their holsters. Two other officers gathered something from their truck bed.

"You make a deal with me right now, no risk to you. Now or never, Morozov. You want the death sentence for treason? Electric chair? Remember the guy they tried two or three times to kill before they got it done? Nursed him back to health just to try it all over again, some kind of experimental method…"

Morozov's face slackened against his skull, his icy eyes watery now, defeated.

The deputies were trotting toward them.

"Now or never."

Morozov motioned for Johansen to lean closer.

Chloe could hear him whispering to the agent.

Johansen stood quickly, turning to the first deputy to arrive. "Get an ambulance for these men." He waved at Morozov and Yazzie. "Right away!"

But an ambulance had already been called, jarring across the open field, its siren blending with the others. Doc helped Chloe stand up.

Smoke rose like dust devils from the Cessna's engine, spectral whisps that warned of fire below. Two deputies ran toward the airplane, extinguishers in hand.

Chloe's grandpa raised his free hand in the air and circled it twice. The sheriff repeated the signal and another deputy turned off the shrieking sounds. Paramedics hurried to the Aeronca and quickly examined Morozov, rolling him onto a stretcher.

"He's in police custody," a deputy told the medics and followed them into the ambulance. In moments, it drove back across the field to the gravel road at the end, then turned and sped away, lights strobing.

A bulky man with sheriff stenciled across his black jacket approached her grandpa with a beefy smile and a handshake. Agent Johansen walked to them and introduced himself.

Grandpa smiled at Chloe then moved stiffly toward Doc, his hand outstretched.

"I owe your granddaughter my life." They shook hands.

"I live on the other side of those pine trees," grandpa wagged his chin to the right, "and saw some of it from the ground." He turned back toward Chloe. "That was a helluva dog fight. You're lucky to be in one piece. No more of that tomfoolery on my watch." He cast her a sly smile.

"Oh, Grandpa, you won't believe it! Doc here is a physicist and he's brilliant, absolutely brilliant, and he's found a new way for quantum computers to work that will change our lives, medicine, computers, it's revolutionary."

"So, that's why that guy…" her grandpa waved the machine pistol at where Morozov had lain.

"That man's a Russian spy or something. He's been chasing Doc to get his quantum computer prototype but

Deputy Yazzie got it. It's in his pocket! We have to get it," Chloe said.

"Then we'll get it back," the sheriff said, "at the hospital." He tapped a number into his cell phone.

"But Chloe," Doc raised his arms, hands clasping an invisible ball.

"Yeah?"

"I've been thinking about this. I think there's an even better way to corral the quantum particles. Better than the prototype Morozov and Yazzie were trying to steal."

Her grandpa and Agent Johansen turned toward Doc.

"You said it, Chloe. It's plants." His lungs worked harder now, bellows fanning the fire in his eyes. "The quantum-like process they use every day. We've got to use the same leaf-like structure, the same bioelectric and biochemical processes. Four cells, circular on top, diamond shaped below, focusing the qubits with bioelectric pulses. Mirror how the simple leaf does it each time it converts sunlight into food."

"That's how we get closer to the breathing force of creation?"

"The Tao is unknowable, remember?" He grinned. "But we'll get closer to the flow of it, anyway."

"You're just the guy to do it, Doc."

CHAPTER 77

Chloe reached around Doc's sizeable girth and squeezed. "I sure am glad we're not in some alternate universe."

"The one where Schrödinger's cat is dead?" He returned the hug.

"That's it." She looked up at him.

"Just think of this: there might be a universe out there where none of this happened at all."

"If I hadn't taken the Aeronca."

"If Belle and your parents were still alive."

"God, Doc," a soft pleading entered her voice, "that'll twist me into a pretzel."

"You're right. Sorry."

She stepped back and beamed at him.

"Shame to see this old airplane all shot up." Her grandpa tilted his head at the mangled propeller.

"Oh, yeah." She seemed at a sudden loss for words.

The sheriff rubbed the side of his nose. "We have a BOLO for that plane. Missing, the owner said. Know anything about that?" He looked at Chloe.

"Well…"

"Missing," her grandpa turned to the sheriff, "not stolen. Right?"

"I suppose,"

"Your flight instructor owns this, right? Peter… somebody?"

She nodded, lips clamped tight.

"So, I suppose we'll need to pay for the repairs right away," her grandpa folded his arms, frowning at the crumpled cowling. "We'll get on the phone to Peter this afternoon."

The sheriff looked at Chloe, waiting for her to say something, but she knew when to keep quiet. He wheezed at the sky, capitulation in his breath. "We'll contact the owner tomorrow. See if he wants to pursue the matter."

"Thanks," her grandpa nodded. "I think we'll get her repaired here and find someone to fly her back to Phoenix. No harm, no foul."

"As long as the owner agrees," the sheriff warned.

"He'll probably get a whole new engine and prop. Better than when Chloe borrowed it."

She rubbed her fingers in circles against her forehead, wondering how much of this she was going to have to repay.

A middle-aged woman, blonde hair tied in a bun, strode across the field, file folder in hand. "Chloe Rochelle?" she said, her voice like a school principal announcing detentions.

Chloe stiffened.

"I'm with the Washington Department of Children, Youth, and Families."

"She's with me," her grandpa spoke quickly, stepping closer to Chloe.

"We have a pick-up request from Arizona social services."

"I'm sure you have." Her grandpa looked at the sheriff. "But I'm her grandfather."

"You can file a request with our department."

"She stays here."

"No, sir."

"I said, she stays here." He pointed to the ground they stood on.

Chloe held her arms against her chest, suddenly cold.

"Sheriff?" Her grandpa turned toward the man.

The sheriff cleared his throat. "Mr. Rochelle here has a temporary order from the court placing Chloe with him pending further hearing."

"What?"

Her grandpa whispered to Chloe, "I got a lawyer as soon as I got your phone message."

"And seeing no immediate risk to the safety of the child," the sheriff tucked his thumbs into his belt, "she will stay with her grandfather until the court says otherwise."

The woman huffed. "Why weren't we notified of this?"

"No time," her grandpa said. "But a hearing will be set in a couple of days, I'm told. You're welcome to attend."

She looked at each of them in turn, then settled her

eyes on Chloe, a silent rebuke. "Well, enough." She turned and walked back across the field.

"Oh my god." Chloe wrapped her arms around her grandpa again.

"We'll need to question all of you." Johansen had joined them.

"Of course," Doc said.

"Can't we get something to eat first?" Chloe's brown eyes shined, combusting, it seemed, like micro-suns in the cosmos.

CHAPTER 78

Chloe sat on the steps of her grandpa's back porch, watching a red-tail hawk hover over the adjoining field. The emergency landing, the confrontations with Morozov and Yazzie, the feel of the shotgun in her hands was two days ago but it felt like only minutes.

Agent Johansen had returned to Phoenix but called with updates. Morozov would be prosecuted in Arizona for the murder of Belle Smith and for assaulting Doc and her with a deadly weapon. Washington State would likely prosecute for attempted murder. The United States Attorney was sorting out the federal charges like espionage and treason. Morozov would avoid the death penalty, but he'd be living in prison for a very long time.

Carl, Morozov's pilot and co-conspirator, died in their crash.

Sadly, Yazzie had sold out to the Russians, just like grandpa thought. Yazzie had deep debts and high ambitions, well outside the credo to "protect and serve." He underwent surgery to repair damage from the salt she'd blasted into his stomach, and when he fully recovers, he'll be prosecuted, too.

The National Security Agency had Ivan under heavy surveillance and told Agent Johansen that counterintelligence operations were underway. No details for the ordinary citizens, though...

Grandpa, Doc, and the local sheriff filed affidavits with the superior court and the temporary order granting custody to grandpa was extended. The court stuff felt perfectly bizarre, though. Outlandish, really. Why should anyone else have a say in where she went or what she did? She hadn't been a child in years.

Grandpa said the social services office in Arizona was re-examining the suitability of Mascara Mary and her weirdo husband as foster parents. About time.

The hawk disappeared behind the trees.

Grandpa worked things out with her flight instructor. He would pay for repairs on the Aeronca not covered by insurance. Chloe would find a job and begin partial repayments to grandpa. Probably for the next twenty years. But she'd resume her flying lessons, this time in Spokane in a modified Cub, another tail dragger. With luck, she'd be licensed in a couple of months. She'd work on her driver's license, too.

Doc was flying back to Azteca College in the morning. He'd camped on grandpa's couch and filled a notebook with cryptic symbols and equations and stubby little paragraphs, working on his new theory about how to improve quantum computing. She'd found him staring at a philodendron leaf, turning it in his hands, mumbling now and then. He offered her an internship at the college, whenever she was ready. Once she had her pilot's license, she'd hit the books and take the G.E.D. test then enroll in the local community college. She'd transfer to Azteca later.

She was going to miss Doc, that was certain. But she wanted time with grandpa again, a chance to settle in. She pressed her turquoise necklace against her chest, remembering her mom and her dad, the sound of their voices. She needed one of those settled patterns for a while, just a little while, the ones scattered randomly across the field of chaos.

She felt a tear roll down her cheek, but it wasn't sadness.

The hawk beat his wings against the sky, climbing into the blue, flying against the wind.

AUTHOR'S NOTE AND ACKNOWLEDGEMENTS

Thank you for reading *Against the Wind* – I really hope you enjoyed it! As an author, I depend heavily on book reviews and referrals. If you think others might enjoy the novel, too, please leave a quick review on Amazon or any other internet site you use for selecting books to read. The moment it takes to leave a quick book rating makes a lasting difference for the author!

Quantum physics is a fascinating field, even for us amateurs. The notion that our reality rests on particles that can both exist and not exist simultaneously, or that can directly connect with each other, even light-years apart, suggests how superficial our understanding of the universe has been. And yet, ancient man has touched the unknown, the mysterious, the patterns in creation being rediscovered by modern physicists. Physics and philosophy twirl in a special dance of their own – sometimes, they seem to blend into the very same thing. Quantum computing may be the next big breakthrough in the journey of mankind and will open doors never before thought possible. Enjoy the wondrous possibilities!

Hats off to my lovely and patient wife for all her support while working on this effort. Thanks to her, Dad, Sarah, and Julie for their valued insights and edits. Special thanks to Dad for his technical expertise on the old Aeroncas. Thanks to my friends, family, and colleagues, whose support helped keep my head above water.

I also want to thank my editor, Jim Dempsey, for his

encouragement, careful attention to detail, and insightful suggestions. I thank Daniel Thiede for his beautiful cover art and book design and his much-needed help with the technical aspects of the work.

Thanks to all who understand our kinship with the planet and those who work in the service of their ideals.

"Well, butter my buns…"

He shaded his eyes with the palm of his hand.

There were two pickup trucks in Demon's Roost canyon – one in the deep arroyo at the base of sheer cliffs to the south, one on the upper flats that made up most of the corkscrew canyon. There'd been uranium mining here in the 1950s, but what these yahoos were doing now was a mystery.

Relic tightened his ponytail and stared into the twisting gorge.

Yesterday morning, snow capped the hoodoos – white icing on scarlet cupcakes. By this afternoon, the sun-fired rocks had begun radiating heat near 100 degrees, wringing moisture from the human body like a twisted sponge. The cliffs above him seemed to glow, slivers of clay injected into the blood-red sandstone like fat marbled into raw steak. A pair of crows squawked overhead.

An unlikely descendent of disparate clansmen – one Scottish, one Hopi – Relic wandered these plateaus and chasms, a sometimes-trespasser, recluse, and moonshiner. He'd been called a vagabond, a sasquatch of the desert, but these remote places were home.

He left his pack by a rock and trotted down the trail to the bottom of the canyon. He moved quickly around the first bend to a spot close to the truck on the flats. No one seemed to be around. He walked to the pickup, a silver double-cab, its tailgate down. Topographic maps lay flattened across the truck bed, rocks on the corners to hold them in place. An empty five-gallon container for water sat on the end of the tailgate, neon-orange stripes across its side. A gust of wind slid the plastic canister off the edge and Relic picked it up.

The maps were of Demon's Roost and places to the north. Scribbles and circles were penciled over the contour lines, but he couldn't tell what they meant. The second truck, the one in the dry creek bed, sat around a bend in the canyon, out of sight from this position.

Something made him uneasy. Some distant vibration, maybe. The crows had gone silent. Charcoal clouds hung in the east.

Two men rounded the corner, boots rasping over the sand, heads down, mumbling to each other. He watched from behind the silver truck, some fifteen feet above them and thirty yards away. One wore jeans and a white dress shirt, out of place in this remote canyon. The other wore a red shirt with a leather strap across his shoulder.

Relic took a step back and felt it again – this time a deep rumble under his boots – and suddenly he knew what was coming. Though desperately dry, it was water that had shaped these desert lands, sheer bluffs and jagged drainages wrought by the power of rain. A cloudburst 50 miles away could become a flash flood in these narrow canyons, a deadly blast of water exploding with little warning. The men in the arroyo stood directly in its path.

"Hey, hey!" Relic raised the empty water container above his head, waving it in the air, sprinting past the pickup truck and toward the edge of the ravine.

One of the men looked up.

"Get out of there! Out of there!" Relic shouted, pointing up the embankment, urging them to run from the dry creek bed before it was too late.

The other man straightened, suddenly startled, and reached for his side.

"Flash flood! Flash flood!" Relic waved the plastic canister again and stepped to the edge of the ravine.

The dissonance in his toes became a bellow in his head, an angry groan.

One man began to climb from the bottom of the arroyo, boots slipping up the sandy rise. The other lifted his hand from his side, a pistol in his fingers, aiming it toward Relic.

Relic spiraled backward reflexively, stepping suddenly into thin air, dropping down the slope, skidding feet-first through loose sand all the way to the bottom. He stood and looked at the gunman, who'd holstered his pistol and begun climbing the side of the arroyo behind his companion. In a moment, they both stood above the empty drainage, out of danger.

Now the sound of thunder rolled through the canyon, echoes doubling the alarm. Relic ran down the dry bed, frantically searching its steep walls for a place he could ascend. The rumble became the roar of whitewater, ramjet engines at full throttle, all other sound blasted aside by the urgency and enormity of the coming flood.

Relic turned in time to see a two-foot bank of water rise behind him, precursor to the deluge to come.

He held tight to the empty container and ran toward

the spot the two men had used to climb from the dry bed, but as he began to scramble up the slope, the coffee-colored water, heavy with silt, reached his feet, sweeping them forward, twisting him down into the roiling river.

He wrapped his arms around the canister, his makeshift life vest, and lifted his feet in front of him. A surge forced him underwater – his eyes closed, mouth shut – then lifted him rapidly toward the top of the arroyo, shoving him forward faster than a man could run. He kicked to keep his feet downstream, buffers against rocks, trees, or cliffs. The newborn river hurtled him around the bend, a choleric infant wailing at the world.

The second pickup truck lay directly in his path.

He wiggled and twisted, paddling his boots as fast as he could, but the truck came swiftly closer, closer, his feet about to smash into the rear window. If he were forced through the glass and into the cab of the truck, the river would pin him there and drown him. But as he approached, he seemed to slow, then slow some more. His boots touched the window. He bent his knees and pushed away, then he realized he hadn't slowed at all. The truck had been lifted from the ground and shoved forward with him. The water carried them both through the flood together.

The deluge raged around another bend in the canyon, rocks clacking violently against each other along the bottom, tumbling into the flow from the sides, debris that could crush him in a second if he got caught between them. The truck separated from him, rolling to its side. A wave suddenly tossed his head and chest above the flow, his feet pulled downward. He flipped forward and under the rapids, no time to take a breath. Despite the buoyancy of the canister, the swirling river forced him downward, somersaulting into the dark. He lost all sense of direction, what was up or down, dizzy in the swirling storm, helpless under the unyielding, raging current. Pressure rose in his lungs to near explosion, his diaphragm tensing, preparing to blow his final breath from his chest, when finally he spun upward, his head breaking through, and he gasped.

He pushed on the container, lifting his head as high as he could, hungrily sucking in air. The sides of the arroyo sped by, bending left, then right, disorienting him. His boots struck something hard, and he realized his legs were dangling below him again – a dangerous position. He pulled himself into a back float, feet downstream, arms clutching the canister. Waves splashed into his eyes and mouth, blinding him for seconds at a time, forcing him to take quick, shallow breaths. The current threatened to spin him again, so he paddled his feet, twisting to keep his face above water.

The waves began to spread farther apart and his sight improved when he squinted. The truck was behind him now, spinning slowly in the current as he passed another bend in the gorge.

The sky seemed to lighten as the canyon walls receded. He felt his elevation lower as the flood spread across more open ground, closer to its destination in the Colorado River.

He spun to his left and kicked as hard as he could, moving out of the current. In moments, his bottom touched hard ground. He pushed farther away from the receding water until he could sit up. A three-inch flow continued to swirl around him, but he knew he was safe.

He took full, deep breaths, clearing the adrenaline from his system, regaining a sense of balance.

The flow of water slowly turned to mud. The truck had rounded the last corner, then gotten stuck behind a rock and buried nearly a foot deep in the sandy bottom. He dropped the empty container and wiped the water and hair from his eyes.

"This is the worst thing that's happened since the last thing," he told himself with a grin. It was the second time he'd been caught in a flash flood and nearly drowned. The first time, it'd been his own damn fault. Well, hell, he thought, maybe it was his own fault this time, too.

If the swim hadn't been so deadly, part of him, at least, could have admitted to the thrill.

He sat for a moment, staring into the clear sky. Who were those guys and what the hell were they doing in this canyon? And why did one of them draw his pistol when he'd warned them about the flood?

"I guess no good deed goes unpunished," he scolded himself. He stood slowly, shaking out his arms and legs. He removed his shirt, wrung it out, and put it back on. "I'll dry you out later," he spoke to his pants and boots.

It was time to get the hell out of there.

RAPTOR CANYON

The tent became a dome of light, then began to smolder and burst into flame near the back, near the kitchen stove.

"Hey, we just cleaned the grill back there," Relic said, making Wyatt laugh.

The fire spread slowly, casting a halo of light across the camp. Security guards hollered, workers yelled their curses and questions, and everyone rushed to see what the commotion was all about.

"Is she really crazy enough to do that?" Wyatt asked.

"Yep," Relic nodded.

"Well, shee-it," Wyatt did his best imitation of Faye.

Relic smiled. "Don't let her hear you or she'll knock your block off."

"No doubt."

"Would you see what you can do to slow down that backhoe up ahead of us and anything else with a lock and key? Then work your way north, swing back toward the staircase and we can meet up there."

Wyatt nodded.

"Keep a close look out. They'll be searching as soon as the mess is under control."

"What's your next move?" Wyatt asked.

Relic jerked his thumb toward the portable toilets.

"Really?" Wyatt said.

Relic turned and faded into the dark. Wyatt heard footfalls, someone moving quickly toward him. After a moment, he recognized her shape bobbing along. She tossed something and he heard it clacking into the bed of a pickup. She nearly ran into him.

"Hey." He put his hands out toward her.

"Hey," she said, slowing, but only a bit. "Here." She tossed a stick of dynamite to him, the fuse sparkling lit.

"Shit!"

"Throw it!" she shouted as she ran past. "Now!"

Wyatt stared at the tube in his hand. The fuse sputtered and spat and shortened with every second, time compressed with the tightness of his breath, the glowing fuse moving forward immutably until something like a spinning clutch popped in his chest and muscle movement became possible again. He reached his arm back and threw it as far and as fast as he could, then he spun and ran to the side of another truck and turned back to look.

The pickup Faye had tossed something into rose into the air with a smack that washed away all other sound, then fell back to the ground with a nasty twist as pieces of sheet metal dropped from the sky.

"Holy…"

Wyatt's stick of dynamite exploded somewhere beyond another truck, lighting something on fire, sending a second sonic boom through his skull, making him jump in his tracks. He stared at the blaze as it settled into a steady burn and looked the direction Faye had run.

A third, fourth, and fifth explosion erupted in quick succession in the row of portable toilets and Wyatt knew it was Relic's work. Where was Relic's peaceful resistance now? Lord, he hoped no one was in those toilets. Then, he thought, what a mess of shit, and he giggled and smacked his hands together.

Oh, my god, was it possible to have so much fun? He never expected stopping Lord Winnieship from stealing this canyon to feel so damn good.

He stared at the fire he'd started and tried to think. He wanted to follow Faye but there was no telling what other mayhem she had in mind, and he did not want to walk into an exploding outhouse. He tried to regulate his breathing, with only a little luck. He circled away from the path Faye had taken, giving her a wide berth, moving to the outer edge of the parked vehicles.

Wyatt turned and trotted toward a lone backhoe, maybe sixty yards away. Though the electric lights of the compound were out, the kitchen and dining room blaze cast a sallow glow on the tops of the other tents and equipment. The upper arm of the yellow backhoe was lit like a candle.

His shins scraped across brittle sage and he slowed to a walk. He'd lost his own toothpicks, so that trick would not work with the heavy equipment. After Faye's dynamite, toothpicks seemed pretty pathetic anyway. Maybe there was a set of keys kept in the ignition that he could toss away. Or maybe he could flatten its tires or pull wires from under the dash to disable the beast. He turned to watch the bobbing of flashlights all around the burning mess tent a quarter of a mile away. The voices of men rose and fell in a rhythm that was almost musical, like an offbeat composition.

He stopped at the base of the backhoe and stared up at the top, where the boom and dipper attached. He circled the machine to the open cabin and peered inside.

"Stop and turn around." The voice was deep

and familiar.

Wyatt turned and raised his hands. Even in the semi-dark, Lynch's muscled bulk identified him immediately. He held a pistol aimed at Wyatt's chest.

"You!" Lynch said. "You sonofabitch."

Wyatt saw the left hook a milli-second before it struck his jaw, wrenching his head away and toward the ground. He stumbled to the side. A blow to his stomach struck like a rocket and his chest ached, all the veins in his body shut down by a sonic boom. Slivers of light flashed through his eyes, closed tight against the assault. He sensed himself floating to the earth, his muscles turned to liquid. He was out before he hit the dirt.

Excerpt from
WINGS OVER
GHOST CREEK

He sucked a shallow breath of air, pulled his gaze from the dead arm, and looked back the way he'd come. From this perspective, the arm was well-hidden on the backside of the long pile of dirt, tucked close to the low rock face and well out of view from the hangar and the tents beyond. Last night's heavy storm had flushed loose soil from the canyon slopes and probably from the body, too. He tried not to look back at the fragile hand, but he couldn't help himself. Skin shriveled against the tiny bones, stiff leather holding the assembly of joints together, keeping the fingers pointed in confusing, haphazard directions, their owner not sure which way to go. Red nail polish added a cheap party flare, a celebration completely out of place.

Holy eff. Hold it together, he told himself, get back to camp and pretend he'd never seen it. Tell Thomas. No one else. Someone here could have killed this girl, must have killed her. Why? What had happened here?

He turned his eyes to his feet and shuffled across the ground, moving to the edge of the pile of dirt. He peered around the mound and saw the edge of the hangar and the back of the tents. No one seemed to be around, so he hustled away from the dirt, across the hard-packed surface, and into the hangar. He went to the yellow plane again and leaned on the right strut, his breath still shallow and labored.

Owen looked beyond the hangar to the field outside and the Cessna waiting for them. Where was Thomas?

"Did you get that cold drink?"

Panic charged through his brain, a devil's hot wire crackling from one ear to the other. His head jerked toward the front of the plane and he clamped his hands tightly on the strut. Everett's question was smooth but – was there an undertone in his voice?

Owen managed to force a breath.

"No…" he patted the wing support, glanced at Everett, then spoke to the plane itself, too nervous to look at the man again. Squeezing the strut helped him to focus. "I got sidetracked by this old Aeronca. What year is it, do you know?"

"1946, I'm told."

"Oh."

"Are you a pilot?" Everett moved out of the sunlight and into the shade of the hangar. Owen knew the man could see him better now.

"No, no, I'm not. Tried to take some lessons, but…" He struggled to keep his thoughts on the aircraft, away from what he'd discovered. "Just look at this panel, the instrument panel," he pointed. "Not hardly any instruments here, though. It's all metal, too, like the dashboards on old cars." He kept his eyes on the cockpit, still reluctant to look directly at Everett.

"Yeah, I've looked it over myself." Everett's voice seemed more normal now, more conversational. "The owner has a friend who came out here a couple of days ago. He's restoring the old bird, but I don't know how far he's gotten. The fabric looks like a stiff breeze would pull it off." He ran his hand across the edge of the wing opposite Owen. "You wouldn't catch me flying in this death trap." Everett wandered away from the plane, plucked a long blade of grass from the ground and began to twist it absentmindedly.

"Yeah, the cloth on this one needs completely replaced." Owen tried to sound like an authority on the subject and felt his nerves calm a little as he spoke. He ducked under the wing and walked into the sunlight. "Seen my boss?"

"I think he's about done," Everett pointed toward the tents along Ghost Creek. Thomas and Angela were walking slowly back toward the Cessna. Angela was explaining something, Thomas nodding.

"Well, it was nice meeting you." Everett moved quickly toward Owen and offered his hand, his smile showroom friendly, his shake cold and curt.

"Yes. Nice meeting you, too." Owen made eye contact briefly and turned back toward the Cessna. "Better get going."

He strode toward the rented Park Service plane, muscle memory moving his legs, thoughts flowing back to that tortured hand, its ragged movement in the breeze. He tried to be nonchalant about getting the hell out of there. Angela and Thomas came closer to the Cessna.

"Got what we need?" Owen asked Thomas.

Thomas looked up. "Yep. Thanks for the tour and good luck to you," he said to Angela. He shook hands with her and Everett and turned back to the plane.

Owen did not wait to be told to climb in. He adjusted his seatbelt, put the headset on, and waited. Thomas did the same.

How was he going to tell Thomas about the dead

girl's arm? When should he tell him? Angela and Everett positioned themselves to one side and in front of the Cessna. They could see any conversation between him and Thomas, so he stayed quiet.

Thomas spent a moment examining the air map and checking the instruments. Out of the corner of his eye, Owen saw the man with the red hat, Luke, run up to Everett and whisper urgently in his ear. Everett glared at the plane, then gave some sort of order to Luke, who ran out of view. Did they know he'd found the girl's body?

"Clear prop!" Thomas pumped the throttle and turned the key, the engine spitting to life. Owen sat back in his seat, eyes straight ahead, and listened to the engine as Thomas adjusted the fuel mixture and checked the magnetos, turning first one off, then the other, then both back on for flight, Owen wishing he would hurry the hell up. Thomas finally pushed the throttle forward and the engine roared, the Cessna shuddered, and they began to roll down the dirt strip, vibrating, bouncing, jarring over small ruts until suddenly, liftoff, and the ride became smooth and even, the engine solid and throaty, clear air ahead of them, and Owen finally took a deep breath.

Thomas made a gentle turn to their left, flying back toward the creek, the dig site, and the old hangar, circling to gain altitude needed to fly over the plateau above the camp. They rose steadily as they went, Owen thinking how to explain what he'd found, hoping he'd done the right thing by waiting until they were in the air, bound for home base.

They leveled out about two miles past the Quonset hut, aiming for the broad Colorado River as they continued to climb beyond the canyon. A ribbon of dust rose to their right, a truck in motion along the road, soon to be well behind them. Ghost Creek faded from view as they neared the level of the plateau. They could see the bronze river beyond as it wound its way southward, on toward the Grand Canyon, on to the Gulf of California. Owen rubbed his hands on his pants and readied himself.

"Thomas," he spoke into the microphone on his headset.

"Yes?"

"I've got something to tell you, something I discovered down there while you were with the archeologist..."

"Yes?" Thomas checked his GPS and adjusted his heading.

Just then, a hollow thump jarred Thomas forward and he pushed the yoke in, then tugged and released it as he slumped back in his seat. Owen grabbed the yoke and his eyes swelled wide and he stared at Thomas' slackened face and began to scream his name, bobbing the plane's nose up, down, up, when another hollow thump jarred them and oil sprayed into the air and onto the right side of the windshield and he heard the motor cough, and cough again, and felt the Cessna lose its power, dropping in the air, descending toward the ground and he screamed again.

Excerpt from
DIAMONDS OF
DEVIL'S TAIL

"Wicked chickens lay deviled eggs, but this one's rotten, too." Relic took the binoculars from his eyes and stroked his buffalo-beard goatee. Something about the man on the trail below made his skin tingle.

He slid away from the edge, out of the man's line of sight, and looked about. An unlikely descendant from clans of the Hopi and Scottish, Relic wandered the remote reaches of the Green and Colorado Rivers and the high plateaus between them, a weathered hermit at home in the desert outback, roaming ancient trails, brewing his homemade gin at a couple of narrow, spring-fed crags tucked above the floodplains. He tightened his ponytail, errant strands of white flashing through his coal-black hair.

A dried-out branch of cottonwood leaned against the nearest in a row of six Pueblo houses nestled tightly between the floor and ceiling of the cliff, a string of separate rooms, their stone blocks still mortared together in the corners. Inside were mano stones, held in the hand for grinding corn, and metate, wide-bottom slabs used for the same purpose. A child's bow and arrow, chert for making knives and arrowheads, and bowls of corn, squash, and other seeds were set neatly on indoor ledges under a layer of dust; their owners, it seemed, only away for the winter. In the farthest room was a row of large pots painted with white and black bolts of lightning, edges curved and sharp, with handles on their sides, tops still sealed tight, their contents a thousand year-old mystery. Relic meant to keep it that way.

He leaned forward again. The man strode purposefully toward the high cliff with something long, something strangely out of place, glinting in the desert sun. He put the binoculars back to his eyes.

Of all the things to be lugging in this remote country, to be balancing on bony shoulders in the noonday heat, that angular, outrageous shape was an aluminum ladder, designed for the suburban handyman.

"Well, shit on a shingle." Relic tucked the binoculars away, lay flat near the ruins, and waited.

The man struggled awkwardly up the trail, finally dragging the extension ladder to a stop at the base of the sandstone cliff. He wiped the sweat from his forehead and gazed upward at the solid, sloping rock and the extreme measures the Pueblo people had taken to keep their houses and granaries hidden and safe, high in the cliffs and crags, deep in the desert outback. Centuries ago, they carried masonry, mortar, and jars of water up rickety, wooden ladders to build these solid structures; hard, hot work with just one purpose – protection against interlopers. Now the man below had a ladder of his own, and he rested it against the stone and tugged on the rope that extended it upward, the arms squealing in their tracks, each rung clunking into place as it went.

The man shifted an empty duffle bag across his shoulders and began climbing carefully, one step at a time.

The twenty-eight foot ladder shifted suddenly an inch to the side, but it seemed to find a new, more solid base. The man flexed his knees, testing to make sure the aluminum would not slide any farther, and glanced up. The top of the ladder reached just above the lip of the sandstone ledge.

That man must think he'll find a load of artifacts up here, Relic thought, maybe even lower them to the ground by rope from the ruins, then step back down the ladder unencumbered. But the ancient Pueblo had one last line of defense.

Relic rolled away from the ruins and shifted along the ledge until he was directly in front of the top rung of the ladder, waiting. He listened as the man placed one hand on the step above him, then the next, one at a time, rising cautiously higher.

The man reached the cap of the ledge, but when he looked across the level shelf, where the stone walls rested, there, alone in the red dust, sat Relic looking, he knew, like a weathered Pueblo man, a ghost of the ruins, with a black goatee and a ponytail, holding a three foot cottonwood branch as thick as his arm.

"Shit!" the man's foot slid off one rung and down to the next. "Holy mother...who the hell are you?"

Relic's dark eyes squinted, his lips rose at the corners, and he slid the branch toward the man's ladder.

"What the hell?" the man tightened his grip.

Relic placed the branch on the top rung and began to push.

"No! Shit, no!" He raised his hand for a flash then returned it to the ladder. "You'll kill me!"

Relic slowly pushed the ladder away from the ledge, forcing it to twist outward on one end, then the other, as it lifted from the face of the cliff.

The man dropped both feet to the lower rung and slid his hands quickly down the aluminum sides, dropping his feet, holding for a moment, dropping, holding, dropping as the ladder leaned farther and farther away from the cliff, more and more upright above, ready to catapult him into a pile of rocks, and just as his feet hit the dirt the ladder tipped past its balance, dipped overhead and spun out of his hands and onto the rocky ground with a *Clang*, a bounce, and another *Clang!*

Sign up for book anouncements and special deals at:
AWBALDWIN.COM

Also available from Award Winning Author
A. W. Baldwin:

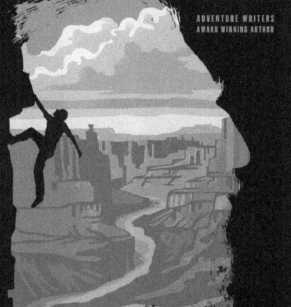

An "ENGAGING ACTION...MYSTERY" - READERS' FAVORITE

A.W. BALDWIN

DESERT
GUARDIAN

ADVENTURE WRITERS
AWARD WINNING AUTHOR

A *RELIC* NOVEL

A moonshining hermit.
A campus bookworm.
A midnight murder.

Ethan's world turns upside-down when he slips off the edge of red-rock cliffs into a world of twisting ravines and coveted artifacts. Saved by a mysterious desert recluse named Relic, Ethan must join a whitewater rafting group and make his way back to civilization. But someone in the gorge is killing to protect their illegal dig for ancient treasures... When Anya, the lead whitewater guide, is attacked, he must divert the killer into the dark canyon night, but his most deadly pursuer is not who he thinks... Ethan struggles to save his new friends, face his own mortality, and unravel the chilling murders. But when they flee the secluded canyon, a lethal hunter is hot on their trail…

Can an unlikely duo and a whitewater crew save themselves and an ancient Aztec battlefield from deadly looters?

Readers' Favorite says:
Desert Guardian is an "engaging action… mystery"

The novel features "tough, credible characters"

Readers' Favorite Five Star Review

Buy now from a bookstore near you or amazon.com

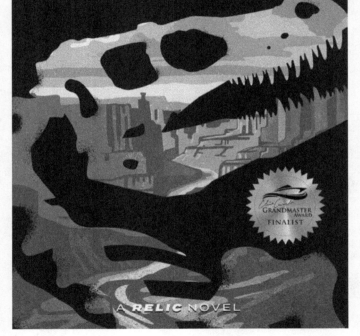

A.W. BALDWIN

RAPTOR CANYON

GRANDMASTER AWARD FINALIST

A *RELIC* NOVEL

A moonshining hermit.
A big-city lawyer.
A $35million con job.

An impromptu murder leads a hermit named Relic to an unlikely set of dinosaur petroglyphs and to swindlers using the unique rock art to turn the canyon into a high-end tourist trap. Attorney Wyatt and his boss travel to the site to approve the next phase of financing, but his boss is not what he seems... When a treacherous security chief tries to kill Relic, Wyatt is caught in the deadly chase. The mismatched pair must tolerate each other while fleeing through white-water rapids, remote gorges, and hidden caverns. Relic devises a plan to save the treasured canyon, but Wyatt must come to terms with the cost to his career if he fights his powerful boss... A college student with secret ties to the site, Faye joins the kitchen crew so she can spy on the enigmatic project. When she hears Relic's desperate plan, she has a decision to make...

Armed with a full box of toothpicks (and a little dynamite), can the unlikely trio monkey-wrench the corrupt land deal and recast the fate of Raptor Canyon?

"A gem of a read…"
– Dirk Cussler, #1 New York Times best-selling author

"[You'll be] holding your heart and your breath at the

same time…"

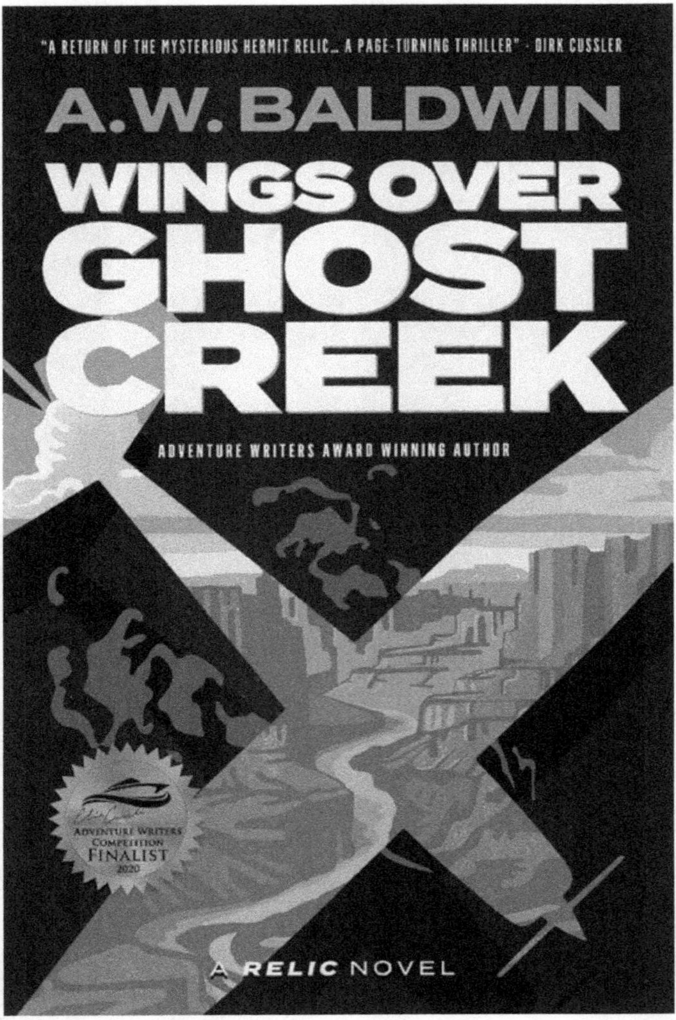
"A RETURN OF THE MYSTERIOUS HERMIT RELIC... A PAGE-TURNING THRILLER" - DIRK CUSSLER
A.W. BALDWIN
WINGS OVER GHOST CREEK
ADVENTURE WRITERS AWARD WINNING AUTHOR
ADVENTURE WRITERS COMPETITION FINALIST 2020
A RELIC NOVEL

A moonshining hermit.
A reluctant pilot.
A $5million plunder.

Owen discovers a murdered corpse at a college-run archeological dig in the Utah outback but when he and a park service pilot try to reach the sheriff for help, their plane is shot from the sky. Owen must ditch the aircraft in the Colorado River, where he is saved by a gin-brewing recluse named Relic. The offbeat pair flee from the sniper and circle back to warn the students but not everyone there is who they seem... The two must trek through rugged canyon country, unravel a baffling mystery, and foil a remarkable form of thievery. Suzy, a student at the dig, helps spearhead their escape but the unique team of crooks has a surprise for them…

Can they uncover the truth and escape an archeology field class that hides assassins and dealers in black-market treasure?

"A beautifully written thriller."
— ***Readers' Favorite Five Star Review***

"[A] humorous, fun, and well-plotted adventure. Baldwin is a master storyteller…"
— ***Landon Beach, Bestselling Author of The Sail***

"Baldwin delivers another gripping Relic tale with

trademark wit and deft expression. This is adventure with philosophy that keeps you nodding your head long after you've put the book down."

— *Jacob P. Avila, Cave Diver, Grand Master Adventure Writers Award Winner*

Wings offers "…action-packed adventure and nerve-racking suspense, with a touch of romance and humor mixed in." Baldwin has a "gift for capturing the reader's attention at the beginning and keeping them spellbound"

— *Onlinebookclub.org review*

Grand Master Adventure Writer's Finalist Award
Buy now from a bookstore near you or amazon.com

A.W. BALDWIN

DIAMONDS
OF DEVIL'S TAIL

ADVENTURE WRITERS
AWARD WINNING AUTHOR

A *RELIC* NOVEL

A moonshining hermit.
An English major.
A $4 million jewel heist.

When diamonds appear in a remote canyon stream, white-water rafters and artifact thieves set off in a deadly race to the source.

Brayden, an aspiring writer, works in a Chicago insurance firm with his ambitious uncle when they embark on a wilderness whitewater adventure. On a remote hike, they find their colleague, Dylan, dead in the sand, a handful of gems in his fist. When thieves charge in, Brayden flees deeper into the canyon, where he encounters a gin-brewing recluse named Relic. Brayden's uncle is cornered and cuts a deal with the thieves, but they each have a surprise for the other… and the rafters have ideas of their own about getting rich quick… Brayden and Relic must become allies, traverse the harsh desert, and beat the thieves to the hidden gems. Brayden must confront his uncle about suspicious payments at their insurance firm and what he was really doing at the stream where Dylan was killed…

Can they discover the truth, find the lost jewels, and protect the rafters from grenade-tossing thieves?

"…an adeptly written thriller…the excitement and tension are superb…the entire plot [is] compelling"
— *Readers' Favorite Five Star Review*

"straightforward and thrilling, with humor inter-mixed...Relic is a unique and intriguing character...passionately interested in preserving the ancient archeological sites and conserving the land and water...[We] enthusiastically recommend it to readers who enjoy thrillers, action-packed adventure, and crime novels."

— Onlinebookclub.org four out of four Star Review

"Another rollicking Relic ride from A.W. Baldwin...a bunch of double-crossing, dirt dealing, diamond thieves run into Relic's trademark wit and ingenuity. Enjoy!"

— Jacob P. Avila, Cave Diver, Grand Master Adventure Writers Award Winner

Buy now from a bookstore near you or amazon.com

A.W. BALDWIN

BROKEN INN

A *RELIC* NOVEL

A moonshining hermit.
A budding reporter.
A $25 million misdirection.

The mob, undercover agents, and secret payloads make Broken Inn a dangerous place for a fresh reporter, a newspaper photographer, and a moonshining hermit.

Hailey witnesses a murder at the enigmatic Broken Inn, but when she learns that the hotel manager and her editor are pals, she investigates on her own. When a corrupt guard finds her snooping, she flees into a box canyon, where she is saved by a gin-brewing recluse named Relic. She reports the murder to a deputy, but for some reason, no arrests are made... She enlists help from Ash, the newspaper's photographer, but they must flee for their lives into the back country with Relic and a four-legged stray with a nose for trouble. They discover mysterious metal drums hidden deep in an abandoned uranium mine, but can't tell what's inside. And just when they're most desperate for help, they learn that not everyone is who they seem...

Can they uncover the secrets of Broken Inn, dodge the syndicate, and head off an environmental disaster?

"Danger scorches in another outstanding mystery by A.W. Baldwin"
  – New York Times #1 Bestselling author Dirk Cussler

"Brilliantly executed... heart stopping excitement"

– Readers' Favorite Five Star Review

Grand Master Adventure Writer's Finalist Award

**New York City Big Book Award
– Distinguished Favorite**

Global Book Awards

Independent Press Award – Distinguished Favorite

Books Shelf Award – Second Place

Buy now from a bookstore near you or amazon.com

"A true delight" - DIRK CUSSLER
A.W. BALDWIN
THE
ANTIDOTE
LITERARY TITAN
BOOK
AWARD
GRANDMASTER
AWARD
WINNER

Can genetically modified seeds provide the antidote for climate change?

A geneticist has developed plants that could stem the tide of climate change, but when grad student Lila finds him murdered, she flees the scene with the seeds. To escape the killer, she hitches a ride with an eccentric duo and a secret payload that could land them all in prison. Chased by ruthless thieves, the three must rely on their wits, uncover the mystery of these potent plants, and deliver the future of the planet to an unknown scientist a thousand miles away…

But the cross-hairs on those million-dollar seeds are on them, too…

"This harrowing techno-thriller is an impressive achievement – timely, and rich with research, intrigue, and a main character you will be rooting for from the beginning all the way to the exhilarating climax. Highly recommended!"

– #1 Amazon Best-selling author Landon Beach (*The Wreck*, Narrator).

"The chemistry between Harry and Keaton is electrifying." "…there is never a dull moment…The Antidote [is] a gripping novel."

– *Readers' Favorite 5 Star Reviews.*

"Baldwin is one of the preeminent authors in the adventure-thriller genre and he showcases that talent in spades with his latest novel, The Antidote. A unique premise, richly drawn characters, and constantly increasing risk makes this science-gone-wrong, Crichton-esque thriller a slam dunk. Readers will delight in the protagonists deftly navigating a tangle of intrigue and mortal threats, surviving assassins and gunfights to ensure a brilliant discovery—one that could impact the future of the planet—isn't lost to corrupt special interests and greed."

— Award-winning author Nate Granzow (Get Idiota, Cogar's Revenge).

First Place – Grand Master Adventure Writer's Competition

Books Shelf Award - Compelling Read

Independent Press Award -- Distinguished Favorite

Buy now from a bookstore near you or amazon.com

"VIBRANT CHARACTERS... WITTY DIALOGUE AND HUMOR" - READERS' FAVORITE

A.W. BALDWIN
MOONSHINE MESA

ADVENTURE WRITERS
AWARD WINNING AUTHOR

A RELIC NOVEL

A moonshining hermit.
An aspiring lawyer.
A $55 million-dollar eco-scam.

Criminal clients, a pollution mitigation scam, and a million-dollar double-cross make Moonshine Mesa a dangerous place for an aspiring lawyer, an intrepid deputy, and a moonshining hermit.

Something is killing bees, crows, and humans at Moonshine Mesa. When Parker finds suspicious readings at a remote pump station, clients of a prestigious law firm prepare to toss him off a cliff. A gin-brewing recluse named Relic saves him and together they must solve the mysterious deaths, outmaneuver armed drug runners, and rescue an intrepid deputy dedicated to solving the crimes. And all is not what it seems between the partners in these lethal schemes...

Can they unravel these baffling deaths and stem the environmental carnage?

"A gripping tale of mystery, intrigue, and environmental peril."
   – – *Literary Titan 5 Star Review.*

"Fascinating from the first chapter...I couldn't put the book down."
   – – *OnlineBookClub.org 5 Star Review.*

"A sleuth murder mystery, crime-drama thriller, and action novel all rolled into one page-turner."
– – *Readers' Favorite 5 Star Review.*

Winner of the Global Book Awards Gold Medal

Gold Medal Winner, Reader's Favorite International Book Competition, eco-thriller

Buy now from a bookstore near you or amazon.com

www.ingramcontent.com/pod-product-compliance
Lightning Source LLC
LaVergne TN
LVHW041700180125
801629LV00001B/135